# THE
# BLUE LADY

# THE
# BLUE LADY

## ELEANOR HAWKEN

HOT
KEY
BOOKS

First published in Great Britain in 2013 by Hot Key Books
Northburgh House, 10 Northburgh Street, London EC1V 0AT

A CIP catalogue record for this book is available from the British Library.

ISBN: 978-1-4714-0090-2

1

Typeset by Palimpsest Book Production Limited, Falkirk, Stirlingshire
This book is typeset in Berling LT Std

Printed and bound by Clays Ltd, St Ives Plc

**FSC**

Hot Key Books supports the Forest Stewardship Council (FSC), the leading
international forest certification organisation, and is committed to printing
only on Greenpeace-approved FSC-certified paper.

www.hotkeybooks.com

Hot Key Books is part of the Bonnier Publishing Group
www.bonnierpublishing.com

*For Luke, thank you for never complaining when I disappear into my imagination. When I come back into the real world, I'll always come back to you.*

Headmistress Beaton
St Mark's College for Girls
Oxfordshire
England
4th May 1786

Dear Brigadier Marshall,
It is with deepest regret that I write to inform you of the sudden death of your daughter, Isabelle. Miss Isabelle Marshall's body was discovered on the steps of the school soon after sunrise this morning.

As you know, Sir, Isabelle was expelled from St Mark's College for Girls only two days ago. I must make it clear to you that despite her recent expulsion from our guardianship, the school accepts no responsibility for Isabelle's death. Given her condition in recent months, we cannot help but feel that her tragic fate was unavoidable.

Isabelle's body is currently with the police pending a post-mortem investigation. Her immortal soul is now in His judgement, and all at St Mark's will pray for her.

With deepest regret,
Headmistress Beaton

I

I was never the sort of girl who believed in ghosts. I never
played with Ouija boards, held seances or felt afraid of the
dark. That stuff was for other people, not me. But that all
changed when I went to live at St Mark's College.

Unlike the other girls at St Mark's, I hadn't lived away
from home since the age of eight. I didn't come from a
posh family who had a house in the country and a yacht
in France. The only time I'd ever been to France was when
Mum and I took a day trip using ferry tokens she'd saved
up from a newspaper. Boarding school wasn't for girls like
me. I ended up there by mistake.

The mistake happened last December, when Mum's
friend Lynn invited her to an army officers' Christmas ball.
Lynn's brother is a major in the army, and had just got
back from a tour of Afghanistan. Apparently his wife used
to write to him every week while he was out there, and
then one week the letters stopped. Two months later he
had another letter from her – only this time all she sent
him were divorce papers. Lynn wanted to set Mum up with
this guy – although I wasn't keen. Mum's had enough loser
boyfriends without adding a jilted army officer to the list.

But that night, at the ball, Mum accidentally sat on the

3

wrong table and chatted to a guy who she thought was Lynn's brother. Turns out the man she was talking to wasn't Lynn's brother, but Lynn's brother's boss. His name was Lieutenant Colonel Phillip Walker. They got married eight months later. And thirteen days after the wedding, Phil was posted to Germany. Instead of taking me to Germany and putting me into a German school, Mum and Phil decided to send me to an English boarding school. So it was all just one big mix-up – if Mum had chatted to the right guy that night, I would never have been sent to St Mark's. If I'd never gone to St Mark's, then I'd still believe there's no such thing as ghosts.

Term started in early September. Mum and I had talked it over and decided it would be best if I said goodbye to her at home and for Phil to drive me to school. Mum's never been good with her nerves. Being the new girl was tough enough without a hysterical parent in the equation.

We barely spoke on the long drive to my new school. After two hours, Phil broke the silence. 'We'll call as soon as we arrive in Hameln next week.'

'Sure,' I muttered back.

'St Mark's is an excellent school,' he reminded me. 'And the new sports hall they're building will mean it has one of the best sports facilities in the country.'

I smiled, trying to put Phil at ease. I didn't have the heart to tell him that I hated sport of any kind.

I spent the journey staring out of the window as the sun sank in the cloudless September sky. Piles of golden leaves were beginning to gather at the side of the road – Mother

Nature's way of reminding everyone that nothing lasts forever. I took out my new sketchpad and pencils, and began to capture the leaves falling from trees. Putting pencil to paper was a good distraction from the familiar knot in my stomach. I imagined the leaves as parts of my old life falling away from me – freeing me to sprout new buds and start again. Drawing was my only real friend, the one thing I could always rely on. Everything else just came and went.

I was only fourteen but I'd already been to a ton of schools, although the others had at least had boys in them. Mum liked to move to be near her latest boyfriend. So going to boarding school was a good thing. It meant I could stay somewhere longer than a few months. I'd finally get a chance to be who I wanted to be, and not have to pretend just to fit in.

Moving around a lot had forced me to be a teenage chameleon. It's the easiest way to survive. In the past I'd tried all kinds of things: I'd dressed as an Emo and a chav, pretended to like horses, followed bad reality TV. There was one school where the only person who'd speak to me was an exchange student from Hong Kong – I'd even learnt a few words in Cantonese. I'd learnt to build walls around myself so no one ever saw the real me. But you can't fake it forever.

I was tired of trying on a new identity as if it were a new coat. St Mark's was the chance for a new beginning. I was wearing black jeans, a black polo neck and a studded metal belt to show everyone that I was serious. I liked art and poetry. That summer I'd started to watch the news and pay attention to politics. I cared about deforestation and war, the melting of polar ice caps and university tuition fees. This was who I was and I wasn't afraid to let people know. As Phil's car got nearer to my new school, it felt like the setting sun was a ticking clock, and as soon as it slipped below the horizon, my life would irrevocably change.

We passed through a small town called Martyrs Heath, which sat at the bottom of a hill. The town was peppered with cobblestone houses, well-kept lawns and an ancient church with a sprawling graveyard. Very quaint, very 'English'.

The road we travelled down forked off ahead. A queue of cars waited to drive through a vast iron gate leading to a winding gravelled path beyond. My stomach flipped. Surely this was it: my new school.

'That's St Hilda's,' Phil said simply. 'Brother school to St Mark's.'

We drove on, and I craned my neck to catch a glimpse of one of the waiting cars. A woman sat behind her steering wheel anxiously chewing her nails as a boy about my age sat listening to his headphones in the passenger seat beside her. He clearly wasn't a new pupil. He didn't look as nervous as I felt.

So St Mark's had a brother school. The prospectus hadn't told me that. I should have known then that the school was keeping other secrets too.

Martyrs Heath, and St Hilda's, lay in the shadow of St Mark's College, which sat upon the hill. St Mark's weathered, grey-stone turrets loomed down over me as Phil's car drove smoothly through the streets and up the winding road.

Finally, after what felt like forever, the car pulled up at my new home – St Mark's College for Girls.

A tall, thin woman tottered towards us as Phil parked up his Mercedes. She was dressed in a shocking purple trouser suit with a mountain of grey hair piled high on her head. Small round glasses framed her bird-like eyes. If I could have drawn a caricature of an eccentric English boarding school matron, it would have looked like her.

'Francesca Ward?' she asked with confidence.

'Frankie,' I corrected her.

'I'm Ms Thurlow.' She shook Phil's hand without looking at me. Phil introduced himself. He always sounded so formal when he spoke.

Ms Thurlow turned away and motioned for us to follow. 'Welcome to St Mark's. I'll show you up to the fourth-year dorm. I'll be your housemistress for this year, Francesca,' she said, walking ahead and not looking back. 'I'm also Head of Latin – although I don't think you're taking Latin, are you?'

'No,' I answered simply. They didn't teach Latin in the kind of schools I'd been to. They'd taught us important stuff: how to roll your skirt up, look a bully in the eye and skip out on swimming lessons by faking your period every week. You don't learn skills like that in a Latin classroom.

Ms Thurlow led us up stone steps and through a grand arched doorway at the front of the building. 'This is the original entrance to the school. Of course the girls aren't normally allowed to come in through this door. There's another entrance at the side of the building for everyday use.' She smiled at Phil. 'But we make exceptions at the start of term, as a special treat.'

The entrance led us into the school's main corridor, which was narrow and paved with ancient, chipped marble flooring. The white walls were lined with dozens of old school photos, documenting St Mark's girls from the time cameras were first invented right up to the present day. An elite club of girls, all of different ages, races and faces, but united by one thing – they were all pupils at St Mark's. I was the newest member of this privileged society. Once again it hit home that life was changing forever.

Our footsteps echoed along the corridor until we reached a small, dark stairwell at the end. The fourth-year dorms were on the second floor. There were three in total, and each dorm slept twenty. The dorms weren't numbered 1–3, or A–C; instead they had names of explorers: 'Raleigh', 'Drake' and 'Columbus'.

I was in Raleigh Dorm.

'You're in the last room on the left,' Ms Thurlow informed me, her eyes darting around like a sparrow, avoiding my gaze. Up close I could see lipstick marks on her teeth and deep creases in her clothes. 'I'm afraid,' she said to Phil, 'Francesca will have to take her bags from here – we don't allow men into the dorms. We don't allow them above stairs normally, but being the start of term we make an exception.'

'That's quite all right,' replied Phil, looking mildly embarrassed.

'I'll be in my flat should you need me,' Ms Thurlow said hurriedly. And without telling me where her flat was, she disappeared back down the dark stairwell.

'You'll be OK from here?' Phil asked. I nodded.

I plonked down the suitcase, gym bag and box of CDs I'd been lugging and gave Phil an awkward hug. 'Don't worry,' I grinned. 'I promise to wait until your car's left the car park before I throw myself out of the window.'

Phil eyed me with horror.

'I'll be fine.' I rolled my eyes, inwardly groaning at Phil's total sense-of-humour bypass.

With a deep breath I pushed my weight into the heavy oak door and it swung open reluctantly. Raleigh Dorm was the size of a grand banqueting hall. Huge, panelled windows lined the mint-green walls and the ceiling was arched high like a chapel. It had probably sat empty all summer, but already it smelled of coconut-clean hair, pine-fresh body sprays and rose-scented lip balms.

The vast space had been divided up into roofless, oak-panelled rooms – each division like a furnished horsebox.

The first door to my left was open as I walked past. Inside, a girl with red hair paced the few steps of space and talked in excited squeals at a girl with bobbed brown hair. The redhead wore skinny blue jeans and an expensive-looking jumper with a patterned scarf draped luxuriously around her neck. I knew then that I wouldn't fit in at St Mark's, even if I wanted to. I wouldn't even know where to buy a scarf like that, let alone afford one.

My eyes focused ahead of me – to the last door on the left, the small room that was to be my home for the next year. I walked to my room without stopping to look around. I hated the fact that my heart raced in my throat and my knees shook with every step. Starting new schools was old news to me, and I was never usually this nervous.

I reached the end of the dormitory and entered my room. There was nothing in there but a bed, a drawer unit, a pin board above a desk, a lamp and a small window that over-looked the school car park and the school sports fields beyond.

The room was small and simple, but it was mine.

The thought of parading around the dorm and intro-ducing myself to my new schoolmates just made me cringe. If someone wanted to speak to me, then they could knock on my door. I began to unpack and stick pictures to the wooden walls. On my pin board I attached a photo of me and Mum taken on a protest against deforestation outside the Brazilian Embassy last summer. Before Phil, Mum went out with a hippy. It didn't last long, but long enough for me to learn all about the world's rainforests being chopped down for the sake of 'human progress'.

Next to my bed I put my new sketchpad, my *Complete Works of Shakespeare* and a framed picture of Mum holding me as a baby – three weeks after Dad had left. Under my bed I hid a green biscuit tin that Gran had given me as a child. The tin was where I kept all my most sacred photos and drawings, which I didn't want to share with the rest of the world on a pin board.

Finally, there was a knock on my open door.

The girl with bright red hair and the expensive scarf walked confidently into my room. 'I'm Saskia,' she said without smiling. 'You're the new girl? Francesca?'

'Frankie,' I told her. 'Hi,' I smiled.

Saskia sat on my bed as I continued to unpack. She

babbled at lightning speed about her summer in the South of France. Apparently she'd drunk champagne 'basically every hour of every day' and hooked up with a French guy called Louis. 'There's something about French men that makes them so sophisticated, you know? Not like English boys, especially the sorry excuses at St Hilda's.'

I waited for her to ask me about my summer, and about the photo of Mum at the protest, but she didn't. Instead Saskia cast a bored look around my room, resting her eyes on a charcoal sketch I'd done of Mum.

'O-M-G,' Saskia snorted. 'This is like, so morbid. Who's the old witch?' She reached to peel the picture from the wall and I instinctively slammed my hand over hers to stop her. She recoiled in shock before a flicker of understanding passed through her eyes.

'Mum was just really tired when I drew her,' I said defensively. 'She was working two jobs at the time.'

Saskia eyed me up and down with curiosity. I could feel her judging every item of clothing, every strand of hair, every shuffle of my Converse trainers. I stood up straight, trying to defiantly meet her eye.

'Where did you get your clothes from?' she said slowly.

'I went shopping in London this summer,' I answered proudly.

'Interesting look,' Saskia said coolly. 'I can really see what you were trying to do.'

I opened my mouth to speak but Saskia got there first. 'Is it true you used to go to a school with boys?'

'PIZZA!' I heard someone scream from the other end of the dorm.

11

Saskia grabbed my hand and pulled me through the dorm like some kind of new pet.

As a beginning-of-term treat we were allowed pizza in the TV room. I sat with Saskia, George (the girl with bobbed brown hair) and a girl called Claire who had nostrils like a horse. Claire looked like a blonde version of Saskia: expensive scarf, skinny jeans and manicured nails. George didn't look as bothered by rich-girl fashion as the others, with her short and simple hair, plain black vest and blue jeans. I offered her a smile when she looked my way, but it wasn't returned.

I silently munched my pizza, and listened to them rattle on about their summer holidays. 'So, Los Angeles was cool,' George said breezily to the others. Saskia eyed her hungrily for more. 'Mum was working a lot, though. So when I wasn't lying by the pool I went riding up in the hills.'

'Daddy bought me a new pony this summer,' Claire boasted. 'I've called him Smartie.'

I pretended I was choking on my pizza as I stifled my hysteria. *Smartie!* Talk about cruelty to animals.

They seemed so uninterested in me, and I struggled to hide my disappointment. I'd been secretly looking forward to impressing new friends with the 'real' Frankie. Even the fact that I'd been to school with boys seemed to bore them after a while. After dinner in the TV room, I followed Saskia and her posse of well-groomed friends back to Raleigh Dorm. I found myself walking alone, at the back of the crowd.

That was when I first saw Suzy.

She was alone too, walking down the corridor towards

us. She was, without doubt, the coolest person I'd ever seen. She had bright red hair (dyed, not natural like Saskia's), a nose piercing and dark eye make-up. She was wearing a dress that looked homemade, ripped tights and big, scruffy boots. Among the sea of perfect St Mark's Barbie dolls she couldn't have looked more like a freak. Suzy looked as out of place as I felt. I knew as soon as I saw her that we'd be friends.

I tapped Saskia on the shoulder and she swung around. 'Who's that?' I whispered as the girl with bright red hair walked past us.

'Just some weirdo from the year above,' Saskia grunted. 'I don't know what her problem is but I bet it's hard to pronounce.'

Claire snorted at Saskia's cruel remark.

The dorm lights were out by ten o'clock. I could hear everyone sneak into each other's rooms to whisper and giggle. No one knocked on my door and came to whisper with me. I tried not to care. I tugged back my curtains, letting the moonlight flood into my small room, and opened my sketchpad. Flattening out the first clean page, I drew black lines onto the whiteness, forming shapes that soon became pictures – pictures of a woman who looked like Mum, standing by a house in a country across the sea.

I sketched for hours, trying to escape my loneliness by disappearing into the endless world inside my own head. As dark clouds passed over the moonlight, lengthening the shadows across my newly decorated walls, I had a creeping sense of unease.

St Mark's was the perfect English boarding school. But

something wasn't quite right. I'd known before I'd arrived about the beautiful old building and impressive academic record. But since stepping into the cold school halls I couldn't shift the feeling that there was more to St Mark's than worn grey bricks and neatly pressed uniforms. There was a dissonance in those halls. I couldn't put my finger on it, but I knew instinctively that the school was not a peaceful place. It wasn't as glossy as the school brochure made it look. There were dark secrets at St Mark's – stories that had been hidden and buried away. And I was now living among them.

## 2

My first school day at St Mark's started with assembly in the hall. Everyone sat on hard wooden benches, apart from the prefects and teachers who sat on plastic chairs lined against the walls. The prefects, all dressed in perfectly pressed blue uniforms and shined shoes, watched us like hawks from the sides of the room. It felt as though all their eyes were soon on me – the newest member of the pack. I swallowed hard and tried to ignore their scrutinising gazes, and listen to Ms West give her start-of-year speech. Ms West was my new headmistress, and she looked like the teachers who might have taught my grandparents. Over her clothes she wore a black teacher's robe, and on her face she wore an expression that reminded me of sucking a sour sweet. I listened as Ms West told us St Mark's girls should 'strive for excellence in everything they do'. I felt a shudder of excitement; no one had ever told me anything like this before.

The morning's lessons were pretty standard: English, French and History. I didn't know any of the girls in my History class, so I walked to lunch on my own. I hung my new school-bag on a hook outside the dining hall and queued up to collect a plate of lukewarm, stodgy lasagne.

I was scanning the room for somewhere to sit when Ms Thurlow, my housemistress, appeared in front of me. Her wild grey hair was clipped back from her face with a bright red comb, clashing with the purple suit she was wearing for the second day in a row. 'Francesca,' she said, looking around as if the sight of me bored her, 'I thought it might be nice for you to meet someone in the same situation.'

'Another new girl?' I asked hopefully.

'Another military boarder,' she answered, pointing to a table at the back of the hall.

I followed Ms Thurlow towards the table, weaving our way through the lunch crowds. Suzy, the girl with bright red hair I'd seen the evening before, was sitting alone with a bowl of soup. My stomach did a small flip as I realised I was going to have to talk to her – the coolest girl I'd ever seen.

'Susanne,' Ms Thurlow said to her, 'this is Francesca. Her father's just been posted to Germany.'

'Stepfather,' I said quickly as Ms Thurlow scuttled away towards the teachers' table.

Suzy's clear green eyes studied me carefully. 'You can call me Suzy. I hate Susanne almost as much as I hate my parents for putting me in this dump.'

'You can call me Frankie,' I smiled at her. 'No one calls me Francesca.' I noticed she'd taken out her nose ring. There was still the faint trace of black eyeliner around her eyes.

'Thurlow your housemistress?' Suzy asked. I nodded. 'She's a total wino. I had to go up to her flat once, and counted seven empty bottles of Merlot on her coffee table.

You're lucky, with Thurlow you can get away with murder. She's too drunk to care.'

I smiled at Suzy's words – the first interesting thing someone had said to me since I'd stepped foot in St Mark's.

'So, Germany, huh?' Suzy raised an eyebrow and studied me for a moment. 'My dad was stationed out there a couple of years ago. We live in Cyprus now.'

'Cool,' I said, feeling instantly envious. I would have put up much more of a fight to stay with Mum if she was going to live in sunny Cyprus.

'It's not cool,' Suzy said sharply, making me feel foolish. 'If it wasn't for the stupid army then I wouldn't be in this place. I mean, who names an all-girls' boarding school after a male saint?'

She had a point. 'This isn't a school, it's Hell with classrooms, right?' I joked. Suzy nodded in approval. 'And St Hilda's down the road,' I added quickly. 'A boys' school named after a female saint? Talk about messed up!'

Suzy leant forwards dramatically, as if imparting words of great wisdom. 'If you know what's good for you you'll stay well away from St Hilda's boys.' She shook her head with concern. 'It's a long story . . . trust me!'

'Yeah?' I grinned, already wanting to hear every one of Suzy's stories.

She put down her soup spoon and studied me again. 'I saw you hanging out with Saskia and her Barbie doll gang last night,' Suzy said accusingly. 'You know those girls are only popular because they're rich? Girls like that don't associate with girls like us.'

I smiled at Suzy's use of 'us'. 'I kinda guessed that much,'

I said truthfully. 'George didn't seem as bad as the others,' I shrugged.

'You know her mum's a Hollywood script writer?' Suzy said with what sounded like envy. 'But seriously, Frankie, if I could give you one piece of advice – don't even bother with girls like that. You're new, you don't know how things work around here.' Her green eyes narrowed, clearly enjoying the sense of power my naivety gave her. 'Take it from me, St Mark's is a battleground – give your enemy any kind of ammunition and they'll obliterate you and dance on your bones.' Suzy sat back dramatically, satisfied. 'So, what kind of stuff do you like, Frankie?'

'Well, I like reading,' I said swiftly, finally glad to have an opportunity to tell someone about myself. 'I like watching the news, politics and stuff like that,' I said proudly. Suzy groaned and rolled her eyes. 'I like art, and drawing too,' I added quickly.

She gave me another nod of approval. 'Art's cool,' she said loudly. 'But I'd much rather listen to music, or read poetry.'

I looked down at my food and prodded it with my fork, searching around in my lasagne for something interesting to say. 'I liked the dress you were wearing last night,' I told her. 'Did you make it yourself?'

'I make all my own clothes,' she answered casually. 'I've even designed my Oscar dress.'

'Your Oscar dress?' I repeated.

'I'm going to be an actress,' she said, as if that explained everything. 'My dad went to uni with Emma Thompson, you know.'

Suzy spent the next half hour talking at a break-neck pace about how she was going to go to drama school one day and then marry a famous film director. 'We do a school play every year with St Hilda's,' she said, her eyes gleaming. 'I played the part of Cobweb in *A Midsummer Night's Dream* last year. That's kind of how I met James Martin, he was playing Peter Quince – but we don't have time for me to go into the whole James Martin thing right now.'

I listened intently, studying her as she spoke. I could see how Suzy would make a good actress; everything she said was theatrical. She threw her hands about and widened her eyes, weaving a web of tales of how she'd one day live in Hollywood, and be the most famous actress alive. Suzy was like no one I'd ever met before.

'People hate me for my ambition,' Suzy said passionately. 'But I don't care. *Ambition should be made of sterner stuff.*'

I laughed to myself. '*Julius Caesar.*'

'Excuse me?' Suzy asked. I looked up quickly, anxious I might have offended her, but she was smiling.

'What you said, about ambition,' I explained. 'It's from *Julius Caesar* – the play, I mean. Mum used to read me Shakespeare at bedtime when I was a kid. It was kind of "our thing", you know?' I'd never told anyone that before.

'I knew I liked you as soon as I saw you,' Suzy smiled, her emerald eyes sparkling with excitement. A huge grin creased my face – finally, a friend who liked the real me.

'Don't be late for your first Chemistry class, Suzy,' said a bald man with a blue blazer as he walked passed us.

'God,' Suzy sighed. 'Mr Desmond is such a freak of

nature. He's always on my case. Maybe he's secretly in love with me?' She twirled her red hair playfully.

Suzy pushed her chair back and stood up. I did the same, sad that the lunch hour was coming to an end. The dining hall was beginning to thin out as people started to make their way to afternoon lessons. We both dumped our trays before walking towards the bag rack. Suzy had the best school-bag I'd ever seen – she'd written quotes from her favourite songs, poems and plays all over it.

'What you doing later, after school?' she asked me, slinging her bag over her shoulder. 'Wanna hang out before prep?'

'Sure,' I smiled.

'Cool. I'll meet you outside Newton at four.'

The rest of the afternoon felt as if I'd slipped into a time vortex. It went so slowly. I watched the clock throughout my Maths lesson and then spent the whole of Biology class listening to Saskia tell the story of kissing Louis for the billionth time.

As soon as the end-of-school bell rang I headed straight back to my room. I quickly got changed out of my school uniform into my new black jeans and a black and white striped top, like the kind you imagine French artists might wear.

I walked proudly past Saskia, George and Claire in the corridor. I didn't need them. I was making friends on my own.

The fifth-year dorms were at the other end of the building. They were all named after famous scientists. I casually leant against the wall of Newton Dorm, trying to appear cool as haggles of girls looked me up and down as they went in.

Eventually, Suzy appeared. She was wearing a purple dress with small beads and mirrors sewed into it and a bright green cardigan.

'I need to get out of this hellhole!' she shouted dramatically, putting the back of her right hand over her forehead like an actress in a silent movie.

'Wanna run away with me?' I joked.

'Can't,' she replied, skipping down the corridor. 'I have a Biology test tomorrow. Can you believe it . . . the second day of term and I already have a test! They're trying to kill us – or make us as mad as Macbeth!'

I laughed out loud and once again felt myself smiling insatiably as I listened to Suzy talk about her day. Suzy was the type of person I'd always dreamed of meeting. She knew how to quote Shakespeare and play with every word as if she were addressing a vast audience. All I wanted was to hear more.

We headed down the stairs and out of the school building. Beyond the sports fields were acres of woodland, which all belonged to the school. Suzy didn't explain why we were heading towards the woods, and I didn't think to question her.

We walked farther into the woods until school was out of sight. Every few seconds, Suzy looked over her shoulder and scanned the woodland around us distractedly. She seemed nervous – I noticed how she kept pulling the sleeves of her cardigan down and wringing her fingers anxiously into them.

'No one's following us,' I reassured her.

But Suzy wasn't worried about seeing teachers or hawk-eyed prefects. There was someone else she was expecting to see.

The woodland floor was carpeted with vividly coloured flowers – twisted yellow buds on bright green stems. The woods smelt like damp earth and bark, and rustled with the sound of insects and birds. I trod carefully as Suzy nervously led me through tangled mosses woven into fallen autumn leaves. We arrived at an old shack in the middle of the woods; the door was falling off its hinges and inside was nothing but rotting leaves and a rusty stool.

Suzy seemed disappointed as we walked into the shack, as if she'd been expecting to find something exciting in there. 'This is one of my favourite places,' she told me. 'I come here when I want to think. I like the flowers – you should see it in spring, the whole forest floor is covered in bluebells. *The violets in the mountains have broken the rocks!*' she said with a large sweep of her arms. 'Tennessee Williams wrote that, you know. It means that something wild and beautiful can crush anything, even rocks. That's what these woods are to me,' she said, 'something wild and beautiful amid the horror of boarding school!'

If anyone could make rotten leaves seem beautiful, it was Suzy. She seemed to live in such a vivid world where everything around her was magical. I was beginning to feel as though all my life I'd only ever lived inside my own head, and that I was finally seeing the world for the first time.

Suzy pulled out a packet of cigarettes from her cardigan

22

pocket and leant against the rotten shack wall. She put a cigarette in her mouth and lit it. I was relieved she didn't offer me one. Mum had a boyfriend once who smoked and I hated it – it had always made the house stink. Plus I knew that if a teacher caught me smoking I'd be kicked out of St Mark's on the spot.

I stood watching Suzy, dramatically puffing away on her cigarette. She fell silent and stared at me. I couldn't tell what she was thinking, but she seemed disappointed somehow.

That's when we heard it. The sound of twigs breaking underfoot and branches being pushed aside. Suzy flew to the shack door and peered out hungrily. 'Oh, no!' she muttered under her breath. My heart skipped as I followed her line of vision. I braced myself for the shrill sound of a teacher shouting as they discovered us sneaking out of the school and smoking cigarettes.

But it wasn't a teacher bulldozing through the woods. There were two boys coming towards us.

They were our age, possibly a year or two above us. I was never good at guessing these things. One of them had short sandy hair, the other scruffy dark hair that covered his eyes. Both were wearing school uniform – shirts untucked, ties loose around their necks and blue blazers embroidered with a school emblem. The St Hilda's school emblem.

'Susanne,' boomed the sandy-haired boy as he strode confidently towards us.

'James,' Suzy replied with what sounded like disgust. 'I'd assumed you'd caught some kind of infectious disease over the summer. I'm surprised to see you here.' One look into Suzy's eyes and I knew she was lying. She couldn't have been happier to see James.

'No infectious disease, I'm afraid,' James smirked cockily. He stepped into the shack and the dark-haired boy followed him in. James casually leant against the wall as his friend walked over to the glass-less window and peered out into the woods.

'So no excuse for not calling me then?' Suzy said, trying to sound indifferent.

'Come on, Suz,' James grinned. He had one of those killer grins you see on teen soaps. A grin that obviously always got him his own way. 'Chuck us a fag.'

Suzy threw him her packet of cigarettes. 'This is Frankie,' she said loudly. My arms instinctively folded across my chest and I nodded shyly. 'This is James and Sebastian.'

'I'm new,' I said, dumbly. I raised my eyes and saw James still grinning at Suzy. The other boy, Sebastian, turned around from the window, reached up and brushed the dark hair from his face. His striking blue eyes locked into mine.

I felt an uncomfortable tightening in my stomach as he looked at me, and I couldn't bring myself to look away. The intensity of his stare burned into me. I'd never seen eyes like that before. They looked as though they should belong to someone much older. Someone who had already seen too much of life.

After what felt like forever, Sebastian's gaze flickered over to Suzy and nodded in acknowledgment. Then he turned to look at me again, his eyes once again unnerving me. His expression gave nothing away. In that moment I'd have given anything to know what he was thinking.

James exhaled loudly on his cigarette, and the noise jerked me out of my trance. I swallowed hard and looked over at James, trying to distract myself from the fact that I could still feel Sebastian's gaze linger on me. James looked a much more natural smoker than Suzy. I reckoned he'd been practising all summer.

He took his phone from his pocket. 'Seb, this was that Youtube video I was telling you about in Maths.'

I watched as Sebastian sauntered over to James, casually leant against the wall next to him, and stared down at the phone. James started to play the video and both boys began to smirk at whatever they were looking at.

'Let's see,' Suzy said. They ignored her and she turned to me, chewing her lip in thought. 'You know Katie Newman?' Suzy asked me loudly, her eyes quickly scanning the boys to see if they'd heard. Neither of them looked up from the phone.

I shook my head at Suzy, I had no idea who Katie Newman was.

'She's a girl in my year,' Suzy explained. 'She had sex with her boyfriend this summer.' She said that bit extra-loudly. 'She was telling everyone about it today after Chemistry. Apparently she thought she might be pregnant and had to take the morning-after pill.'

'Oh,' I replied, not knowing what to say. I'd never known anyone my age who'd had sex before.

Suddenly, whatever was on James's phone seemed to become even more interesting, and the boys both stared in intense silence at the screen. I could tell they were listening to us, though.

'Now she thinks she's so cool,' Suzy frowned, throwing her cigarette butt on the ground and stubbing it out under her boot. 'She's not cool, though,' she assured me. 'I remember when she kept the whole dorm up one night in first year cos she thought she'd seen the Blue Lady!' Suzy snorted.

'Who's the Blue Lady?' I asked.

'The Blue Lady,' Suzy walked towards me, her green eyes twinkling with the opportunity to spin a story, 'is the ghost that haunts the corridors of St Mark's.'

'Girls,' James muttered as he shook his head.

'Suzy, there's no such thing as ghosts,' I chuckled, hearing the edge in my voice. I risked a quick glance at Sebastian. He was studying Suzy carefully. My face flushed again as I realised just how good-looking he was. His dark, careless hair made the pale skin of his heart-shaped face look so smooth and milky.

'I'm serious,' Suzy said sternly, annoyed she wasn't being taken seriously. 'She was a pupil here hundreds of years ago – she died on the steps to the main entrance. That's why no one's allowed to walk through it normally – because you're walking over her death bed.'

A gust of wind blew through the trees and the hairs on the back of my neck stood sharply to attention. 'Believe me, Frankie, there's something dark and terrible in the past of St Mark's. I bet they don't tell you that in the school prospectus.'

Seb pushed himself away from the shack wall and glared

at Suzy. His chest rose as he took a deep breath and then shifted his stare towards me. I felt my heartbeat begin to quicken. His eyes froze into mine, as if he were asking me a question that I didn't understand. But Suzy didn't seem to notice the change in Seb's manner. She was just pleased to have an audience.

Silence fell on the woodland shack. The wind shook the trees outside as Suzy took a deep breath and told us the story of the Blue Lady.

# 3

'She was a schoolgirl, here at St Mark's. St Mark's and St Hilda's were world-famous back then – the first schools of their kind. To be given a place you had to be the son or daughter of a high-ranking army officer. You couldn't just buy your way in like you can today.' Suzy spoke in a whisper. She took her time with every word, searching it for dramatic potential.

'So this happened hundreds of years ago?' I asked, shivering as the autumn breeze rattled through the shack. James leant against the wall, uninterested and texting on his phone. But Seb was curious; his eyes never left Suzy as she told her story. I felt an unexpected pang of jealousy. I wished it were me he was listening to. I wished I knew the story of the Blue Lady. A story he'd obviously been waiting to hear.

Suzy nodded. 'Her father was one of the highest-ranking generals in the British Army – stationed out in India, in the days of the British Empire. Everybody in school knew who she was. Every Sunday they'd all walk to the local church down in Martyrs Heath. They'd see the boys from St Hilda's, and they'd all stare at her. But she wasn't interested in boys. Every week she noticed other women's husbands admiring her. Back in those days girls were meant to be modest and reserved, but not her. She loved the attention. One Sunday she let a man speak to her – he told her she was beautiful, and seeing her in church was the best part of his week. And as time went on, she grew closer to him; he brought her presents and wrote her love letters, which he passed to her in church. Before long, she was sneaking out of school to meet him in the evenings. She believed him when he told her he loved her, and he'd leave his wife and run away with her.

'In those days they didn't have the morning-after pill, or condoms or anything like that. So when she discovered she was pregnant with his baby she couldn't do anything about it. Obviously, there was no way she could let the teachers at St Mark's know, they'd expel her. And her family would disown her if they found out. So she hid it from everyone. No one noticed for months. Apparently she gave birth in one of the fifth-year dorms.'

'Errr . . .' I chipped in, horrified at the idea that anyone would give birth in a school dormitory.

'There was blood and yuck everywhere,' Suzy added, playing on my obvious disgust. 'Once the baby was born her secret was out.'

I hugged myself tightly, trying to keep warm, although I wasn't sure if it was the wind that was making me cold.

'What happened?' Seb asked. It was the first time I'd heard him speak. His voice sounded gentle, thoughtful. Like one of those people who only spoke when they really had something to say.

Suzy continued, 'Well she couldn't stay here at St Mark's. The teachers expelled her, threw her out as quickly as they could. Told her to leave and never come back. It was winter and freezing outside, and the girl ran through the wind to her lover's house with her screaming baby. It was cold, and rain beat down on her as she banged on his door. But he wouldn't even open it – he pretended to his wife he didn't know who she was. He left her out there in the cold, holding a wailing baby with nowhere to go. So there she was – newborn baby, no money, no home and no one who cared.

'So she came back here, to St Mark's – she was desperate. But they still wouldn't let her in. She lay down by the main entrance with her baby in her lap. She fell asleep there and never woke up. She froze to death.'

'The baby too?' I gasped.

Suzy nodded. 'And that's why she's known as the Blue Lady, because she was blue with cold when they found her. For the last two hundred years, she's haunted the school. Some people hear her baby's cries carried on the wind, others see her walking up and down the school corridors. Sometimes people look out of their windows at night and see her walking through the grounds. And sometimes people wake up in the night and see her standing at the end of their beds . . . staring straight at them.'

We were silent for a moment, each of us lost in our own thoughts. 'Well, we all know what you spent your summer doing, Suz,' James smirked at Suzy. 'Is that a new monologue you've been practising?'

Suzy shook her head and grabbed my arm, pulling me towards the shack door. 'You are such a jerk, James Martin!' She dragged me out of the shack and back into the woods. The light was fading and the branches around us shook in

31

the wind. I dared a glance back towards the little wooden hut. Seb was standing in the doorway like a statue, his ice-blue eyes following us as we slipped through the trees.

I fleetingly wondered when I would see him again.

'I don't believe in ghosts,' I turned and whispered to Suzy, feeling the hairs on the back of my neck prickle at the words.

'Neither did I,' Suzy said slowly, her grip on my arm tightening for a moment before she let go completely. 'Until I saw the Blue Lady with my own eyes . . .'

At that, Suzy let out a manic laugh and started to run through the woods, back towards the school. I ran after her. It was getting dark and I didn't want to be left alone.

'Where, when?' I called after her, as we burst out of the woods and into the sports fields.

'In second year,' she shouted back. 'But you don't believe in ghosts, remember!'

Suzy's laughter carried on the wind and I laughed along with her. Although, I wasn't sure if she was joking or not.

As we approached the school Suzy turned and stared at me. 'I didn't think they'd turn up.' I assumed this was some kind of apology for not telling me James and Seb would be there. 'The woods divide our school with St Hilda's. The shack is kind of a halfway point. James and I used to meet there last year when we . . .'

'And Seb?' I asked, trying my hardest not to sound like I cared. 'You know him too?'

'I only know Sebastian through James,' Suzy shrugged. She started to walk towards the school again. 'He helped design the stage set for *A Midsummer Night's Dream*, so

I got to know him a bit then. He doesn't ever say much. And he asks really weird questions all the time.'

'Like what?'

Suzy's green eyes narrowed as she smirked. 'Frankie! You don't fancy him, do you?'

My face flushed red and I stumbled over my words, 'Of course not. I don't even know him.'

'He's single,' Suzy winked.

I felt mortified, wanting desperately to change the subject. 'So what's the story with you and James then?'

Suzy gave me a knowing nod. Suzy was happiest when she was talking about herself.

I spent every moment I could with Suzy, those first few weeks at St Mark's. I don't remember ever trying to make friends with the other girls. I just wasn't interested. It was all about Suzy. Each morning I'd meet her for breakfast, and we'd talk about the day ahead and which lessons we were dreading. I ate every lunch and dinner with her too. She taught me everything I needed to know about St Marks and the world beyond it – nothing I could have learnt in a classroom. I knew all about the girls in Suzy's year, which ones had boyfriends and which ones Suzy hated, which seemed to be all of them.

She gradually drip-fed me information about James and Sebastian too. I hung on every word she said. I wanted to know everything, to be a part of her world.

James's dad was a banker, Suzy told me, and they lived in Hong Kong. He liked reading crime novels and watching action movies. 'I can't see what else he and Sebastian have in common besides a mutual love of Tarantino films,' Suzy said wisely. She told me James always kept a notepad and pen by the radio so he could write down the names of songs he liked.

'That's really cute,' I smiled.

'Don't be fooled,' Suzy tutted as we scraped our leftover food into the bin one lunchtime, 'just because he pays attention to music doesn't mean he's a decent person. I'm sure there are sea anemones with a stronger moral compass than James Martin.' I'd noticed that Suzy loved to call him by his full name. I could only guess that this was because it sounded more dramatic.

I wondered what Seb's last name was. But Seb wasn't the one Suzy wanted to speak about.

'James has been texting me again,' she admitted over breakfast one morning.

'Saying what?' I asked, reaching for her phone as she thrust it in my direction. '*Your green cardigan makes you look fit,*' I read aloud and rolled my eyes. 'Who said romance was dead?'

If the days were all about Suzy, then the evenings were all about the boys. Every day after school we'd run through the woods until we came to the secret shack – the midway marker between our school and the mysterious world of St Hilda's. James Martin and Seb soon became a regular feature of our evening escapades.

I'd been at school with boys all my life, but I'd never really made friends with them. Speaking to them was like learning a new language, and Suzy was my teacher. I noticed she dressed a certain way, said certain things, lit her cigarette seductively like they do in old movies and twirled her hair around her fingers in a way that she never did in the lunch hall. Suzy made no secret of fancying James. And he loved the attention.

'Couldn't stay away, could you, Suz,' James teased her as we arrived at the shack towards the end of the first week. He was already leant against the shack wall, cigarette in mouth. Seb was next to him, studying something on his phone. His eyes didn't even rise to greet us.

I tried to see James through Suzy's eyes – his flashy grins and cheesy compliments, and the way he ran his fingers through his hair when he thought she was looking. He was handsome, I suppose – that much was obvious. James was obvious. There was nothing mysterious or intriguing about him.

And Suzy was right; it was hard to see what James and Seb had in common. They couldn't have been more different from one another.

While James was easy to understand – he came to the woods to smoke, smile and flirt – Seb was an utter mystery to me. James was never short of a story to tell, or a joke to crack. But Seb was always so silent. I wished I knew what to say to him, how to start a conversation. More than anything I wanted a way to distract myself from Suzy and James. But something about Seb unnerved me, and made me feel so awkward.

He wasn't silent in the same way that I was. He didn't seem awkward or lost for words. He just always seemed so distracted by his own thoughts. And I had no idea what he was thinking. His blue eyes gave nothing away.

Seb didn't even seem that interested in speaking to James. I got the impression he'd be happy if no one ever spoke to him. But as Suzy and James busied themselves flirting for England I had no choice but to make conversation.

'Where do your parents live?' I asked Seb, nervously, one evening. He stared at me as though I were speaking Cantonese and then looked away.

'The South of France,' he replied, after what felt like an hour.

'Whereabouts?'

'It's a small town. You wouldn't have heard of it.'

'I've always wanted to go to the South of France,' I said, beginning to feel self-conscious about the fact he still wasn't even looking at me. 'The French Riviera especially – it seems so glamorous.'

He finally turned and looked at me, casting his eyes over my Converse trainers, drainpipe jeans and big woollen jumper, 'You don't seem like someone who cares about glamour.'

The ground could have swallowed me up right then and there. 'You don't seem like someone who cares about anything. I'd probably have more luck talking to a tree,' I spat back without thinking.

Seb smiled.

It was the first time I'd ever seen him smile. His blue eyes lit up and creased around the edges, small dimples appeared in his cheeks and he just looked gorgeous. And I had done that; I had made him smile. I found myself blushing and smiling back at him, feeling strangely pleased.

I thought, maybe, after that first smile, I had broken

down some kind of barrier around Seb. I hoped that the next time I saw him he would be warmer towards me. But Seb wasn't even there the next day. James came on his own. It was awful. I stood and watched Suzy giggle as James taught her how to blow smoke rings for a full ten minutes before I made some lame excuse to leave and head back towards school.

'Frankie, where do you think you're going?' Suzy caught up with me, annoyed, as I plodded up the cold stone staircase to my dorm. 'You just left me with James. You're meant to be my wing girl – you can't just skip out on me.'

'Sorry,' I mumbled in apology. I didn't want to upset her – she was the only friend I had.

'And you just left me to walk back through the woods on my own,' she scolded, looking slightly smug and wanting to press her point further. 'Anything could have happened to me – who knows what's lurking in there: serial killers, rapists, the Blue Lady herself.'

'Ghosts can't hurt you.' I rolled my eyes and smiled. 'Besides, there's no such thing as ghosts, remember?'

Suzy frowned. 'Just don't run off like that again.'

So the next day I dutifully went back to the woods with her, silently dreading the possibility that I would be the awkward third wheel again. But this time Seb was there too, much to my relief. As James leant in unnecessarily close to Suzy to light her cigarette, I plucked up the courage to speak to him.

'So, did you have some kind of after-school club last night?'

Seb looked at me as if I were crazy, and I suddenly realised that it looked as though I was.

'Are you keeping a log book?' he said. I tried to hide my embarrassment and pretend that I had been joking. 'No, no club, Frankie.' He shook his head and didn't elaborate. I frowned and wanted to press him further, but I just wasn't brave enough. I wondered what he'd been doing that was better than hanging out with us.

I found my thoughts wandering back to Seb more and more. During lessons I would imagine conversations with him. He'd ask me, with interest, about myself, and would listen, captivated, as I told him who I was. But those conversations remained in my daydreams and any dialogue we ever shared was strained and fraught.

Every evening our strange little foursome would talk about everything, and nothing at all.

'When's your birthday?' Suzy asked James playfully one Friday night.

'Eighteenth of September, why?' He blew smoke rings into the autumn dusk.

Suzy grinned and sucked on her cigarette, 'Just wondering what star sign you were.'

'All that stuff is rubbish, you know that, right, Suz?' James laughed.

'You would say that, you're a Virgo,' Suzy said, as if accusing him of a terrible crime. A smile split across his face and he lunged towards her. She skipped away from him, eyes shining with happiness. He caught up with her and clamped his arms around her, pulling her away towards a nearby bush. I heard the smack of a rough kiss and Suzy chuckle, 'James Martin, get off of me!' She stomped back towards me, feigning indignation, although her glee was clearly etched across her face.

'What star sign are you, Seb?' I asked quickly, feeling strangely embarrassed by James and Suzy. Seb's blue eyes shot up and met with mine.

'Scorpio,' he shrugged.

'I'm a Cancerian.'

'What's that supposed to mean?' Seb asked, his blue stare fixed on me.

'Like a crab,' I said, a little awkwardly. 'Hard on the outside, soft on the inside.'

Seb slouched comfortably into the shack wall as if he were a part of the ivy growing through the cracks. A flicker of what looked like amusement passed through his eyes, but he said nothing.

'I've always liked crab,' James said, overhearing and lifting his eyebrows. 'Baked slowly in white sauce and breadcrumbs!'

Suzy laughed, and then quickly changed the subject to something that James would find interesting.

'What do you think of Seb?' Suzy asked as we walked back to school one night.

I shrugged as I thought carefully about my answer. For some reason I didn't want Suzy to know how curious I was becoming about him. 'He's not exactly easy to get to know.'

Suzy considered this and nodded. 'Maybe we could set you up with one of James's other friends?' she suggested.

'I don't need setting up with anyone!' I said with horror.

'I think James and I are getting back together. You're my best friend, Frankie, I don't want you feeling left out and –'

'Trust me,' I laughed. 'I'm happy as I am.'

And I was. I was happy. The walls I'd spent years building up around myself were beginning to crumble, and it felt liberating. I was proud to be me. Being me didn't make me popular. I had Suzy, though, and right then she was all I needed. But just like leaves on the woodland trees, friendship can bloom and blossom and then be ripped apart by raging winds. And there was a terrible storm about to head our way.

# 4

The confirmation that I was the most unpopular girl in my year came when I was voted fourth-year fire marshal – a position that no one wanted. It became my duty to evaluate the dorms for possible fire hazards and tell Ms Thurlow if anyone was burning candles or incense in their rooms. Not that Ms Thurlow would have noticed a blazing fire tearing through the school. One night she left the door to her flat open, and when I walked past I saw her passed out on the couch next to an empty bottle of wine.

Suzy rolled her eyes when I told her that I'd been voted the fourth-year fire marshal. 'I wouldn't worry about it. I've been a fire marshal ever since I can remember.'

'It basically makes us the most unpopular girls in school,' I joked, pleased that we had yet another thing to bond over.

'Who cares?' she shrugged. 'I'd rather be hated for who I am than loved for who I'm not.'

Besides an ability to quote poetry at random, Suzy was also a fount of knowledge about everyone and everything at St Mark's. She delighted in telling me every last scrap of gossip she could think of. They say knowledge is power, and Suzy's knowledge of the school gave her great power over me, and she knew that. She loved that I was a clean slate that she could paint with any colour she desired.

'See that girl sitting on her own over there.' Suzy nodded towards a nearby table in the lunch hall one day. 'Don't be so obvious, Frankie!' She kicked me under the table as I turned around to stare.

There was a small girl with white-blonde hair sitting on her own and picking at a salad. I hadn't noticed her before, but I guessed she was a first year, she was so tiny.

'Her name's Sarah Niever. She's in third year,' Suzy said seriously.

'She doesn't look that old,' I commented.

'Her growth is seriously stunted,' Suzy snorted unkindly.

'Why?' I asked.

'They say grief can do funny things to you,' she said knowingly.

'Grief?'

'Her sister, Laura, was in fifth year when she jumped out of her dormitory window a few years ago.'

I frowned in confusion – this wasn't the usual harmless gossip that Suzy liked to share.

'She died?' I asked, feeling uncomfortable.

'Not straight away – she broke nearly every bone in her body and died three days later. No suicide note. Although, she *was* crazy. Said she kept seeing the Blue Lady . . .'

I shivered at the memory of Suzy describing the Blue Lady – her frozen body lying on the steps of the school. I turned around and stared once again at the small, frail-looking girl sitting alone. She was prodding a soggy tomato around her plate and swinging her feet below the table.

I don't make a habit of feeling sorry for people; I've always hated it if someone felt sorry for me. But I couldn't help pitying Sarah Niever – no one should have to live through something so horrible.

The knowledge that someone had killed themselves at the school was sickening, but strangely unsurprising. I briefly wondered if Laura Niever had been the first person to take her own life at St Mark's.

'Don't stare, Frankie!' Suzy kicked my feet again sharply.

'Right . . .' I mumbled, turning back towards her.

Suzy and I spent every day together. The days turned into weeks, and as the weeks passed they grew colder. Soon every tree in the school woodland had lost its leaves. The bare branches rattled and swayed with the winter wind, but that didn't stop us going there each day. The woods were more than just the backdrop for our evening meetings with the boys. They were our refuge from the everyday bore of boarding school – our sanctuary away from the real world. In a funny way it felt like James and Seb were a part of the woods themselves, and not of the world beyond. It was like they existed in between the trees just for us. I couldn't imagine them sitting in a classroom and queuing up in the lunch hall whenever we were away from them.

The evenings got so dark that James and Suzy's cigarette ends would glow like hot coals as they puffed away. 'Tomorrow's Saturday,' James pointed out one Friday night. 'We should all meet back here tomorrow and hang out – make a day of it. At least then I'll actually have daylight to look at you in.' He winked at Suzy. Even in the darkness I could see her grinning.

I wasn't thrilled at the prospect of an entire day making awkward conversation with Seb while Suzy and James smoked and flirted themselves into oblivion.

'What's that in your hands?' Suzy asked as we made our way to the woods on the Saturday morning.

'My sketchpad,' I replied. She frowned and rolled her eyes at me but didn't say anything else. I wished she understood that I needed some way to avoid Seb and his silence.

We arrived to find James and Seb walking through the trees towards the shack. Seb had a heavy, old-looking book in his hands. My heart sank a little at the sight of it – maybe he'd brought his book for the same reason I'd brought my sketchpad.

The four of us sat down in the shack and James produced his phone from his pocket. 'I thought we could listen to some music.'

'Oh God, James, must we really suffer your taste in music?' Suzy teased playfully.

Seb opened up his book and started reading, and I took that as my cue to open up a blank page in my sketchpad. I tried to ignore the sound of James and Suzy squabbling, but after a while I heard James say, 'Fancy going for a walk, Suz?' I looked up to see Suzy smile and twist her red hair between her fingers. She bit down on her lip and looked up through her eyelashes at him. I almost felt embarrassed at how brazen she was being.

Suzy didn't even look my way as she took James's hand

and left the shack. I watched them walk off into the bare-treed woods, hand-in-hand.

'Mind if I change the music?' Seb broke the silence, picking up James's phone.

'Sure.' I shrugged casually, as if I wasn't interested in what he might choose. Secretly I couldn't wait to find out what kinds of things he liked. He chose soft guitar music. I didn't recognise the voice which sang over the mournful chords. I liked it, and it seemed to fit well with the creaking shack walls and the soft moaning of the wind.

Silently, I looked back at my sketchpad. I absently drew lines onto the page as I listened to the melancholy music.

I kept stealing glances at Seb – he was engrossed in whatever he was reading. I longed to talk to him, to ask him about his book and the music he had chosen. But so far it had always been me trying to start a conversation with him – conversations that had gone nowhere. Why was he always so quiet? Why wouldn't he talk to me? Why did he make me feel like I was grovelling for his attention? Why bother sitting there with me if he didn't even want to talk?

One song bled into another and soon my angry thoughts ebbed away and my mind wandered back to the drawing taking shape in front of me. With my pencil I created a twisted woodland scene, branches entwining and mosses and flowers scrambling over each other. I don't know how long I sat there drawing for – minutes, hours. I'd almost forgotten that Seb was there. I'd gone from feeling so self-conscious in his company to being weirdly at ease. As I drew more knotted vines onto the page I became aware of his eyes boring into me.

Taking a deep breath, I raised my eyes to meet his. He blinked quickly, as though I'd somehow caught him out, as though he didn't want me to see him staring. I bravely stared back at him until he allowed himself a smile.

'What are you drawing?' he asked simply.

'Just the woods,' I shrugged.

'You're really talented,' he mumbled, looking back down at his book and ignoring me once again.

My face burned up and I muttered, 'Thanks,' under my breath before returning to my sketch. I hated that he had me so lost for words.

'Frankie, we're going,' Suzy announced, poking her head into the shack. Her lips were very pink and she had bits of leaves and twig in her hair. Casting a furtive glance at Seb, I closed my sketchpad and got to my feet. James walked into the shack with a smug look on his face. 'Until next time, James Martin,' Suzy smiled.

I glanced over at Seb by means of goodbye and caught him staring at me intently. I frowned at him and silently followed Suzy into the woods. As I walked away from the shack, and from Seb, I eagerly wondered when the 'next time' in the woods would be.

But we were soon to discover that the school woods were about to vanish from our lives forever.

In assembly on the Monday morning, Ms West's speech took on a particularly serious tone, 'After several years of school fundraising and some exceptionally generous donations from parents . . .' Saskia was sitting in the row in front of me. Her back straightened and she looked around smugly.

'. . . Building work is finally getting underway for our new sports hall, which we will of course share with the pupils of St Hilda's, who have also been raising funds these last few years.'

Excited whispers and squeals erupted throughout the school hall.

'Girls, quiet please.' Ms West didn't need to shout; she was one of those people who had a natural, cold authority. 'From now until further notice, the woodland beyond the sports fields will be out of bounds for all pupils while work on the new hall gets under way. Under no circumstances must anyone trespass into the area that is currently woodland. It will soon be a building site and unsafe for wandering around.'

So that was it – no petition, no votes, no warning. The woods were about to be ripped down forever.

'I have a plan!' I said enthusiastically as I met Suzy at lunch. 'We'll start a protest campaign. I'll design the posters, draw them up in charcoal so they look more dramatic. We could get the boys involved.' My heart lifted at the thought of an excuse to speak to Seb. This was something we could share. 'Seb and James can lead the protests from their side of the woods. And how about we call up a local radio station and . . .'

Suzy blinked slowly and I noticed she'd painted her eyelids a shocking shade of purple. 'This is my protest,' she explained. 'Homage to all flowers, and the trees and all the animals that live in the woods.'

'Susanne Baker!' Ms Thurlow swayed up to us. 'You're to go back upstairs and take that hideous make-up off now.'

I could smell gin on her breath; I'd recognise the smell anywhere. One of Mum's ex-boyfriends liked to drink gin before lunchtime, too.

'It's a protest,' I said proudly.

'I'm wearing violet make-up in honour of the hundreds of violets that are going to be savagely mowed down to make way for the new sports centre,' Suzy added.

Ms Thurlow rolled her eyes and I noticed that other girls were staring and laughing at us. 'Do as you're told, Susanne. Otherwise you'll come and see me at four o'clock for detention.'

I was expecting Suzy to argue back but she stayed quiet. 'No way I'm giving up my free time so Thurlow can make me sweep out the Latin classrooms,' she muttered to me. 'Stay here? I'll be right back. Don't go anywhere – there's something I need to talk to you about when I get back.'

'I'll have a think about a campaign logo,' I shouted after her.

There was a loud snort from behind me and I spun around to see Saskia and Claire smirking.

'Freak,' Saskia said flatly.

'Been shopping recently, Saskia?' I said quickly. 'I heard they're selling lives on Oxford Street – maybe you should go buy one and stay out of other people's.'

I stormed away from them and sat on my own in the dining room, waiting for Suzy to reappear. Desperate to ignore the sniggering coming from Saskia's table, I took out my sketchbook and started to doodle ideas for a campaign logo.

Only a few pencil strokes in, a loud voice rung in my ear.

'Frankie Ward?'

I looked up, surprised that someone other than Suzy was calling me Frankie, and not Francesca.

'I'm Ms Barts,' smiled a frizzy-haired woman that I'd somehow never noticed before. 'I'm the fifth-year house-mistress.' Her lips looked too big for her face, like some kind of beak. She reminded me a cartoon platypus – a caricaturist's dream. I tried not to snigger at the thought.

'Er, hi,' I said, letting my pencil drop. Apart from her large mouth, Ms Barts was one of those people that could blend into grey wallpaper. She looked younger than most of the other teachers at St Mark's. She must have been in her late twenties, even though she dressed much older – ugly flat shoes, grey tights and a shapeless dress that didn't seem to be any colour at all.

'I see you're already friends with Suzy,' she said with a quiet lisp, once again drawing attention to her overlarge mouth.

'Yeah,' I nodded, trying not to stare at her rudely.

Ms Barts smiled. 'Us military gals should stick together!'

I stared blankly at her.

'I was an army brat too in my day,' she explained hastily. 'I'm a St Mark's old girl – I was here in the 80s when my father was stationed out in Russia. Of course there were more of us then, military gals, I mean . . .'

'Yeah,' I muttered, glancing at the sea of glossy hair and manicured hands around me. Saskia watched me, nudging

Claire and whispering something in her ear. 'Too many freaks and not enough circuses,' I muttered quietly.

'Pardon?' Ms Barts asked.

'Nothing.'

'Did Ms Thurlow make Suzy take off her make-up?' Ms Barts asked, looking around.

'We're protesting about the woods being cut down,' I said proudly.

'Vive la révolution!' Ms Barts smiled, her eyes bulging slightly as she spoke. 'Don't listen to Thurlow, that woman's as mad as a hatter!' She caught the smile that flashed across my face and quickly smiled back. 'Anyway, I just thought I'd come and say hi. If you need anything, at any time, don't hesitate to bother me. My flat's just upstairs. I like to think I'm more approachable than most of the other teachers here,' she smiled.

I smiled back, trusting her instantly.

'Anyway, toodle-oo!' She waved, heading off. I watched as she walked away. It seemed strange that I'd never noticed Ms Barts before. I'd been in the school for several weeks by that point. Despite her dull appearance there was something about her that didn't fit in, something that was slightly off key.

I returned to my sketchpad and drew for some time, allowing lines and shapes to sculpt themselves into campaign logos.

'I've been thinking,' Suzy's voice interrupted me, mid pencil stroke. I looked up and saw that her face was red from where she'd scrubbed at her make-up.

'About the protest?' I swung my sketchbook around. 'I've started to design a campaign logo . . .'

'No. I've been thinking . . .' she lowered her voice and looked me in the eye, 'about ghosts.'

'You've been thinking about ghosts? What? Why?' I asked, confused.

Suzy turned my sketchbook around and studied my doodles briefly. 'We're reading *Wuthering Heights* in English,' she said, by means of explanation.

I cast her a blank look while she closed my sketchbook and pushed it back across the table towards me.

'God, Frankie, you know nothing about the Classics, do you?'

I shrugged, making a mental note to read *Wuthering Heights*.

'*Wuthering Heights* is amazing,' she said, sounding animated. 'It's a tragic, beautiful love story – it's also a ghost story.'

That's when I noticed she was holding something in her other hand. A book.

'Check this out.' She pushed the book into my hands. 'Turns out this school copy of *Wuthering Heights* was used before me by Laura Niever. The girl who threw herself out of a window and died. Remember?'

I nodded grimly. 'You've been thinking about Laura Niever?'

'Look what she wrote in this book.' Suzy carefully turned the pages until she reached a chapter called 'A Ghost at the Window'. There were five words scrawled manically onto the side of the page. They looked almost like the scribbles of a child, or the etchings of a madman. But they clearly spelt out a sentence:

# THE BLUE LADY IS COMING

'Everyone says that Laura Niever was crazy. That she was obsessed with the Blue Lady. But when we were talking about ghosts in class, it made me think . . . maybe Laura Niever was being haunted by her . . . by the Blue Lady.'

I shook my head, annoyed. Suzy hadn't mentioned the Blue Lady since she'd told me about Sarah Niever's sister killing herself, and I wasn't keen to start talking about that again.

Suzy picked up my glass, took a long sip of water and then looked me straight in the eye. 'I think we should try to investigate.'

'What, the Blue Lady? How? Try to sneak a peek at school records or something?' I suggested, dreading the idea of breaking into the school office and snooping around.

'No, like investigate ghosts!' she grinned.

'You don't actually believe in ghosts?'

'Of course I do! If she really does haunt the school, maybe there's a reason she's haunting it, maybe we can help her . . . you know . . . move on.'

'And how exactly are we meant to help a ghost "move on"?' I used my fingers to draw quotation marks in the air.

'Ouija board,' Suzy said with a sparkle in her eye. 'My cousin showed me how to make one last Christmas.'

'What's a Ouija board?' I asked, clueless once again.

'It's a way to contact spirits, and it's guaranteed to work. Meet me after school this evening.'

'Today?' I asked, disappointed to be missing out on our trip to the woods.

'Why not?' Suzy said, her green eyes glinting at me. 'It'll do the boys some good to miss us for once. Besides, you're not scared are you?'

'No, of course not. Ghosts aren't real.'

'We'll see,' Suzy said knowingly.

# 5

Secretly, I wished Suzy had given up on the idea of doing a Ouija board after school. I didn't like the thought of the boys waiting for us in the dim, damp shack. I wondered how long they'd stand there before they knew we weren't coming. They must have heard about the plans for the new sports hall – maybe like us they wanted to find a way to stop it. Maybe this would be my chance to finally find a way to say something meaningful to Seb.

But Suzy was waiting for me outside Gibson Dorm after dinner.

Gibson was an unused dormitory on the top floor of the school. I'd never been in there before but I'd heard Claire describe it as 'spooky' once.

As I walked up to Suzy I noticed she was shifting her weight from one foot to the other, her fingers trembling as they clutched a folded piece of paper. In those first few weeks of knowing Suzy, the only times I'd ever seen her nervous were when we were in the shack. I was used to her anxious glances at James, chewing the inside of her mouth as she waited for him to answer when she spoke. But I'd never before seen Suzy nervous in school. If Suzy were a queen then school was her kingdom, and nothing and no one here had ever made her anxious, until now.

'Did you bring a pen, like I asked?' she said. I nodded and held up one of my drawing pencils that had been new at the beginning of term.

'That's a pencil, not a pen,' Suzy pointed out, annoyed. 'I guess it'll have to do.'

Suzy pushed open the oak door and reached her hand inside the dorm to feel for a light switch. Bright fluorescent white light flickered inside the room as Suzy pushed the door wider.

The dorm was empty apart from a few old lockers, all of which had broken doors and battered sides. 'What's this place used for?' I whispered, unsure of why I felt the need to keep my voice down when we were completely alone.

'Nothing,' Suzy replied. 'Typical St Mark's – leaves huge rooms like Gibson unused while they bulldoze down the woodland to make way for new buildings.'

Claire was right, Gibson did feel spooky. The old strip lights flickered and strobed, and our voices echoed off the high ceilings as we tried to whisper. Gibson didn't look like my fourth-year dorm – there were no horsebox-like rooms. Instead there were plain walls with chipped paint and scuffed skirting boards. I could see why Suzy had chosen Gibson in which to do a Ouija board. Not only was it completely deserted but it was by far the creepiest room in St Mark's.

Suzy walked to the end of the dorm, and looked around uneasily. She sat down awkwardly, settling her back against the wall and gesturing for me to sit down opposite her.

As I sat down, Suzy laid the paper she'd been carrying

flat on the floor. I handed her the pencil and watched in silence as she wrote the letters of the alphabet anticlockwise around the paper. In the middle of the letters she drew two small boxes. In one box she wrote the word YES and in the other she wrote NO.

I crossed my legs and got comfortable as Suzy pulled a coin out of her pocket and placed it between the two boxes, in the middle of the paper. It felt like watching someone prepare an important ritual. It reminded me of going to church with Nan as a child, and how I'd watch as the vicar lay things for communion and mutter sacred words.

Suzy lifted her hands away from the board slowly, and anxiously nodded her head in approval. 'This is what a Ouija board looks like,' she informed me. Her nervousness began to melt away as she spoke and the Suzy I knew sparkled beneath her green eyes. 'Ouija boards are used to contact spirits of the dead, spirits that are stuck on Earth and doomed to walk among the living.'

'Are you sure you know what you're doing?' I asked. The Ouija board looked so makeshift – it was just a scrap of paper with letters written on it in pencil. Hardly something powerful enough to channel the spirit world – if there even was such a thing.

'I told you,' she replied, sounding annoyed that I'd question her authority on the subject. 'My cousin showed me how to do this. Here, take my hands.'

I reached out and took her hands in mine, and we stretched our arms out and held them above the newly made Ouija board.

There was a moment of quiet, where the hum of the

lights and the whistle of the wind outside seemed to thump at my eardrums and make me nervous. I caught Suzy's eye and something about the look she gave me told me that she felt it too.

Suzy broke the silence. 'First we need to call the spirits.'

'How?' I asked.

'We close our eyes and say "Spirits come to us" three times.'

I tried not to snigger at how ludicrous it all sounded – as if summoning the spirits of the underworld was as easy as muttering a few words. 'And then what?' I asked playfully, widening my eyes and smirking.

Suzy chewed on her lip and looked down at the Ouija board she'd just drawn. 'And then we each place a finger on the coin and ask the spirits questions. If it works, then the coin will move.'

Suzy drew in a deep breath and seemed to steady her thoughts silently. Then her eyes locked into mine and gave me that mischievous glint that I'd come to know so well, 'Ready?' she asked. I nodded. 'Close your eyes.'

I closed my eyes and squeezed Suzy's hands in mine.

We both chanted at the same time, 'Spirits come to us. Spirits come to us. Spirits come to us.'

I prised open one eye and Suzy did the same. We opened our eyes fully and looked at each other.

Something had changed. The world around us seemed so silent – the kind of silence that burns your ears. I watched Suzy, waiting for her to speak, but she stayed quiet and just stared into my eyes. I was suddenly aware of my heart beating, thumping furiously inside my chest as if I'd just run for hours.

Then Suzy gave me a huge smile and winked her green eyes at me, and I felt stupid for feeling so strange. She let go of my hands and wiped her sweaty palms on her ripped jeans. She placed her right index finger onto the coin on the paper. I did the same.

'Is there any one there?' Suzy asked. Her voice was trembling slightly, and I wondered if she felt like I did: short of breath and thinking that maybe this wasn't such a good idea, after all.

The coin didn't move. It stayed completely still.

'Is there anyone there?' Suzy asked again. Her voice was louder, and less shaky.

Still nothing.

I felt the sudden urge to stand up and run away. 'Suzy, maybe we should –'

The coin moved beneath my fingertips. My heart leapt in my chest and I lowered my eyes and watched the small coin drag towards the box that said YES.

I looked up at Suzy. 'You moved it!' I accused her.

'No I didn't,' she said, her voice sounding shaky again. 'I told you this worked.'

Suzy pulled back her shoulders and drew in another deep breath. I could see her getting lost in her game, playing along with the drama of it all. I was sure it was her that moved the coin – she was doing this as some kind of elaborate show. Life was just one big stage to Suzy.

'Are you the Blue Lady?' Suzy asked the Ouija board.

The coin moved again, only this time it pulled towards the box that said NO.

A flush of disappointment swept over Suzy's face. 'That's

not her name though, is it?' I pointed out. 'Maybe she doesn't know we call her the Blue Lady?' The words coming from my mouth sounded so bizarre, it was as if I were already beginning to believe that there was someone waiting beyond the board, waiting to get through.

'You're right,' Suzy muttered to me. 'Are you the spirit of the girl we call the Blue Lady?' she asked confidently.

The coin didn't move. It stayed where it was, on the word NO.

A small chuckle rose in my throat. 'Look, this is stupid –'

The coin shifted again, and we both gave each other a nervous nod before looking down at the board to eagerly follow its movements.

This time it didn't move towards one of the boxes, it moved towards the letter T. It stayed there for a while before moving again, this time to the letter R. Then it moved again, and again, spelling out a word as it went . . . T-R-A-P-P-E-D.

As soon as the coin arrived on the D Suzy flung her hand in the air. 'You moved it!' she shouted at me. 'Frankie, that's not funny!'

'I didn't!' I shouted back.

Suzy bolted to her feet. Her sudden movement made my flesh jump from my bones and I leapt to my feet as well. It felt like all the blood in my body had rushed to my head and the world seemed hazy as I watched Suzy pick up the coin and walk towards the nearest window. Lifting up the heavy sash, she tossed the coin out as hard as she could.

'Destroy the board,' she instructed, panic clear in her voice.

'We could burn it?' I suggested.

'You're a fire marshal, Frankie, don't be stupid,' Suzy said in a poisonous tone. Panicking, she started to rip the piece of paper into small pieces. 'We'll flush it down the toilet.'

I followed Suzy out of Gibson Dorm. Relief flooded through me as the door to the old dorm slammed behind us, and I swore to myself that I'd never go back there ever again. We hurried down the corridor to the nearest toilets. I didn't take my eyes off Suzy, waiting for her to break the spell and say something witty and light-hearted. But she didn't say a word.

'I'll see you at breakfast tomorrow,' Suzy said as the last piece of ripped-up Ouija board flushed down the toilet bowl. She walked off without so much as a glance in my direction. I watched her go, feeling utterly confused. I hadn't moved the coin.

I walked down the stairs to the fourth-year dorm alone. At that moment, the corridors of St Mark's were an alien place. The stairwell banisters seemed ice cold as I ran my hands over them, and my footsteps made chilling, haunting plods as I shuffled down the stairs. I couldn't bear the thought of being alone.

I felt so stupid. I didn't want to believe it had worked. There was no such thing as ghosts.

That night, after lights out, as everyone else in my dorm crept into each other's rooms to share their secrets, I lay in bed thinking about what I could do to make everything seem normal again. Suzy was so angry with me, and I couldn't understand why. It was the first time I'd ever seen her mood change so suddenly, as if a thunderous storm cloud had descended around her.

I lay in bed wondering how difficult it would be to break into the school office and look through the old school records. Maybe that way we could really find out the truth about the Blue Lady, and not bother wasting time with Ouija boards. And then I remembered that the Ouija board coin had moved to NO when Suzy asked it if we had contacted the Blue Lady.

As these thoughts filled my mind I became aware of an unusual smell flooding my room. The smell of flowers. It reminded me of the school woods the first time Suzy had taken me there. The smell was so strong it almost burnt my nose. It smelt like freshly cut flowers, wet grass and tree bark. The sudden scent in my room was so bizarre, I bolted upright in bed. I had no idea where it had come from – the window was shut and no one inside the dorm was spraying perfume. But then the strange smell started to change. It no longer smelt fresh and clean and floral, but musky, old and rotten. It smelt like the time a mouse had crawled into our garage at home and died. My room stank of death. But before I took another breath, the pungent smell disappeared – vanishing as quickly as it had appeared.

I sank back into bed, feeling my heart race inside my chest. There was a sense of rising panic creeping through my veins, across my skin, like someone was trying to squeeze the air out of me. I closed my eyes and worked to steady my breathing. I couldn't bring myself to open my eyes again. I kept them scrunched closed and pulled my bed covers tight over my head, as if they could somehow offer me protection.

I lay restless for hours, longing for sleep to come and snatch me away. I tried desperately to shift that awful feeling. But all I could think about was that strange smell, and what it might have meant, and what Suzy and I had awoken that night in the Gibson Dorm.

# 6

The next morning I waited for Suzy outside the dining hall. I stood across from the entrance and watched as first-year girls funnelled and yawned their way into breakfast. They looked so tiny. I struggled to remember ever being so small.

I was so deep in thought I almost missed Suzy walking past me.

'Hey, Suzy,' I called after her. She kept walking without looking back.

I lunged forwards and pulled on the back of her blue school blazer. 'Suzy.'

'What?' She jolted. I flinched with surprise as she turned around. Suzy's usually crystal-green eyes were red and sore, as if she hadn't slept all night. Her tangled hair lay matted in un-brushed clumps on the side of her head, and her skin looked pale and clammy.

'Err, I think the grunge look kind of died out in the 90s, Suzy?' I laughed, pointing at her hair.

'This isn't a joke, Frankie,' she replied curtly. Her eyes darted about the dining hall nervously, and she lowered her voice. 'I know it was you. If you're trying to freak me out it won't work.'

'What?' I mumbled.

'Just stay away from me, OK?' She spat each word like poisonous darts.

'Fine!' I retaliated, shocked. I felt all the blood in my body rush to my face and my cheeks begin to burn as Suzy stormed away. She charged purposefully towards the coffee, poured herself a mug and then took it over to a table full of fifth-year girls. She sat down at the only empty seat and barged her way into the conversation.

There was a sniggering noise and I looked around to see Saskia and Claire laughing at me as my only friend walked away. 'Aw, don't worry, Frankie,' Saskia said loud enough for everyone to hear. 'If you need another friend you can always get a dog.'

'If I had a lower IQ I might even enjoy your company, Saskia,' I hissed back, trying to hide my embarrassment.

Glancing around, I quickly spotted an empty seat on a table with other girls from Raleigh. I headed over, casting an anxious glance towards Suzy. She was throwing her head back and laughing wildly at something the girl next to her had said. As I came towards the empty seat, Saskia bumped me out of the way. She mouthed a patronising *Sorry* in my direction before sitting down, leaving nowhere for me to sit.

It felt like all eyes were on me. Everyone could see that without Suzy I had no one.

Resolve kicked in. I tilted my head high, shrugged my shoulders, muttered 'Whatever,' and walked away. I hoped that no one could see how much I was shaking inside. Walking out of the school dining room, I felt my chest begin to tighten in panic. I should have known that everything had felt too good to be true. Life had never stayed the same for long before – why should St Mark's be any different?

I couldn't give up on Suzy so easily. Suddenly, life without her seemed so bleak. There was no way she could be mad at me over the stupid incident with the Ouija board. There had to be a way to convince her that it wasn't me that moved the coin.

The workmen arrived at school that morning. There were scores of them, each wearing bright orange jackets and cement-stained jeans. They hauled in vehicles and dangerous-looking machines, which clanked and rattled outside the classroom windows. Of course no one could concentrate on lessons, and Mr Desmond struggled in vain to make us learn about ions and electrons in Chemistry. All anyone wanted to do was stare out the window and watch as the workman circus wheeled in.

After half an hour of futile lecturing, Mr Desmond made the mistake of leaving the classroom for a moment, which meant that the room erupted into excited squeals about the workmen.

'Did you see the guy with the blond hair?' asked Claire to anyone who'd listen. 'He was gorgeous!'

'Honestly,' Saskia snorted as she scrolled through her mobile phone, looking bored. 'Stick a pig in a fluorescent jacket and you'd probably want to snog it. You're so desperate, Claire. You need a proper man!'

'He had buff arms,' Claire defended herself as Saskia started texting. I was lost as to why anyone was friends with Saskia. Besides her parents' money I couldn't see what else she had going for her.

'I guess they must be cutting down the woods on the St Hilda's side as well?' mused George, rising from her seat and peering thoughtfully through the window. 'I heard they planned to chop down every tree between here and there before they started to dig the foundations.'

I looked out on the trees that swayed happily in the autumn sun, oblivious to the fate that awaited them. I wistfully wondered what Seb would think about them being chopped down.

By lunchtime the school woodland had been cordoned off. The workmen put a fence made of bright yellow plastic around the outskirts of the woods so no one could get in. As I walked to lunch on my own I realised that Suzy and I hadn't done anything special to mark the last time we'd ever be able to go into the woods after school. It was too late now. I wish we'd scratched our names into a tree trunk, or picked a bunch of woodland flowers to press and keep forever. And we'd missed our last ever chance to meet with James and Seb in the shack. Instead we'd spent the previous evening playing with the stupid home-made Ouija board.

Suzy was nowhere to be seen at lunchtime. And after school I didn't even bother looking for her. I'd got the hint by then. Instead I headed straight up to my dorm.

There was a note stuck to my door with a blob of chewing gum.

*If you want to make it up to me then meet me in the woods after school. Bring something that means a lot to you.*
*Suzy*

I mulled over the note as I entered my room. As I looked up, something out of my horsebox window caught my eye. There was a person crossing the school car park with purposeful strides. I walked closer to the window and stared out. It was Suzy.

I pressed my face up against the window and chewed the inside of my mouth as I watched her march across the car park in the cold. She was heading towards the sports fields, and the woods beyond them.

She wanted me to join her.

My pride wanted me to rip up the note and let Suzy freeze outside in the woods waiting for me. But I hated not speaking to her, and I needed to make everything OK. Looking around, I grabbed the charcoal sketch I'd done of Mum from my wall before throwing on my coat and running outside.

'Suzy!' I called into the wind, chasing across the school sports fields.

Suzy looked around and stared straight at me. She was shaking violently, her teeth chattering and her eyes flaming with fear.

I ran towards her, relieved that she'd at least acknowledged me. 'What are you doing out here with no coat?' I shouted. 'It's freezing.' She was still wearing her school uniform. Her shirt hung loose from her skirt and she had some kind of ketchup stain on her jumper. I'd never once seen her wear her uniform to the woods before – she always jumped at the chance to show off her rainbow wardrobe.

'I wanted to be here when they started tearing this place down.'

I could barely hear Suzy through the howl of the wind. A single tear trickled down her pale face, a windswept salty ribbon glistening in the sinking sunlight.

'This isn't right, Frankie.' She swept her hand wildly towards the diggers. 'We have to do something. Did you bring something to burn?' She narrowed her eyes with purpose.

'Burn?' I echoed. I wrapped my hands around my chest and hugged myself tightly, hiding the sketch of Mum from Suzy's view. There was no way I wanted to set that alight.

'We need to make offerings to the Earth Goddess,' Suzy said flatly, as if it were obvious.

I felt a jolt of annoyance grip my gut and my teeth clenched together. First Ouija boards and now the 'Earth Goddess'. Suzy's constant dramatics were wearing thin. Her mood swings, like everything else in her life, seemed volatile and theatrical, and just an excuse for attention.

'You owe me big time, Frankie,' Suzy added angrily, sensing my lack of commitment to her latest crazy scheme. Without explaining what I might owe her for, she stormed towards the woods and clambered over one of the barriers.

'You can't come through here, love,' shouted a fat man in a neon safety jacket. Suzy ignored him, running into the woods. 'We're firing up the diggers in ten. I can't have you here then,' he shouted after her.

I cast the man an apologetic smile as he shook his head at me. My feet sped over the woodland floor, thrashing through the fallen leaves. Suzy ran ahead, slipping between the trees, like a terrified fox running desperately from a hound. I chased after her as fast as my legs would take me.

'Suzy!' I shouted.

'Frankie!' I heard my name. 'Frankie, wait!'

My name carried on the wind like a song. It wasn't Suzy's voice. The sound was coming from behind me. It sounded like a boy. Like Seb.

My heart froze.

I spun around, catching my breath. Seb burst through the trees and stopped in front of me, his cheeks burning pink from running. He wasn't wearing his school blazer and his creased white shirt flapped in the wind. I fought the urge to run away. Being alone with him made me feel slightly sick with tension.

'Suzy's gone to the shack,' I managed to say, edging away. 'Tell James he'll find her there.'

'James isn't here.' Seb stepped closer to me, seeming agitated. 'He isn't coming. Where were you yesterday?'

I didn't answer him. His blue eyes locked into mine, flooding me with familiar unease. My gaze darted nervously over his flushed face, the smatter of freckles on his nose, the hole in his ear where he must have worn an earring over the summer, the untamed curls in his hair.

He moved towards me and I instinctively stepped back. My pulse raced as the air between us crackled with anticipation. 'Can I?' he asked. Before I knew what he wanted, he reached forwards and gently pulled the drawing I was holding from my hands. He studied it. 'This is great,' he muttered. 'You did this?' He looked at me and I gave him the slightest of nods. 'Really dark, interesting. She looks like you . . .'

I snatched the drawing back from him, suddenly feeling embarrassed and exposed. 'I need to get to Suzy.'

'Wait.' He gestured for me to stay. I cast a desperate glance in the direction of the shack. I'd spent hours imagining this kind of conversation with Seb, but now that it was happening, I wanted nothing more than to run away.

'Once the woods are gone we won't be able to meet here.' Seb spoke so gently I could barely hear him.

'So?' I challenged.

'So I need someone I can trust. From St Mark's. I need . . .'

'Trust?' I flinched as I repeated his word. Trust with what? A secret? His life? His heart?

Seb wanted my trust, and I knew instinctively that I would give it to him. I wanted to hate myself for that – for giving a part of me, my trust, away so easily. There was no guarantee I would get anything in return.

'I don't even know you,' was all I could think to say. 'You don't know me. We don't know anything about each other. I don't even know your last name.'

'Cotez,' he said gravely, as if it should mean something.

'Ward,' I responded quickly. 'Frankie Ward.'

Seb nodded seriously. He brought his hand up to sweep hair from his forehead, revealing half a dozen bright cords and bands tied around his wrist.

'OK,' he mumbled. 'You need to go. I'll speak to you

soon.' And then he turned and ran, leaving me empty as I watched him slip away. I shivered in the cold air, clutching my drawing until my fingers were numb. I had no idea what had just happened, or what he wanted from me. I picked up my feet and sped through the woods, my heart thumping in my chest and my head aching with confusion.

# 7

Suzy was waiting for me alone at the shack.

She'd collected a pile of twigs and leaves, assembling them into some kind of bonfire in the middle of the floor. 'This will only take five minutes,' she said gruffly, without even questioning why it had taken me so long to join her. 'Give me that drawing, Frankie.'

'What drawing?' I pretended.

'The picture you brought with you,' she glared at me. 'Hand it over.'

'Suzy, I really don't want you setting fire –'

'Frankie, the woods as we know them are about to be taken from us.' Suzy flung her arms into the air dramatically and opened her eyes as wide as she could. 'The trees, the plants, the animals that call this place home – all gone forever! We can't let this happen without offering something up to the Earth Goddess. Besides . . .' Suzy lowered her voice, unsure of herself, 'we need her protection.'

'I've never heard you talk about any Earth Goddess before,' I said flatly. 'What next, Suzy? Fairies, Easter bunnies and goblins?'

'Do you want to be my friend or not, Frankie?' Suzy challenged me.

'Of course, but –'

'So hand over the picture and stop being such a bitch. We don't have a lot of time.'

I reluctantly handed over the picture of Mum, silently apologising in my head for what we were about to do. 'Why do we have to burn a picture of *my* mum?'

'I brought this.' Suzy pulled a badly drawn sketch of a woman in a long gown out of her coat pocket. 'It's the design for my Oscar dress. It's the most precious thing I have.'

'Then why burn it?' I asked, watching as Suzy put her sketch next to Mum's picture on the shack floor.

'Don't you know anything about sacrifice, Frankie?' Suzy muttered, sitting down on the floor and taking a cigarette lighter from her pocket. 'A sacrifice is worth nothing unless it's something you care about. It would be an insult to the Earth Goddess if we sacrificed our Chemistry textbooks.'

I sat down opposite Suzy. 'I'm sure she'd still appreciate the gesture . . .'

Once again I found myself in one of Suzy's twisted games. Like the Ouija board, we sat and faced each other holding hands, only this time we had the two pictures between us instead of the board.

'Close your eyes,' she instructed.

I was vaguely aware of the sound of workmen in the distance, laughing and hauling around machinery. But drowning out the workmen was the sound of the wind. It howled through the trees, rushing urgently between the branches as though it knew it would be for the last time. The smell of earth and leaves crept up my nose and I suddenly felt so sad. The woods seemed so alive at that moment. I could feel the pulse of the trees thudding through the shack floor and the breath of every living creature whisper in my ear. Suzy was right, destroying the woods was a tragedy, and there was nothing we could do to stop it.

'Earth Goddess, hear our prayer,' Suzy called into the moaning wind. 'We come to make a sacrifice to you, to acknowledge the sacrifice you are giving us. We thank you for the trees and the creatures of this wood, and pray for their souls once they are gone.'

I prised my eyes open and felt annoyed at the expression painted on Suzy's face. Her stupid incantations seemed to dumb down the tragedy. She let go of my hands and sparked up her cigarette lighter.

She held the flame to the pictures but they wouldn't set alight. 'Stupid wind,' she mumbled. 'Frankie, go and close the shack door.'

Rolling my eyes, I stood up and walked towards the rickety old door. I reached outside for the rusted handle.

Something in the woods caught my eye. My heart leapt into my throat unexpectedly, and I felt myself gasp for air.

There was someone running between the trees. It wasn't James, or Seb, or one of the workmen, or anyone I recognised from school.

It was a slight figure, slim and delicate. Darting between branches and running desperately from something. Running for her life.

It was a girl.

Long, dark hair swayed behind her as if she were underwater. As if she belonged to another world.

The image was gone in a flash, but still lingered haunt-ingly. As if whoever she was somehow stood outside of time.

The wind blew at me, shaking my bones. I was aware of someone shouting at me but all I could really hear was the sound of the woods. The way the fallen leaves rustled on the ground, the creaking of the shack door on its hinges, the strain of the branches billowing in the gale like an eerie symphony. The woods' final concerto before they disappeared forever.

'Frankie!' someone shouted. 'Frankie, shut the door.' I felt Suzy's hand reach over me and grab the door handle. I flinched as her skin brushed against mine. 'What is wrong with you? You've been standing here like a lemon.'

'I thought I saw –'

Before I could finish I was cut off by the sound of Suzy screaming. She rushed back into the shed and started to stamp wildly on a small fire that was raging on the floor.

'It must have caught fire without me noticing,' Suzy panicked as the last lick of flames were stamped out. 'The Goddess came for the sacrifice, after all . . .'

'Suzy!' I bent down and studied the ashes of the fire, nausea creeping up in me.

Suzy let out a terrified whimper.

There was a word charred into the shack floor. Four letters, as clear as a heading in a textbook:

NEXT

Suzy pulled on my shoulders, dragging me backwards. I scrambled to my feet and threw myself at the shack door.

We didn't stop to pick up the remains of our pictures. The Earth Goddess was welcome to them.

My feet didn't stop moving until we broke out of the woods, nearly tripping over the workmen as we entered the safety of the sports fields.

'What was that?' My voice trembled so badly I sounded like I was singing.

'Nothing,' Suzy whispered in denial. 'Nothing.' She turned to look at me, her eyes burning fierce with defiance. 'Smoke and mirrors, Frankie . . .' I shook my head, wanting an explanation. She tried to smile at me, but couldn't. Resilience hardened her face. 'There's no such thing as ghosts . . .'

I couldn't hear any more; she was drowned out by the sound of a digger revving up at the edge of the wood. Confusion pulsed through me as I tried to make sense of what we'd seen. I wanted to run back to the shack, to get another look at the letters burnt into the floor. I wanted to believe we'd imagined it. It couldn't be real.

But there was no going back. The woods were about to disappear forever.

Suzy brought a shaking hand to her mouth and suppressed a sob, as we watched one of the workmen climb into the digger and stretch himself out at the controls. He stuck his head out and nodded as a younger man below gave him a thumbs-up signal. With a sharp jolt, a huge metallic claw began to scrape away at the trees, pushing and pulling them over as if they were nothing but paper figures made by a child.

Suzy's head shook sadly from side to side. 'I dreamt

79

about this place last night.' Her voice trembled and cracked. 'It was awful. I was stuck there, in the woods, and I couldn't move. The trees started to fall down and I wanted to run away but I couldn't – it felt like I was going to die with them.'

'It's horrible,' I agreed, watching as a grand chestnut tree was ripped from the soil. The digger lifted it up high into the air and roots dangled below like veins ripped from a body. Dust and mud carried into the wind as the digger carelessly flung the tree to the ground. A feeling of utter hopelessness crept through me and I suddenly felt like crying. I wanted so badly to run over and stop the workmen, to stick a flag in the soil and claim it as my own: mine and Suzy's. But I was frozen to the spot. It was all I could do to stare at the horror scene unfolding before me.

I slipped my hand into Suzy's and squeezed her cold fingers gently. Suzy sniffed up the tears streaming down her face and used her free hand to wipe her red cheeks.

'Don't think I'm talking to you again, Frankie,' she said suddenly.

'What?' I asked in shock, quickly snapping my head towards her. She still couldn't bring herself to look at me.

'I know it was you, Frankie.'

'What?' I asked again, feeling helpless.

'That prank you pulled back there in the shack. And the tapping and scratching at my door in the middle of the night. I got up to let you in and then there was no one there. Did you run off and hide?' She shook her head. 'You're trying to freak me out – make me as mad as Macbeth. Well it won't work.'

Then she turned and stormed off. She didn't look back as she ran. My throat tightened and I felt like I was going to vomit into the roaring wind. I wasn't sure what had just happened but I couldn't have felt more bereft than if all the trees in the world had suddenly died.

I called Suzy's name into the wind but she didn't turn around, she just carried on running. My knees trembled beneath me and I wanted to lie down on the grass and sob.

I turned and marched to school without once looking back. I couldn't bring myself to catch a last glimpse as the woods vanished into nothing but memory. I didn't know what we'd just witnessed in the shack, but I knew it wasn't good, and I knew I had no way of explaining it.

## The Times
### 15th November 1940

### *Schoolgirl Dies in Unexplained Circumstances*

The body of a Greater London schoolgirl who went missing during yesterday's nationwide air raid was discovered soon after the all-clear sounded.

Susan Montford, fourteen, was found with a broken neck in the driveway of St Mark's College, the prestigious military-affiliated school which she attended, in circumstances which are assumed to be suspicious.

Teachers and pupils were unable to account for the girl's movements between two p.m. and ten p.m. yesterday as they sheltered from the threat of bombs.

Like many St Mark's pupils, Susan's family are of a military background and her father, Major Simon Montford, is currently serving in France with his artillery regiment.

No member of staff at St Mark's was available for comment at the time of going to press.

# 8

I didn't want to be alone. I needed someone to make sense of it all with. There had to be a rational explanation, but I needed help getting there.

I couldn't trust myself to speak to Suzy. I was shaking too much to talk sensibly about anything. So I wrote her a note instead.

*Hey Suzy,*
*It wasn't me. I promise you. Whatever we're dealing with,*
*we need to deal with it together.*
*Frankie*

I slipped the note into Suzy's bag as it hung on the racks outside the dining hall.

Adrenalin still coursed through me after what had happened in the woods. I skipped dinner that night, I felt too anxious to eat. Instead I took myself upstairs, revved up my laptop, connected to the school wifi and logged onto Facebook. I needed to distract myself from whatever I'd just seen.

I'd collected a menagerie of friends from my various schools. None of whom were really 'friends', of course.

I hadn't spoken to them in months, and I wouldn't dare phone them up or rely on them for anything, but I still liked to look through their pages every now and again. So far at St Mark's my only Facebook friend was Suzy – her page was full of quotes from films, tagged pictures of herself in school plays and the occasional catty status about other girls at school.

My stomach lurched when I saw I had a friend request. Seb Cotez.

He wanted to be my friend. My finger hovered over the 'accept' button as I wondered when he had found me on there. Had it only been that night, when I'd told him my full name? Or had he been looking at my page for a while, looking through my profile pictures and wondering what knowing me would be like? I felt my cheeks burn red as thoughts raced through my head like the howling wind.

He didn't use a photograph as his profile picture. Instead it was some kind of comic-book character. Although, it wasn't all bright colours and strong lines like Superman or Captain America. It was dark, sketchy, gothic and sad. My heart pounded as I clicked 'accept' and started scrolling through Seb's page. But there was nothing much on there. A few other comic-book pictures, all equally as dark and mysterious. Only one tagged picture of him, painting the stage set in the background of a school play rehearsal. Under his favourite quotations he'd written:

*The murdered do haunt their murderers. I believe – I know that ghosts have wandered on earth. Be with me always – take any form – drive me mad! Only do not leave me in this abyss, where I cannot find you!* Wuthering Heights

Most people quote songs or *Family Guy* on their Facebook page. I didn't know any other teenage boys who'd quote a book like *Wuthering Heights* – especially something so depressing and dark. Why would anyone wish that someone would haunt them?

I sat, staring at my laptop for what felt like hours. Was he going to message me? Did he want me to message him? He'd told me he needed someone he could trust, someone at St Mark's. I had no idea what that meant.

But the weekend came and went without a message from Seb, Suzy or anyone else for that matter. It was a horrible feeling to be so alone. I wanted so much to escape the thoughts inside my head. They kept pulling me back to the shack in the woods, the strange figure I'd seen running between the trees and the warning singed into the shack floor. There had to be a rational explanation for it, but no matter how long I spent trying to figure it out, I only drew blanks. It was easier to pretend it hadn't happened.

I kept logging into Facebook, looking for clues as to what Suzy and Seb were doing. But there was nothing. No new status updates, pictures or messages. I was early to bed each night, but lay awake staring at the high dormitory ceiling. I waited for Suzy to come and find me, to apologise for her stupid behaviour and make friends again. I'd written her the note, I'd done enough. It was her turn now. But she made no effort.

Finally, on the Sunday night, as everyone around me was getting ready for bed and I was scanning the pages of Facebook once again, I jumped as someone knocked on my horsebox door. 'Frankie?' I heard Claire's voice.

'Yeah?' I called back.

'Suzy from the year above wants to speak to you. She's outside the dorm.'

My stomach lurched into my chest at the thought of the inevitable showdown with Suzy. Claire was swanning back to her room as I opened my door and walked through the dorm.

Sure enough, Suzy was standing outside.

'Frankie, hi.' She shifted her weight nervously from one foot to the other. She tilted her chin as she waited for me to say something. I had no idea what she wanted to hear, and all I could do was stare at her. She looked worse than dreadful. Her red hair hung lank around her face and her skin was sallow and clammy.

My arms swung limply at my side, unsure what to do. 'It wasn't me, Suzy,' I said, trying not to sound too desperate. 'The coin, what happened in the shack . . . and I've never even been inside Newton Dorm.'

Suzy lifted her palms up to stop me talking. 'Please, Frankie, we don't need to talk about that.' She crossed her arms over her chest and anxiously scanned the empty corridor, searching for something. 'If we don't talk about it then we can pretend it's not true,' she mumbled. 'I'm sorry, my head's just all over the place at the moment.'

'It's OK,' I said, relieved.

'Of course I knew it wasn't you.' She nodded her head but I didn't believe her. In that moment I wished that it had been, then she could just forgive me and we could move on. 'But . . .' her voice trailed off and she looked around nervously. 'Come with me a second.'

She took hold of my hand and pulled me into the TV room, which was dark and empty. My eyes squinted as Suzy flicked on the light. I'd been too distracted before to pay any attention to what she was wearing. Her once coordinated, colourful clothes now looked like a rainbow of insanity – like she was destined to become one of those crazy women who lived on the streets and carried their lives around in plastic bags.

Suzy started talking; her voice ran at an impossible speed. 'I guess I always knew it wasn't you. How could it have been? No one could just disappear into thin air. But you believe me, don't you, Frankie?'

I nodded, not really sure what I was agreeing with but just relieved that Suzy was speaking to me again. The more she spoke, the more relaxed she became, as if the sound of her own words were calming her.

'I can't sleep, and I need my sleep, Frankie. I'm not like you – I don't have good skin genes. If I don't get my beauty sleep then I come out in spots – and how many actresses have spots? None! But how can I sleep? I keep hearing noises in the night. And there's this . . . this . . . smell . . .'

She took my hand and led me to a nearby armchair. She sat herself down in the chair and I perched on the arm, leaning in to listen. She opened her mouth to speak, and then closed it again. Like a goldfish gulping for air. Confusion passed through her eyes as she tried to find the words to explain herself. She absently picked at the skin around her nails. I noticed they were red-raw. She must have been doing that for days.

'Since doing the Ouija board, I've heard noises.' Her words were slow and tense. She looked at me carefully, trying to gage my reaction, seeing if she could trust me with more. I gave her an encouraging nod. 'It comes in the middle of the night. First there's this smell, like flowers and earth, like the woods after it's rained. It's so strong it makes me want to throw up.' All the heat in my body seemed to evaporate at her words. I had smelt the woods in my room that first night after we'd done the Ouija board. 'Then come the noises. Scratching. Tapping. Shuffling. Knocking.' Suzy's eyes widened, reminding me of the time she told me the story of the Blue Lady, as if she were an actress reciting a monologue on stage. 'I got up the first time, to investigate. But as soon as I opened the door there was nothing there. Impossible, right?' She let out a nervous chuckle. 'But when it happened again, I didn't move. I couldn't, it was like I was glued to my bed. But the stiller I stayed the louder the knocking got. I was sure someone else in the dorm would wake up. I held my breath waiting for someone else to speak, waiting for someone to yell 'Shut up!' But no one did. No one else heard. And then after what happened in the woods . . . in the shack . . .' She shook her head slowly and chewed the inside of her mouth. 'I'm sorry I blamed you, really, I am. But I guess I was just angry.'

'Why?' I managed to interrupt.

'Because it was you and me together.' Anger filled her eyes. 'The Ouija board, Frankie. We've awoken something, something terrible. And what happened in the shack . . .'

Suzy stared into my blank face, waiting for a reaction, but

I said nothing. I knew I'd find a rational explanation for what I'd seen eventually. But at that moment, I had nothing.

'I want to do it again,' she said, challenging me.

'No.' I shook my head, my mood suddenly darkening. I'd always loved Suzy's dramatics, but the picture she was painting for me now left me feeling deeply uneasy. I took her hand in mine, trying to soothe and distract her. I was certain I wanted nothing more to do with Ouija boards. I'd only done it the once and I still didn't believe in them. But I knew – I knew as well as I knew cutting down trees was wrong – I never wanted to touch a Ouija board again.

'Something . . . someone is haunting me, Frankie,' Suzy said without a hint of sarcasm.

I shook my head and looked away. 'I don't believe in ghosts.'

Not the reply Suzy wanted. She sprung to her feet in frustration and began to walk away. I heard the beeping of a phone and Suzy pulled hers from her pocket. She read a text message distractedly. 'He's annoyed with me.' She snapped her phone shut and looked down at it with disgust.

'James?' I asked, relieved that the conversation was steering away from ghosts and haunting.

'I haven't been texting him back. But how can I think about James when all this is going on? Frankie, there's something in this school . . . something that shouldn't be here. We need to do something.'

I shook my head with steel-like determination. No way did I want to get any more involved in Ouija boards and fire rituals than I already was.

Suzy began to storm off once again.

'Wait.' I grabbed hold of her jumper. 'Of course I believe you. It's just, I've never believed in ghosts before now.'

'I wouldn't lie about something like this,' she said quietly. And at that moment, I couldn't tell if she was telling the truth or not. But I didn't want to lose her, so I played along with the game.

'If we need to find a way to get rid of whatever it is,' I said, humouring her, 'maybe more Ouija boards are a bad idea. If you think the board started it all off, then another one won't do much good.' I was so relieved she was speaking to me again, I didn't dare challenge the ridiculous notion that something, or someone, was haunting her.

'We could ask Father Warren to bless my room?' Suzy suggested in earnest.

I felt my nose crinkle up in objection. The school chaplain had better things to do than preach incantations in the room of the most over-dramatic girl in school.

'We could do it ourselves?' I replied.

'In case you hadn't noticed, Frankie,' she said with sarcasm, 'neither you nor I are priests.'

'No, but we can say prayers,' I said quickly. 'We could even go to the chapel, steal some holy water?'

A familiar mischievous glint sparkled in Suzy's eyes. 'Now you're talking!'

The chapel was dark when the door creaked open. Pale moonlight found its way through the faded stained-glass window high on the back wall.

'There's a light switch by the first set of pews,' I instructed

Suzy, remembering how I'd studied it intently while Father Warren gave his most recent sermon. The chapel lights flickered on, illuminating the small, stone room packed with pews and hymn books.

'Where do you think he keeps the holy water?' Suzy asked nervously, walking towards the altar and lifting up the large, golden cloth that lay draped over it.

'We can just take some from here,' I suggested, pointing to the small font by the chapel entrance.

'Bingo,' Suzy smiled, hurrying over to the font. 'What can we carry the water away in?'

I looked around and spotted a dying pot plant sitting in a small, grubby dish on one of the tall windowsills. I made my way towards it, clambered onto the nearby pew and lifted the plant out of the dish. 'It's a bit dirty, but this'll do.'

'It's holy dirt,' Suzy smiled. 'It's in a church, gotta be.'

After scooping the water from the chapel font into the plant dish, we made our way back upstairs.

'I'll take it from here,' Suzy said, taking the dish out of my hands and nodding at the Newton Dorm door. 'People will only get suspicious if they see a fourth year in our dorm.'

She was right.

'Do you know what you're gonna say?' I asked eagerly, wishing I could follow her.

'Maybe a bit of the Lord's Prayer,' she answered.

'Good luck!' I gave her a quick hug, careful not to spill the water. 'Suzy, you'll be OK, you know that?' I said seriously. 'I'm here for you.'

She gave me a warm smile before disappearing into the dorm.

As I lay awake in bed listening to the sound of other girls whispering, I realised that life at St Mark's really wasn't worth living unless Suzy was there. Without her I was nothing, lost to the world inside my own head. I knew that, and it hurt deeply. Without Suzy by my side I recognised a feeling that you read about in books – the feeling you have when you're small and you wake up screaming from nightmares. A feeling I came to know so well that first year at St Mark's. The feeling of fear.

General Edgar Palen
Royal Sapper and Miner's Corps
Africa

1st February 1815

Dear Headmistress Wilson,

I desperately still await news of my daughter, Hetty, who disappeared quite suddenly from St Mark's College grounds now two months ago.

The police have informed me that since the body of my daughter has not been found, I must not assume that she is deceased. However, with knowledge of my daughter's pious nature, it is most unlikely that she could simply run away. I can only fear the worst.

The sheer negligence and utter incompetence of your school's staff, which has allowed a child of fourteen years of age to disappear from her school, is clear for all to see.

No compensation offered to myself or to my wife (who, being of a nervous disposition, has been nearly killed by these ghastly events) can replace the loss of our only child. However, someone must be brought to justice for

*this terrible crime, and that person, Miss Wilson, must
be you. My only consolation will be the knowledge that
both St Mark's College and your personal reputation will
be forever ruined.*

*Yours sincerely,*
*General Edgar Palen*

# 9

Suzy wasn't at breakfast the next morning.

I sat on my own. As Saskia, Claire and the other Raleigh girls came to sit down I quickly finished my toast and left.

'Leaving on our account, Frankie?' Saskia smirked.

'Don't flatter yourself,' I grumbled back.

'And don't think we don't know about you and Seb,' she said quickly, a tone of delight in her voice.

I swung around and stared at her incredulously. It stung to hear her speak his name. There was nothing to know about me and Seb. And even if there were, it had nothing to do with Saskia. She whispered something in George's ear and I felt my face flush red as George shook her head in what looked like disgust before muttering something back.

I couldn't get out of the dining hall quickly enough – I had no desire to know what they were saying about me.

I walked back to my room via Suzy's dorm, just in case she was hanging around outside. I still hadn't been inside Newton Dorm at that point. The dormitories of other years were like mysterious countries – places on a map that you hear tales about but never see first-hand.

I made a quick stop to Raleigh to pick up my bag before heading to class. I'd forgotten to shut down my laptop and my Facebook page was glowing on my desk. There was a message in my inbox. My heart pounded – it was from Seb. It was the message I'd been waiting days to receive. I hurriedly clicked it open and read:

*Frankie,*
*Can you do me a favour?*
*Seb*

It was short, too short. But it was something. I messaged back at lightning speed:

*What?*

Taking our mobiles into the classroom was strictly forbidden. But I knew I wouldn't be able to log back into Facebook until lunchtime, and I didn't want to wait until then to read Seb's reply. I picked my phone up from my desk, and put it on silent before slipping it into my blazer pocket. The minutes stretched into hours and all I thought about was hearing back from him. I checked my messages in the toilets after assembly, then under the desk in my Maths lesson, but still no reply.

I hid in the toilets once again on my way to lunch. I logged onto Facebook and sure enough, there was a reply from Seb:

*Hey,*
*I need you to check out a book from your library for me. If your library is anything like ours it'll have a book*

*on the history of the school. I need to look at that book
– about St Mark's. Can you do that for me? I'll owe
you.*

    *Seb*

I don't know what I was expecting Seb to ask me, but it
certainly wasn't that. Nothing he did made sense. Checking
out a library book for him? What was that about? And not
even an interesting book – it was a book about my school's
history. I put away my phone in confusion without replying.
He'd waited all morning to reply to me; two could play
that game.

I was dying to speak to Suzy – she'd know what to make
of Seb's strange request.

But Suzy wasn't at lunch either. I knew then that
something was up. First she'd skipped breakfast, and now
lunch. She obviously had a point to prove.

'Don't you own a watch, Frankie?' smiled Ms Barts as I
burst into my first afternoon lesson. Ms Barts wasn't my
normal Biology teacher. I'd forgotten all about her since
the time she'd introduced herself to me in the dining hall.
'Mr Desmond has had to go home. I'll be taking your class
today,' she explained.

'Sorry, Miss,' I muttered, sitting down in the only empty
seat, next to George.

George quickly put her hand over her workbook, but
not before I'd noticed she'd got 100% on our last test.

'Don't be nosy,' George said under her breath, casting a
nervous glance in Saskia's direction.

'Afraid Saskia will dump you if she knows you've got

more than one brain cell?' I said flatly. George just stared at me, her brown eyes blinking quickly. 'Don't worry,' I snorted. 'Your secret's safe.'

'Respiration!' Ms Barts shouted loudly, clapping her hands together. My attention was once again drawn to her duck-like lips. 'Turning oxygen into energy. What organ do we need to breathe?'

Everyone sat in silence, staring at Ms Barts blankly.

'Anyone? Breathing? What can't we breathe without?' She looked around the class expectantly; no one put up their hand. 'Frankie?'

I wished she hadn't called on me. I glanced about at the uninspired faces around me. Maybe one of them would rescue me. Of course, they didn't.

'Er, lungs?' I said obviously.

'Exactly!' Ms Barts clapped her hands together again. 'And today, girls, we're going to get up close and personal with lungs and see how they really work.'

Ms Barts walked up to the long desk at the front of the class, on which lay large silver trays covered with paper towels. Ms Barts whipped off the paper towel from the first tray, revealing two lumps of whitish-grey meat. An audible gasp rung out around the classroom.

'These, girls, are pigs' lungs, fresh from the butchers.'

Comical retching noises filled my ears. I peered over the contents with intrigue – I'd never seen a set of lungs before.

'Disgusting,' George muttered under her breath.

'One pair of lungs between two, please,' instructed Ms Barts. 'Please take a pair of lungs, a scalpel from the cupboard and a plastic straw to inflate the lungs with.'

Ms Barts passed me a silver tray as I approached her desk. 'For you, Frankie. Now, please don't cut into the lung until I give the go-ahead.' The wild twinkle in Ms Barts' eyes reminded me how young she was. Older people never seemed to get that excited about anything, and I'd never seen anyone look so thrilled about the prospect of dissecting lungs.

'On page seventy of your textbooks you'll see a diagram of human lungs. Now, these are pigs' lungs in front of you – they're smaller, but not too dissimilar to human lungs. Now, the first thing we're going to do, girls, is to place the plastic straw in the end of the windpipe, here.' She demonstrated on the pair of pig lungs in front of her, positioning the straw between her trout-pout lips. I offered the straw to George. She violently shook her glossy bobbed hair and I noticed she'd turned a funny shade of grey. I placed the straw just inside the windpipe, as Ms Barts had done.

'Now, place the other end of the straw in your mouth and blow, like this.' She demonstrated again. 'You'll see the lungs inflate and deflate as they fill with air. See? Then, if you take your scalpel and place it at the top of the lung, like this, we're going to slowly pull it down the side of the lung, opening it up to reveal the alveoli inside.'

There was a thud to my left.

'She's fainted!' shrieked Claire behind me. I heard another girl scream as I watched George's eyelids flutter open.

Ms Barts darted towards us and bent down over George, who lay limp on the floor. 'Frankie, help me get her up.' I bent down and hooked my hands under George's right shoulder as Ms Barts took the left. Together we heaved her up into a sitting position.

'I'm sorry, Miss,' George said quietly, as tears welled in the corner of her eyes.

'It's OK,' Ms Barts replied gently, pushing George's school jumper up to feel for a pulse in her wrist. 'Nothing I haven't seen before. You're not the first and you certainly won't be the last to go weak at the knees at the sight of a pig lung. Frankie, can you please walk George up to the San and see that Nurse Pippa examines her? I'm sure you'll be fine,' she said kindly to George. 'But you'd be getting me in trouble if you didn't get checked out by the nurse, OK?'

George nodded and let out a small whimper. I helped her to her feet and left my books and school bag in the classroom. Together, we headed out of the science block and towards the school San.

The Sanatorium was in a separate block from the main school. It was a warren of rooms covered from floor to ceiling in bile-green tiles, which made it seem colder than anywhere else in the school. Anti-smoking posters had been tacked to the walls, and a few plastic chairs edged the corners of the waiting room.

'George collapsed in Biology class,' I informed Nurse Pippa as she poked her head out from behind her office door. Our school nurse had short grey hair that was cut like an old-fashioned monk – it looked like someone had placed a bowl over her head and snipped. The noise of a TV game show was blaring from her office, and Nurse Pippa looked annoyed at having to tear herself away.

'Not pig dissections again.' She shook her mop of grey hair. 'What was it this time? Eyes? Hearts?'

'Lungs,' I told her.

'Ms Barts?' she tutted. I nodded. 'I've told her before, just because they dissected animals ten years ago when she was a pupil . . . Just sit in the waiting room, girls,' Nurse Pippa instructed us. 'I'll be in there shortly.' She ducked back into her office and closed the door heavily behind her.

'There's no one else in there with her, you know?' George said, sitting down in one of the creaking plastic chairs and rubbing the side of her head. 'She sits in there all day watching crappy daytime game shows. She won't come out and see me until she knows who's won. She's obsessed.'

I couldn't help but smile at the thought of Nurse Pippa sitting on the edge of her plastic chair waiting to see who'd won some rubbish game show. 'Everyone has their vices, I guess.'

Pleased that I had a moment away from teachers, I pulled my phone from my pocket to check if Seb had messaged again.

He had:

*Frankie, will you do that for me? Please? X*

That little cross on my screen made my heart pound against my ribs and I knew then and there that I would do anything Sebastian Cotez asked of me.

'Texting your boyfriend?' George teased, leaning back in her battered plastic chair and studying me.

My grip tightened on the phone. 'He's not my boyfriend.' Even I could hear the tension in my voice as I spoke.

She shrugged and looked at the ceiling. 'I saw that you made Facebook friends with him.'

'You stalking me now?'

'Chill out.' She rolled her eyes. 'I hardly know Seb. He's friends with James, right?' I nodded. 'My older brother was in the same year as James's brother. I've known James for years. We've been texting recently.' I stayed quiet. What would Suzy think about James texting other girls? 'I've seen him a couple of times this year. That Seb guy always seems to tag along.'

A pang of jealousy stabbed at my gut. I wondered what other St Mark's girls Seb had doing favours for him; if he ended messages to them with kisses.

'He's weird, though,' George said thoughtfully. 'It's like he wants something . . .'

'What?' I asked, regretting the words as soon as I'd said them. I dreaded George telling me what Seb might want from her, or Saskia, or any other one of those girls I could never compete with.

'He's got some kind of creepy fascination with St Mark's – he wanted me to tell him everything I knew about it. He freaked me out if I'm honest. I only saw him a couple of times.'

I stared at George in silence. I hated the thought that Seb might confide in someone else. But I'd known from the beginning that he wasn't like James, or other boys his age. He didn't speak to girls so he could practise his flirting. He wanted something else, he wanted someone he could trust. I'd seen it the first time I looked into his clear blue eyes, eyes that were so deeply clouded with sorrow. I'd spent too long wondering why.

I looked down at my phone and quickly typed a message back to Seb:

*What is your obsession with St Mark's?* X

I sat back and waited for a reply.

## 10

'I thought I heard your voice,' said Suzy from the doorway of the waiting room. She was leaning against the doorframe, her hair a mess. She was wearing a long, white, old-fashioned nightdress – on anyone else it would look ridiculous but Suzy could pull it off. It made her look like a tragic heroine from a Victorian novel – the crazed Woman in White.

'What are you doing here?' I asked with a smile, happy to realise she must have been in the San all day and not just avoiding me.

Suddenly Nurse Pippa appeared in the doorway. George stood up shakily when Nurse Pippa beckoned her. 'You can have five minutes,' she said to me as she ushered George out of the waiting room. 'Then you have to go back to Biology.'

As Nurse Pippa left the room Suzy came and sat down on one of the chairs next to me, closing the door so we were alone. 'What's up?' I asked.

'They brought me here last night,' she said. I studied her face closely. She almost didn't look like Suzy – her skin was unusually pale and her normally twinkling eyes were glassy and lifeless.

'Why?' I asked, feeling a twinge of concern.

She smiled, but her eyes told a different story. 'Apparently I was keeping people awake.'

'Why?' I asked again.

Suzy's eyes glazed over as she stared at me for a long moment. She bit at her lip anxiously. Absently, she started to scratch the back of her left hand. I waited for her to speak, but the sound of her scratching her flesh, and the sight of her fingernails dragging through her sore skin made me feel sick. I lunged forwards and put my hand over hers to stop her from harming herself any more.

'Hey,' I whispered, putting my other arm around her. 'It's OK.'

Suzy was silently shaking beside me, and I felt my stomach twist into a painful knot. I hated seeing her looking so ill, so tired, so unhinged. I couldn't bear the thought of something upsetting her and changing her, stealing away her magic and leaving nothing but a hollow shell.

'It's OK,' I repeated, desperate to drive her away from whatever had made her like this.

'It's not OK,' she whispered to me, her lips trembling as her words hung on them. 'We shouldn't have done it.'

'Done what?' I asked.

'The Ouija board,' she said so quietly I could hardly hear.

'Not this again, Suzy?' I said, feeling irritated. Once again I found Suzy's penchant for the dramatic lighting a short fuse within me. This wasn't fun. I couldn't shift the feeling that Suzy's story was luring me into something very dark, somewhere I didn't want to go. I couldn't humour her forever. 'What about the prayers and holy water – didn't they work?'

Suzy shook her head violently and let out an exhausted gasp. 'Oh, Frankie!' She started scratching at the backs of her hands again and I reached out, putting my hands over hers to make it stop. 'It's so much worse. When I got back to my room last night, I felt like someone was watching me.'

'You're imagining it,' I said, trying my best to sound kind.

'No,' Suzy said sternly, her voice echoing off the tiled walls. 'When I got back I said some prayers and sprinkled the water about, like I said I would. I did it properly, I made signs of the cross and everything. But when the lights went out, I saw shadows. Shadows creeping over the dorm walls, over the ceiling and at the end of my bed. I closed my eyes tightly, like if I couldn't see what was there then it couldn't hurt me. But then I felt something at the end of my bed.'

I didn't believe in ghosts. But I had ice running through my veins.

'I was drifting off to sleep. I felt something cold, ice-cold hands sweep through the end of my bed – under the covers. That's when I screamed the first time. I couldn't help it.' Her eyes pleaded with me. 'Then it happened again. Only this time the hands grabbed hold of my ankles and shook them. It was so dark, I couldn't see – but I could *feel*, Frankie, I could feel cold hands close in around my ankles. I screamed and screamed but they wouldn't let go. It felt like they were burning my skin, they were so cold. I wanted to get out of bed, I wanted to run away, but I couldn't. Those hands, those cold, cold hands, they wouldn't let me go. Then the dorm lights went on and someone came into my room – I can't even remember who. They tried to hold me still, but I didn't want anyone touching me. I just screamed and screamed. But I wasn't the one who noticed it, Frankie.'

'Noticed what?' I asked quickly.

She started to scratch at her hand again. I was too transfixed by her words to stop her. 'The burn marks. Where I'd sprinkled the holy water – there were small burn marks. Like someone walked around my room with a cigarette and singed holes into everything. On the carpet, on the walls, on my bed – everywhere.'

A sick feeling lurched in my stomach and my mind spun, trying desperately to rationalise what Suzy was telling me. There had to be some kind of explanation for the marks. Had to be.

'That's when they called for a teacher,' Suzy continued. 'And then they called for Nurse Pippa, and she brought me up here.' Tears began to gather at the corners of her eyes and she violently blinked them away. 'I haven't slept, I can't sleep. I'm so tired, I'm so scared she'll come back.'

'Who'll come back?' I asked.

'Her, whoever we contacted – she's haunting me. It's not the Blue Lady – I don't even think there's such a thing as the Blue Lady. This is something else . . . something worse. Something, someone, is trapped here – and they're angry. The scratching, the burn marks, the word "Next" burnt into the shack floor, the cold hands in my bed. It's coming after me.'

I felt my eyebrows pull together in confusion. Suzy

110

inhaled a sharp, ragged breath as coldness swept over her eyes.

'You think I'm mad,' she said bitterly. 'Just like everyone else. Nurse Pippa even called my mum in Cyprus and told her I need to see a doctor.'

'Maybe you do?' I said gently.

'I don't need a doctor!' Suzy shouted. 'I need a priest, that's what I need. And I need something more than stupid water from the stupid school chapel font!'

At that moment the door swung open and Nurse Pippa stood in the doorway, tapping at her watch. 'Biology,' she said to me.

'I'll come and see you later,' I told Suzy. 'After school.'

'Biology,' Nurse Pippa reminded me sternly.

I gave Suzy a quick hug before slipping out of the room and heading back to class, leaving George with her head between her knees in one of the San rooms.

I paused before entering the Biology classroom and quickly checked my phone. There was a reply from Seb. There was no kiss this time, but that wasn't what made my blood run cold.

*My sister died there.*

How could I possibly reply?

I couldn't concentrate on anything that afternoon. My mind was in a thousand places at once, not one of them in the classroom. Suzy's story haunted me – the scratching at her door, the cold hands and the burn marks. And Seb. I wanted to see him again, desperately. I wanted him to know that he could trust me, that I'd help him in any way I could. But I wanted more from him. I wanted to know how his sister had died, and why that made him so obsessed with the school. And why me – why was he telling me?

Just before the bell rang, one of the school secretaries slipped into the classroom and passed a note to the teacher. He studied it silently before reading it aloud to the class.

'Listen up, please. Everyone is to head to the school hall for an emergency assembly after the end of this lesson.'

Curious mumbles rumbled through the classroom.

'Maybe school's being shut down?' grinned Saskia.

'Maybe someone's going to make a film about the school?' Claire added hopefully.

As the bell rung, we all packed our bags and headed towards the school hall.

I spotted Suzy hovering at the hall entrance, and it made me wonder what could be so important that Suzy was pulled from her sickbed and forced to attend along with the rest of us.

'What's going on?' she asked, as I approached.

'No idea,' I replied. She still looked awful, but there was a resolve in her eyes that made me hope she was ready to move past whatever had happened to her the night before. 'I guess it must be serious, though. Suzy, I need to tell you something, it's about Seb –'

'Girls, silence and sit down, please!' called the headmistress from the side of the school hall stage.

We sat down as Ms West slowly climbed the steps to the stage, a look of deep sadness etched between her brows. Everyone fell silent as she cleared her throat to speak.

'Thank you for coming here at such short notice,' she said gravely. I knew instantly that something was wrong; teachers never thanked us for anything. 'I'm afraid I have some very upsetting news. As you know, work has been under way to dig and lay the foundations of the new sports centre. The workmen made a very grim discovery today – they uncovered a body, buried in a shallow grave in the woods.' Suzy slipped her hand into mine and squeezed it so tightly it hurt. 'A very thorough investigation will soon be taking place to establish whose body it is and why it was buried in St Mark's woodland. I urge you all to be as patient and as helpful as possible during the investigation. Further to this discovery, the school will be closed tomorrow as a sign of respect for the deceased and to allow the police to exhume the body and seal off the area. Construction work will be suspended until further notice. All boarders are to stay in the main school building as soon as they leave this hall and we ask that all day girls stay at home tomorrow. We have written letters for all parents to read – please can day girls collect them from the prefects standing at the back of the hall and ensure that they are passed on to their parents and guardians to read. Thank you.'

Ms West left the stage, and exited the room in stone-faced silence.

As the crowd of girls around us erupted with hurried chat, I looked over to Suzy, whose face was the only still and calm thing amid a storm of chaos.

'It's her,' Suzy said, so quietly I had to lip-read. 'They found her.'

## II

The next day at St Mark's felt as though we were living on some kind of Hollywood movie set. Reporters and TV crews crowded around the front gates of the school, desperate to get a sound bite from Ms West, or a picture of the woods where the body was found.

There was a sense of mania, as if we were living from one second to the next. Everyone held their breath and waited for the next big announcement: who did the body belong to? How did they die? How long had they been there? Why had no one found it before?

Rumours spread through the school corridors like wild forest fires. Girls who had never noticed each other before would stop as they passed in the halls, eyes wide with morbid joy as they shared the latest stories as if it were gossip from the pages of a shiny magazine: 'I heard that the body had bullets in it', or 'Apparently there was a baby buried with it – two bodies, not one. Just like the Blue Lady'. The tragedy was bringing us together as a school. Everyone talked to everyone. I even saw one girl in the sixth form walk over to a table of second years at breakfast and say, 'If I were you I wouldn't go walking around on your own. Apparently the body was of a girl about your age. The killer might strike again – you never know.'

I nearly crashed into Suzy as I left the dining hall that morning. She didn't register me, and marched past, distracted. I was keen to know what she thought about the body in the woods. When we'd first heard about it she'd seemed so certain it had something to do with the strange events she'd recounted to me in the San. The last thing I wanted was to indulge Suzy's imagination, but I was curious. I opened my mouth to call after her but I felt a tap on my shoulder and turned around.

Saskia stood facing me. 'You hung out in the woods,' she said with intrigue. 'Didn't you smell anything weird?'

'No,' I replied, honestly, as Suzy slipped further away from me. Even I speculated on the nature of the body. 'It must have been there for a while. Dead bodies lose their smell after a certain time.'

Of course none of the rumours turned out to be true. But the buzz that they brought to the school that day when lessons were cancelled made it seem as if we were living in some weird alternative reality. It felt so exciting – I don't think anyone stopped for one moment to actually consider how horrible the situation really was.

The national papers wasted no time in sensationalising the events that were unfolding at St Mark's. That morning, only a day after the body was discovered, there were headlines on practically every paper and news site. One of the workmen who uncovered the body gave an interview to a national newspaper. He said that the school was like a prison and that it had a dark history. The body was only the tip of the iceberg, he said. Usually the teachers encouraged us to read the newspapers (well, the newspapers they deemed fit for St Mark's girls to read) but on that day they were banned. But everyone knows that when something is forbidden it only makes it more valuable. Ripped-out articles were traded through the dining hall and dormitories like money. By the end of the day every girl in the school had read the account of Jim the workman.

I checked my Facebook constantly, to see if Seb had messaged anything again. But there was nothing. The gruesome discovery must have stirred up all kinds of horrible memories for him. I felt so sorry for him. No wonder he was always so lost inside his own head. I knew that I had to see him again, soon. And doing what he'd asked of me – finding that book – was my only way. Maybe doing that would tell him everything I couldn't write in a Facebook message.

I went to the school library alone.

Sure enough, there was a book in the library about the history of the school. The librarian raised her eyebrows as she scanned *The History of St Mark's College for Girls* into the computer. She must have thought I was foolish enough to look for clues on the body in there.

There was a copy of *Wuthering Heights* lying on the nearest table. I picked it up and handed it to the librarian, 'This too, please.' Maybe reading it would help me understand Seb better. Help me understand ghosts too.

I sent Seb a message at lunchtime:

*I have the book for you.*

He messaged back instantly:

*Meet me outside your school gates after dinner. X*

Dinner seemed like an eternity away. Throughout the day parents of boarders started arriving at the school and demanding to speak with Ms West. I guess no one wanted their daughter to be schooled at a murder scene. I watched out of my horsebox window, my head rested in my hands, my elbows propped up on the windowsill, as the endless stream of cars swamped the school car park. I thought it strange that other people's parents lived so close that they were able to arrive at school so quickly – why bother sending your children to boarding school?

Mum didn't seem to mind, though. She didn't jump on a plane and demand that I leave for Germany with her that afternoon.

'Awfully sad business,' she said when I called to tell her what was going on. 'Phil says not to worry, though. Lightning never strikes twice.'

'Well, so long as Phil doesn't mind . . .' I said feeling slightly cheated.

'You know I'd love to have you here with me in Germany.' Somehow Mum's tone wasn't convincing. 'But a military base is hardly the place for a teenager. You'd be bored stiff.'

'Aren't you worried that I'm living and going to school at what was once a brutal murder scene?' I interrupted, trying to provoke her.

'Frankie, stop being so dramatic. There's no proof that anything was brutal. And, yes, while I agree that the situation is upsetting, there's no way I'm going to take you out of school.' Mum's response was the one I'd wanted. St Mark's was where I needed to be. It had become the centre of my universe, my world filled with Suzy and her theatrics, and Seb and his sad past.

'Look, Frankie, I need to speak to you about something,' Mum said seriously.

I held my breath, hoping she wasn't going to change her mind about taking me out of school. 'What?'

'I know half-term is coming up,' she said carefully. 'But Phil and I have hardly had any time together since coming to Germany. He's been working such long hours. Anyway, we thought we'd take a holiday to Spain . . .'

'Oh, cool,' I said, feeling excited about the prospect of a holiday in sunny Spain.

'I knew you'd understand,' Mum said cheerfully. 'I've already spoken to your housemistress and she says it's fine for you to stay in school over that week. Apparently there's always a teacher there to look after the few girls who have to stay.'

'Stay in school?' I nearly shouted down the phone.

'Well, yes, of course. Where else could you go?'

I tried not to care. It wasn't like it was the first time Mum had put a man before me. 'I could stay with a friend?' I suggested, already earmarking Suzy.

'I think it's just easier for you to stay at school. It's only a week, after all.'

'Right,' I agreed. 'Only a week'.

119

The thought of staying at St Mark's over half-term filled me with mixed emotions. I knew without asking that Suzy wouldn't be sticking around in school over the holidays – no way she'd suffer such a tragedy.

I finally caught up with Suzy in the dinner queue that night. 'Mum's making me stay in school over the holidays.'

'Is she mental?' Suzy said, rather too loudly. 'Every other parent can't get their daughters out of this graveyard quick enough and your folks want you to stay here over half-term?'

'I bet it was Phil's idea,' I explained bitterly. 'Maybe if I had somewhere else to go, a friend to stay with.' I looked at her hopefully. 'Then I wouldn't have to stay here.'

'I'll have the beef, please,' Suzy said to the dinner lady, ignoring my subtle attempt at an invitation.

It wasn't just my hints at a half-term invitation that Suzy ignored. She ignored nearly everything I said to her over dinner that night. Her mind was somewhere else entirely. She said nothing as I told her about meeting Seb after dinner, or about the newspaper articles that were doing the rounds of my dorm. The only thing I said that interested her was about Seb's sister.

'She died here, at the school.'

What looked like terror shot through Suzy's eyes and she flashed me an unconvincing smile as she said slowly, *'All that lives must die. Passing through nature to eternity.'* Suzy's ability to quote Shakespeare at random always impressed me, but doing it when I told her about Seb's dead sister just left a sour taste in my mouth. Suzy could smile and throw quotes at me all she wanted, but I could see in her eyes that she thought the same as me – that whatever had happened to Seb's sister was beyond horrible.

'So you and Seb, huh?' Suzy smiled but it didn't touch her eyes. 'Seems like you guys are quite an item now.'

That annoyed me. Suzy had never been interested in Seb before; she wasn't much interested in anything beyond herself and the events surrounding her. I had no idea what Seb and I were, but we weren't an 'item'.

'We're just friends.' I shrugged dismissively.

'You seem to know a lot about him and his dead sister,' she said, almost as an accusation.

'How's James?' I asked, wanting to change the subject. 'Have you heard from him since . . .'

Suzy glared at me for a long, cold moment.

'I need to go,' she said absently. Her eyes studied everything in the hall apart from me. As if I weren't there.

'I'll come and find you later,' I told her. 'After I've seen Seb and –'

Suzy didn't wait to hear what I had to say. She just walked off. I hadn't even had the chance to ask her opinion on the dead body, or whether she'd had to go back to see Nurse Pippa that day. Suzy was really beginning to annoy me. Everything was always about her. About her and James, her and some stupid ghost. What about me, and my opinions, and the things inside my head? What about Seb?

I was so nervous to see him I was almost dreading it. I

had no idea what I was getting myself into by going to meet him. I felt physically sick with anticipation. I looked at myself in the mirror, taking a brush to my dark hair and trying to sweep it into some kind of style. I wonder if he'd notice that I'd gone to so much trouble, if he'd laugh at me for wanting to impress him. I stared into my reflection, willing myself to be cool. Aloof, unaffected, breezy, that's what I needed to be.

I took my time putting on my coat and walking to the school gates, trying to slow down the minutes and delay the moment when I'd see him and feel my heart lurch in my chest and beat furiously within me.

He was waiting just outside the cast iron gates of St Mark's. As soon as I saw his figure in the darkness, any sense of coolness I'd tried to talk into myself back in the dorm packed its bags and fled. He was wearing ripped blue jeans, battered old trainers and a faded Led Zeppelin T-shirt underneath a black zip-up hoodie that flapped about in the breeze. He looked older in his own clothes. It was the first time I'd ever seen him out of his school uniform and he looked like a totally different person.

'You came.' He smiled at me as I walked towards him. It felt wonderful to see him smile.

I stood about a foot away from him, grinning shyly. I fought the sudden urge to throw my arms around him and hold him close to me.

'I picked up that book for you,' I said, handing over the heavy library book I'd been clutching against my chest. The book shook in my hands. I raised my shoulders to my ears and let my breath escape in little white clouds, trying to pretend it was the cold night air that was making me shiver.

Seb cast his pale blue eyes over the book's cover and nodded in gratitude. The ghost of words danced on my lips as we stood there in silence. There was so much I wanted to say to him. I had no idea where to begin without sounding ridiculous.

He smiled again, and I beamed back, feeling my cheeks flush red. 'Yeah, it's been a weird old day, hasn't it?' he said thoughtfully. I nodded as I tried to think of something clever to say. 'Your lessons cancelled too?' he asked.

'Yeah,' I replied. There was an awkward pause and we stood watching each other. He stared at me curiously, waiting for me to speak. 'Seb.' I stepped closer. 'I'm really sorry about your sister. That she died, I mean.'

Seb's eyes softened, as if a weight had somehow been lifted from him. 'Thanks,' he said quietly. I noticed his expression change as darkness swept through his eyes. 'Well, we don't know for sure that she died.' He spoke slowly, choosing each word with care. 'She went missing from the school nearly twenty years ago. I never knew her – it happened before I was born. But, they never found a body.'

A body.

Horror lurched in my stomach. Seb must have seen the look on my face as he gave me a slight nod, telling me that he was thinking the same thing. The body in the woods. It was his sister. I felt tears prick at my eyes. My voice was barely a whisper. 'What was her name?'

'Marina. It's kind of a long story . . .' He trailed off, as if the words were causing him pain. He flashed me a look that suggested he wanted to tell me. But he looked down, and ran his hand through his shaggy hair. 'I have something for you too,' he said, reaching into his back pocket.

He pulled out an old, battered comic. Only it was thicker than a normal comic. 'It's a graphic novel,' he said, sounding tense. His eyes widened. 'It's called *The Sandman*. It's by my favourite writer. I think you'll really like the pictures in it. You can give it back to me when you've read it. No rush. I've got his others if you like it. You can borrow those too.'

He sounded nervous, and hearing it put me at ease. He was giving me what I'd longed for since I first met him. He wanted to share a part of himself with me. Maybe whatever I felt for him, he felt for me too.

'Thanks,' I smiled widely, reaching for the book. Its spine was creased with age and love, and the pages weathered and frayed at their edges. I flicked open at random and saw the picture from Seb's Facebook profile staring back at me.

'This guy.' Seb pointed to the character, his fingers so close to mine I felt on fire. 'That's Morpheus. He can travel through dreams.'

'That's so cool,' I said quietly.

'I thought you might like it. I mean, I don't really know you, but I wondered if you might like this sort of thing.'

'I do,' I admitted, although I'd never seen anything like it before. I thought comics were for young kids who liked to read about superheroes. This was different – it was deep and dark and wonderful. Everything I knew I had inside of me. And Seb had seen that. Somehow.

'I need to go,' he said. My heart sank. 'They'll kill me if

they know I've snuck out. Especially after everything that's happened today. Thanks.' He held up the library book and tapped it. 'See you soon, yeah?'

I stood stone still, wishing I had a reason to make him stay. Seb seemed to be waiting for me to say something, but the words just wouldn't come. His eyes didn't leave mine as he took a step towards me. I held my breath as he came closer. His breathing seemed to quicken, as if he were nervous, and before I knew it his hand reached out and grabbed mine. The cold night had made my fingers numb, and the warmth of his skin burned into me.

'Thank you, Frankie,' he whispered. He gave my hand a quick squeeze before letting it go. It dropped down at my side like a dead weight and I instantly wondered if I'd imagined the whole thing.

We stood looking at each other, nervously. 'I'd better go.' he said softly.

'Yeah,' I let out the breath I'd been holding as I watched him walk off into the night. I stood there for a moment, watching as he pulled the hood of his jumper over his mop of brown hair and set off down the dark, narrow road back into town, back to St Hilda's. I was still staring when he turned around and flashed me a smile in the darkness.

## 12

I spent the rest of the evening alone in my room. I didn't look for Suzy. I didn't want to break the spell that seeing Seb had cast upon me. I wanted to stay in my daze, only thinking of him. Around me I could hear the constant chattering of the other girls, reading the contraband newspaper articles aloud and exchanging theories about who the body might belong to.

Blocking out the sounds around me, I turned the pages of *The Sandman*. I loved everything about it: its sparse and delicate prose, its dark and haunting pictures, the story it told about the Lord of Dreams. I must have read for hours, before I knew it the dorm lights were switched off and I was plunged into shadow.

Putting the book next to the copy of *Wuthering Heights*, I lay down in the darkness. My mind was too busy to sleep. All I could think about was the body in the woods, and about Mum making me stay at school over half-term. I thought about Suzy, and about ghosts and what it might feel like to die and come back to haunt someone. And I thought about Seb. I wished I was the Sandman, able to travel through dreams. I wondered what kind of things I'd see in Seb's dreams.

As I lay awake thinking, the chatter of girls slowly died out as everyone went to their rooms and fell asleep.

It must have been gone midnight when I noticed the smell.

It crept under my horsebox door and danced around my nose. It was the same as I'd smelt that night Suzy and I had played the Ouija board. Flowers and rot, like the carpet of a vast forest floor.

I ignored it at first, and when it became stronger I pulled the bed covers over my face to try to block it out. It made my tongue itch; it was so strong, so rancid.

The smell started to fade, and was replaced by something else. Something more familiar, something I could put a name to.

Cigarettes.

'Is someone smoking in here?' Claire shouted from the other end of the dorm.

No one answered. Everyone else was asleep.

'Frankie, Frankie,' she called.

I pulled my duvet off, crept over to my horsebox door and creaked it open. I tiptoed across the dorm towards Claire's room.

Ribbons of cigarette smoke danced in the air, heading towards the dormitory door.

'Frankie!' Claire said loudly. 'You're the fire marshal. Do something about it!'

'OK, OK!' I whispered back. 'I'll go check it out.'

I dashed back in my room and grabbed my dressing gown and slippers. Wrapped up warm, I headed out of my room and stood still for a moment, watching the last wisps of smoke thin out into the air around me. It was definitely cigarette smoke, although what it was doing in Raleigh Dorm I had no idea. There was no one stupid enough in my year to smoke cigarettes so brazenly. If they were caught they'd be expelled on the spot.

I opened the dormitory door and peered out into the moonlit corridor. I instantly saw trails of smoke leading to the staircase. Tiptoeing in the moonlight, I followed the trace of smoke. The corridor was freezing cold and so silent I could hear the soft tread of my slippers on the worn carpet.

As my feet crept down the cold stone staircase, I wondered if I'd find Suzy at the bottom. This could be her idea of a joke, an act of rebellion or a way of getting my attention.

But Suzy wasn't standing at the bottom of the staircase – no one was.

In the darkness I could smell the pungent stink of cigarette smoke. I pulled open the door to the main school corridor and stepped into the cold hallway. There was no moonlight. It was pitch black. I couldn't see my feet on the floor or the walls either side of me. I waited, hoping my eyes would adjust quickly.

As I stood there in the darkness, it felt as if someone were standing just in front of me, and that if I reached out I'd grab them. I thought I could hear breathing in the silence, but not my own breathing, someone else's. It was rasping and shallow.

I heard a click, like a lighter being pulled down. Then I saw a flash of light ahead of me and a coal-red dot in the darkness – someone was lighting another cigarette, right there in the main school corridor.

My voice caught in my throat. I wanted to scream out and shout at whoever it was. This was stupid, they'd get caught. And I'd be brought down with them for standing there and not doing anything about it.

The red dot in the darkness began to move away. And as my eyes adjusted to the blackness I could make out a figure in the gloom, someone walking with the cigarette carelessly by their side.

They were leaving muddy footprints behind them.

It wasn't Suzy.

My heart froze.

'Hey,' I managed to whisper into the darkness. The sound of my own voice shocked me. It didn't sound like me – it sounded like some creature living in a dark cave who hadn't spoken a word for centuries: rasping, croaking, petrified.

'Hey,' I managed again.

Whoever it was didn't answer; they just carried on walking. My eyes were well adjusted to the darkness, but the figure remained a shadow, slipping away like sand through fingertips.

My feet trembled as I began to take small steps towards the shadowy shape. My heart was racing and every scrap of sense inside me was telling me to turn back.

I carried on. Tracing the muddy footprints further along the corridor.

'You can't smoke here,' I whispered in the darkness. Still no reply.

My legs started to work faster, taking me nearer and

nearer to the mysterious silhouette in the black of night. I heard a door open ahead of me and I watched as the figure walked into the school office. I was sure that the office was always kept locked, but I'd heard no keys jangle, no lock click open.

My feet brought me outside the school office door. I could hear my heart beating in my ears and my stomach curdle its last meal. My hand rested on the doorknob as emotions wrestled within me. I could have run away, back to the warm safety of my bed and pretend I hadn't seen anything. That would have been the best thing to do, the sensible thing. But I was always sensible, and I wanted to be reckless. I wanted to be the girl that turned the door handle and walked into the unknown.

I felt the doorknob twist in my hand, as if someone was opening it from the other side. The decision was made for me.

The door swung open.

I took a step into the dark office.

The smell of cigarettes burnt my nose and I wanted to retch.

A single beam of moonlight shone through a small window on the far wall, illuminating a tall metal cabinet. The kind of cabinet that contains school records. The kind of cabinet that's always kept locked. But there was one drawer wide open.

Ribbons of smoke poured out of the open drawer and spun towards me like streamers in the wind. I inched over to the cabinet, my heart thumping so hard I wanted to be sick.

I pulled open the drawer.

A stubbed-out cigarette simmered at the bottom of the cabinet drawer. Next to it was a wad of paper, tied together with ribbon. My shaking hands reached into the drawer and pulled out the papers. I untied the ribbon and I began to read . . .

## St Mark's Guild Newsletter
### 28th April 1995

### *Missing Pupil: Marina Cotez*

It is with great alarm that we report the disappearance of one of St Mark's most celebrated pupils, Marina Cotez.

Marina was last seen on Friday 28th October, leaving her final lesson of the day. Marina was due to catch a flight that evening to visit her parents in Northern Ireland, where her father, Colonel Cotez, is currently serving with his Rifles Regiment. However, Marina never boarded her flight to Ireland.

No trace of Marina has been established since her disappearance, and her parents urge anyone with any information to please come forward and share it with either the school or the police.

Colonel Cotez is offering a very generous monetary reward for any information that may lead to the return of his daughter.

# 13

There were four documents in total. All of them photocopies of originals: two letters, one time-stained newspaper clipping and the page from the St Mark's Guild newsletter. Every one of them was dated: 1786, 1815, 1940 and 1995, and each about something tragic that had happened to girls at St Mark's College – Isabelle, who'd died while her father was serving in India; Hetty, who'd vanished without a trace; Susan, who died at the school while everyone else sheltered from Nazi bombs; and Marina Cotez, who'd vanished in 1995.

Marina Cotez, missing for nearly twenty years.

Marina, Seb's sister.

There was a picture next to the article about her: she had dark hair, just like Seb's. But instead of his cold blue stare she had deep brown eyes.

I read those four photocopies over and over again that night, and again the next day and the next. I didn't know why someone wanted me to see them, and I had no idea what they meant. Jim the workman had been right when he spoke to the press – St Mark's really did have a dark past, and the body in the woods was only the tip of the iceberg.

And Seb had somehow known this all along.

That was why he seemed so obsessed with the school. His sister had vanished here, long before he was even born. Her disappearance was haunting him, and he needed to find out why. Something wasn't right – all these girls had gone missing or died while in the school's care. But that wasn't the only thing that deeply disturbed me. The figure that had led me into the school office that night; it was like smoke, a shadow, a dream. It wasn't one of the teachers, or another girl. I'd searched for hours for the figure again that night. Up and down the cold marble corridor, my breath puffing in the cold night air. But there was no sign of their muddy footprints or the smell of cigarette smoke. They'd simply vanished.

At first I didn't tell anyone what had happened, not even Suzy.

'How was your hot date with Seb?' she asked as we were queuing up for our breakfast that morning.

I spun around and glared at her, 'It's not like that.' Suzy's shoulders tensed as what looked like panic passed through her eyes. I realised I'd never snapped at her before, and she didn't know how to deal with it. 'Just leave it, OK,' I warned her. I walked away and sat with the other girls in my dorm, leaving Suzy to sit alone. I felt cruel but I just didn't want to be near her. I didn't want to avoid her questions or have to lie about what had happened.

And I wasn't ready for her to know yet. I'm not sure why – maybe I was scared I'd imagined that night, that I was going crazy.

I wished I had imagined it. I didn't want to be involved

in whatever I was being led into. But as much as I pushed that night to the back of my mind, I knew it was real. The four pieces of paper were real. I could hold them in my hands and run my fingers over the words and pictures. I just couldn't make sense of them.

As I walked down the main school corridor, thinking about how I would tell Suzy what had happened, the old school photographs on the wall caught my eye. There were dozens in total, one taken every few years. I found the 1938 and 1994 pictures and stared at them. I studied the faces of each girl from 1938, wondering which one was Susan Montford, who'd been found dead just two years later. Marina's face jumped out at me as soon as I looked at the picture from 1994. I couldn't look for long. Her dark stare was like a cold hand around my heart, squeezing and tightening my chest. I noticed that the St Mark's uniform had changed three times since 1938. I didn't need to think too long to realise the change wasn't brought about by the evolution of fashion. It was St Mark's way of reinventing itself, shedding its skin and distancing itself from the grim events that haunted it.

I sat down opposite Suzy with a plate of salad and tried to pick my words carefully.

Suzy spoke first. 'You've been ignoring me,' she said accusingly, lifting an apple to her painted lips. 'You're hooking up with Seb and now you're ditching me. *Words are easy like the wind. Faithful friends are hard to find . . .*'

I took a sharp intake of breath and tried my hardest not

137

to roll my eyes. 'You have a Shakespeare quote for everything, don't you?'

'And you're a deserter,' she shrugged back.

'No,' I said simply. 'I've just had stuff to think about, that's all.' I felt guilty as I realised there was some truth to what she was saying. I didn't need Suzy in the same way that I once did. I sighed. 'Is everything OK?'

Suzy did that thing she always did where she looked around dramatically, checking that no one was watching – which they never were – before leaning in and whispering, 'It's getting worse.'

'What's getting worse?' I asked, feeling a twang of irritation.

She leant even further across the table and mouthed, 'The haunting.'

I put my fork down on the edge of my plate gently and looked at her, annoyed. I was getting so sick of always talking about her.

Suzy gave me a sad smile and absently started scratching the backs of her hands. 'Do you remember your first week at St Mark's? I told you I'd seen the Blue Lady.'

I shrugged.

'I was lying.' She nodded and sucked in a deep breath. 'I'd never seen her before. I'd never seen any kind of ghost. I thought it would be funny to scare you and tell you that I had. But I shouldn't have said that, Frankie.' Her fingernails scraped at the flesh on the backs of her hands, making me feel sick. 'It's like the boy who cried wolf. Whatever's after me, I've brought it upon myself. I joked about ghosts and played with Ouija boards like it was some kind of game. But it's not, Frankie. And now I've dragged something out of hell and back to St Mark's, and it won't leave me alone, it won't . . .'

'Shhh.' I reached over and put my hand over hers, trying to stop her drawing blood from the back of her hands. Her eyes searched mine, begging me to say something kind and sympathetic. But I was sick of being sympathetic. So far in our friendship it had nearly always been about Suzy, but for once I had a loaded gun that could make everything about me.

'I have something I need to show you,' I said slowly, enjoying the power more than I ever thought I would.

Suzy's eyebrows crinkled together. 'Don't you want to know what's been happening to me each night?'

'Meet me after school.' I picked up my lunch tray and stood up. 'I'll come to your dorm at four.'

I walked off without another word, startling myself with my boldness. I didn't look back as I walked out of the dining hall, but I imagined Suzy sitting behind me, her head turned to watch me slip away, her mouth hung open in bemusement.

At four o'clock that afternoon I went to Newton Dorm and knocked on the door. A tall girl with jet-black hair opened it and screwed her nose up at the sight of me.

'Is Suzy there?' I asked.

'Third door on the right,' the girl said back, shrugging her shoulders and opening the door wide.

Newton Dorm didn't look as special as I'd imagined. It looked just like Raleigh, with vaulted ceilings and horsebox rooms. None of the other fifth-year girls paid me much attention as I walked through the dorm – the dramatic events of the last few days had made people immune to the scandal of a fourth-year girl in a fifth-year dorm.

I walked into Suzy's room without knocking. I carried the photocopies in the green biscuit tin Gran had given me as a child, the tin I kept under my bed – the safest place I had. The window was wide open and Suzy perched precariously on the windowsill. I sat myself down on the bed next to her, determined not to react to the dramatic gesture of her practically hanging out of a fifth-floor window.

She didn't say anything; she didn't even acknowledge me. I stared at her for a few seconds, my eyes burning into her face, begging her to look at me, but she didn't.

Eventually my eyes began to wander. It was the first time I'd ever been in Suzy's room, and it was just as I'd imagined. The walls were lined with posters of plays she'd seen, pictures of her family and an old black and white photo of her dad with what looked like a much younger Emma Thompson.

My eyes ran over the room as though they were reading the pages of a book. The walls of Suzy's room told the story of her life as well as any words. As my gaze travelled I noticed small burn marks. The corners of posters had been singed and eyes burnt out of photos. The tiny burns were everywhere; it looked like someone had sprinkled acid all over the room.

'Is this where the holy water burned holes?' I whispered, fingering a small hole in Suzy's bed cover. I didn't believe that that's what had happened, but I didn't have another explanation for how they got there. Suzy could have singed them herself for all I knew.

'Yeah,' she answered, her voice hollow as she turned to look at me. Her eyes were red raw; she must have been crying. 'What did you want to show me?'

I opened the beat-up old tin, took out the four documents and spread them out on the bed. Suzy climbed down from the window and reached for the papers. I noticed that the backs of her hands were streaked with sore, bloody scratches.

'What are these?' she asked, distracting me from her hands.

Taking a deep breath, I told her my story.

I didn't tell it as well as she could have. There were no pauses or dramatic crescendos in my voice. But I told it, word for word. I told her about the cigarette smoke and the figure in the hallway and about finding the papers in the drawer. Suzy listened patiently, mindlessly scratching at the backs of her hands as I spoke.

'The oldest document reminds me of that story you told me,' I finished, gently putting my hand over Suzy's to stop her doing herself any more harm. 'The Blue Lady. The girl who was expelled and died on the school steps with her baby in her arms.'

Suzy ignored my observation and snatched one of the other papers from the bed and studied it closely. 'This is her, Frankie,' she said quietly, trying and failing to hide the tremor in her voice. She turned the page around so I could see it, and pointed a shaking finger to the picture of Seb's missing sister, Marina Cotez. 'This is her, Frankie, the girl who's been haunting me.'

'What?' I asked, annoyed that Suzy had somehow managed to make this all about her again. 'Suzy, that's Seb's sister. What are you talking about?'

'I dream about her every night, Frankie.' Her tone was cautious, as if testing how much to reveal.

I must have rolled my eyes without realising it, because Suzy slammed the piece of paper down on the bed and snarled, 'You don't believe me! No one believes me! You all think I'm mad!'

'Calm down –'

'How could I imagine this?' She pointed to one of the many burn marks in the room. 'It's killing me, Frankie. Every night I can hear whispering and scratching and I swear someone's coming for me . . .' Her voice trailed off and she closed her eyes and tipped her head back.

'No one's coming for you, Suzy.' I wriggled closer to her on the bed and put a sympathetic arm around her.

'You don't believe me.' She shook her head and pinched the bridge of her nose. 'You saw those words burned into the shack floor – I'm next!'

I stayed silent, unable to summon the words to express the storm of thoughts raging inside me. Of course I didn't want to believe her. Ghosts only existed in stories, they didn't haunt school corridors. But trying to find an explanation for everything was exhausting. And I could feel myself slipping way, way out of my depth and into the unknown. The thought terrified me. I believed in things I could touch and see in front of me, like the four bits of paper that sat between us on the bed. I wanted to talk about those. I couldn't bring myself to accept that Suzy could be right. That whatever we were dealing with was unnatural and dangerous, and that we had lost all control.

Suzy must have seen the confusion etched on my face. 'Come with me to the graveyard tonight,' she pleaded, her eyes firing up like flames.

I forced a nervous laugh. 'Can you hear yourself speak, Suzy? You sound insane!' But even I could hear the doubt in my voice. Suzy stared at me, her earnest gaze a dangerous invitation. I pulled back my shoulders and tried to stay calm. 'What does a graveyard have to do with anything?'

'It's Friday night,' Suzy said, as if that explained everything. I shook my head, not understanding. 'All the day girls and teachers have gone. Half the boarders have gone home for the weekend. And everyone that's left here is too caught up in the dead body to care what we're doing, right? It's perfect. We can slip out to the graveyard tonight and no one will notice. And we won't be gone long – it'll only take an hour. Maybe Seb could meet us there and he could –'

'Suzy –' I argued.

'Trust me.'

'Why are we going to a graveyard? If this is about doing another Ouija board then I don't want to get involved . . .'

'You won't have to,' she said quickly. 'Not in the graveyard, not tonight, anyway.'

'Then what exactly are you planning to do there?'

Suzy took a deep breath. 'I need to collect some soil. Hear me out,' she said, seeing the look of protest on my face. 'I've been reading about ghosts on the internet and in any book I could find the last few days. And ghosts are trapped spirits,' she explained. 'Spirits that won't accept that they're dead. Apparently, if you sprinkle graveyard soil near an area that's being haunted, it helps cleanse that area of unwanted spirits. The soil acts as a reminder to the spirit – it makes it realise that they're dead and have no place in this world.'

I'd never heard anything so absurd in all my life.

'Where did you read this?' I spluttered. 'I'llbelieveanything.com?'

'I'll go on my own,' Suzy snapped, wriggling away from the arm I still had wrapped around her. 'I'll call Seb and ask him to meet me there, maybe he can tell me more about his sister –'

'Wait,' I said quickly. 'Suzy, please don't involve Seb in all of his,' I begged. The very last thing I wanted was for Seb to know we'd tried to raise the spirits of dead girls with Ouija boards. The thought of him finding out made me feel sick.

'Either you ask him to meet me or I will, Frankie,' Suzy threatened.

Her words felt like a dagger in my gut. I couldn't let her see Seb without me. I didn't want to share him. 'You can't go wandering around graveyards on your own,' I said petulantly.

'So you'll come with me then?' she said hopefully. 'You'll message Seb, tell him to meet us there? And tell him to bring James.'

I pulled out my phone from my pocket and typed a message without stopping to think. I didn't want Seb to know what we were up to. I didn't want Suzy to ask him questions about Marina. But I wanted to see him, and I knew I had to find a way.

*Meet me in the graveyard in town tonight?*

He texted back almost straight away.

*Of course. X*

# 14

The local church was in Martyrs Heath, only a short walk from school. The church was called St Mark's, just like the school, although the church was much older. A narrow road wound down the hill from the school – the only connecting road to the tiny town at the bottom.

St Mark's church was on the outskirts of Martyrs Heath, close to St Hilda's. The church was a small, medieval-looking grey building with one bell tower and a small stained-glass window facing west. Like all churches that old, St Mark's sat in the middle of a vast graveyard. Every grave was ancient – the headstones lopsided, faded and covered with green moss. There was a gate at the bottom of a path that led into the graveyard from the street. It groaned as Suzy pushed it open. I followed as Suzy's footsteps crunched down on the pebbled path.

I could hear Suzy's breathing as she walked towards the church. It was ragged and rasping, as if she was exhausted. Then the sound got louder, and I realised that the noise of my own strained breath was joining Suzy's. Harmonising like some kind of twisted melody, played out in the darkness. I felt the sudden urge to turn and run. I didn't want to be there – I wanted to be inside, in the warm, investigating the four documents. That was what was important to me, not being in a graveyard.

Suzy walked off the path and began to wind her way between the graves. My eyes glared down at the ground beneath me, straining in the moonlight, making sure I wasn't walking over anyone's final resting place. I tried to walk on the spaces between the graves, zigzagging a longer path for myself, losing Suzy as she marched on ahead.

'Frankie, hurry up!' she called back at me.

I ran to catch her up. She was crouching by a cross-shaped headstone. The words *Mary Gasket, 1787 – 1821, Daughter, Wife, Mother* were barely visible.

'So what's the plan?' I asked, standing next to her, my breath dancing on the cold air. I glanced around for Seb but he was nowhere to be seen.

Suzy pulled a clear sandwich bag from her coat pocket. 'No plan,' she said. 'Just need to shovel up a load of dirt into here.'

'So this is where you want to meet from now on?' came Seb's voice from the shadows. 'Now that the woods are gone.'

I spun around, a stupid smile escaping onto my face at the sight of Seb standing in the darkness.

'Where's James?' Suzy asked straight away, quickly pocketing the bag of soil she'd collected. 'He hasn't texted me in a while.'

Seb came closer, his blue eyes glistening in the moonlight. Every inch of me prickled with excitement. 'Er, he's busy.' Seb shuffled his feet. It was obvious there was something he wasn't telling us about James. But I didn't care, and

I didn't care that Seb was so bad at lying. It only made me trust him more.

I looked across at Suzy, wishing she'd just disappear. There was so much I wanted to say to Seb that I didn't want to say in front of her. But Suzy was there, right next to me. And there was no getting rid of her.

'How are you?' I asked Seb nervously.

'Um,' was all he answered. His eyes flicked warily to Suzy, and I wondered if he felt like I did. I wondered if he wished we were alone.

Suzy looked between us, trying to understand the shift in dynamic between Seb and I. She lifted her eyebrows teasingly, and I knew she was on the verge of making some dumb comment about the two of us.

Desperate to stop her, I said the first thing that came to my mind. 'I've been reading that graphic novel.' My breath left white clouds in the night air. 'I really like it. I'd definitely like to read the others you've got.' Seb stared down and kicked at the ground. He seemed on edge, more guarded than he'd been lately. 'And I've been reading *Wuthering Heights*,' I added, trying to fill the silence.

He raised one eyebrow. 'Why?'

I felt my cheeks burn up and I was so thankful for the thick blanket of darkness around us. He'd never mentioned the book to me before; I'd only ever seen him quote it on his Facebook page. Now he was bound to think I was some kind of stalker. I could never admit that I'd only read the book because he had, and I wanted to know more about him.

'What's that?' Suzy grabbed at the book in Seb's hands.

I silently thanked her for coming to my rescue. 'Why do you want to read about St Mark's history . . . oh . . .' She paused and small puffs of warm breath erupted from her mouth. 'I heard about your sister, that she died at St Mark's. Actually, I wanted to ask you about her . . .'

'Suzy!' I warned.

'You must know something about how she died?' Suzy quizzed Seb without an ounce of compassion. I shuffled uncomfortably.

Seb looked at me intensely, as if I somehow knew the answer to Suzy's question. My heart quickened. I looked desperately at Suzy, wordlessly begging that she wouldn't mention anything about hauntings. Seb would probably never want to lay eyes on either of us again if he knew the disgusting truth about how we'd tried to summon up the spirits of the dead in some kind of sick game.

A gust of wind sent a cold shiver through me. I felt the hairs on my arms and the back of my neck stand to attention. My eyes swept around the graveyard, watching as mist clung to the countless tomb slabs.

That's when I saw her.

There was a shadow on the other side of the graveyard. A cloaked figure in the darkness.

My breath caught in my chest like a wild animal blasted with a stun gun. I struggled to breathe, my mouth hanging open, and I gasped. The look on Seb's face changed as he noticed my expression and he turned to see what had caught my eye.

The figure was walking towards us, weaving between the gravestones with grace and purpose. It was a woman. Slender legs hugged tightly by trousers and a long hooded coat flapping as she walked. I opened my mouth to scream, but only a strange gargle escaped. Suzy looked up at me, her eyes confused and scared. She followed my frightened stare and spun around, freezing rigid on the spot.

The woman was coming nearer, moving silently among the weed-covered graves. In the moonlight I could see her eyes sparkle with delight, as if she were a hunter walking towards the prey she'd just snared.

'What are you doing here?' she asked. Her voice was as soft as silk on skin. Loose, sandy curls peeped out from her hood, framing a heart-shaped face and eyes that smiled at the corners. I found myself breathing a little easier.

'What are *you* doing here?' Suzy said promptly, her voice accusing and sharp.

The stranger let out a small chuckle into the night air. 'I'm the church warden. I live in the cottage over the road.' She pointed to a tiny thatched cottage beyond the graveyard. Warm light shone from the windows and smoke billowed from a single chimney. 'I was just locking up the church for the night.'

Suzy shuffled sheepishly and cast me a worried look.

'We were just out for a walk,' I said quickly.

'In a graveyard?' the woman asked with a smile. She seemed friendly, and I instantly felt foolish for feeling scared of her. 'You're from St Mark's College?' she asked.

I nodded and Suzy cast me an angry glance, as if I'd just betrayed a sacred secret.

'I won't report you, don't worry,' the woman said. 'I was a schoolgirl there once. I know what's it's like – you need to get away every once in a while.' Her attention moved to Seb and she gave him a shallow smile of acknowledgment. 'Sebastian.'

Seb nodded in recognition, but his eyes gave nothing away. I wondered briefly how they knew each other.

The woman regarded Seb warily. 'I heard about the discovery in the school woods. Your family must be so relieved that your sister –'

'I've gotta get back to school,' Seb said curtly. 'I was here to meet up with my girlfriend to give her a book back.'

Suzy smiled and hugged the school library book to her chest. My stomach did a sick little flip of jealousy.

'We're just heading back now,' I said, too briskly. Seb must have heard the hurt in my voice; he gave me a shy smile.

The church warden rubbed her hands together for warmth. 'Good idea, it's getting late. I'm not sure it's wise to be walking alone so late at night.' She started to walk towards the gate leading back to the village, gesturing for us to follow her. 'Next time you feel you need to escape, you can always come to the church. You're always welcome there if you need a place to think. If it's not open then you can knock on my door. I always have a key.'

'Yeah, thanks.' Suzy pulled sharply on my arm, leading me away.

Seb threw me an anguished look, as though he wished he could follow us. Suzy jerked me away from him and the church warden, but my eyes stayed on Seb. I watched as he made his way to the other side of the graveyard and leapt over the small stone wall, disappearing into the night beyond.

My insides clenched with disappointment as every step took me farther away from Seb. Suzy and I ran along the narrow path that wound up the hill, back to school. I never once looked behind me. But if I had done, I would have seen the woman standing there, watching as we slipped away.

## 15

'What exactly are you planning to do with the soil?' I asked Suzy, as we walked into Newton Dorm.

I caught sight of myself in a passing mirror and hardly recognised the tangled bird nest staring back. My cheeks flushed at the thought of Seb seeing me look that deranged.

As other girls walked about in fluffy pyjamas, I whispered over the sound of burring hairdryers, 'Aren't you worried that it might . . . you know . . .'

'What?' Suzy looked at me blankly.

Unexpected excitement rose within me. 'That it might burn the place up, like the holy water did?' The exhilaration of the past few days had sent my imagination into overdrive.

Suzy replied with absolute sincerity, 'Well, if it does then at least you'll be here to watch this time. You'll know I'm not crazy.' In the harsh strip lights of Newton Dorm Suzy couldn't have looked more unhinged. Her hair stood windswept to attention and her eyes shone with anticipation.

I sat on Suzy's bed as she frantically pulled a book from the shelf. She urgently leafed through it. 'Here,' she said, thrusting the book at me. 'This is where I read about graveyard soil. All we need to do is scatter the soil around the room and ask the spirit to leave.'

'OK,' I said, peering sceptically at the book.

Suzy put the bag of soil on her desk and unknotted the top. She reached in and took a handful. Closing her eyes, she concentrated on something deep within herself. She took several long, slow breaths and exhaled with control, 'Spirits come to us, spirits come to us, spirits come to us.'

It was just like the Ouija board, only now we had dirt and not paper to summon demons. Even in my newfound state of co-operation it all seemed ridiculous.

Suzy opened her eyes slowly and looked around the room, as if she were expecting to see something. My eyes followed hers but saw nothing unusual. As she held out the handful of soil and opened her mouth to speak, someone burst through her bedroom door.

'Got to go to the chapel now,' a girl with curly blonde hair said, slightly out of breath.

'Haven't you ever heard of knocking?' Suzy replied bitterly.

'It's ten o'clock at night,' I added. 'Why would we need to go to the chapel now?'

'They've identified the body,' the girl said with a wicked smile.

She didn't need to say anything else. Suzy shoved the handful of soil back into the plastic bag, leaving it on her desk. We followed the blonde girl into the corridor, which was bustling with excitement. Every boarder in the school streamed towards the small chapel in a long line, like worker ants scurrying towards their queen.

Animated whispers filled the air as we found our way

to an empty pew. Saskia and Claire sat on the pew in front of us. They'd been in the middle of applying facemasks when they'd been called away, and their faces were caked in thick green clay, making them look like cheap Halloween ghouls.

Eventually, Ms West entered the chapel, followed by two policemen. The look on her face was the same as it had been the day she'd broken the news of the body – solemn, exhausted, regretting every word she had to say.

'Thank you for coming, girls.' Her voice rung out through the chapel. 'I know that it is late, but we have had some news this evening and it's important that you hear it now, from me, instead of reading something incorrect in the papers tomorrow morning.'

She took a moment to draw breath. The silence of anticipation prickled in the air, as if her words could light up all the candles in the chapel. 'I have been informed by the police that a positive identification has been made on the body that was found in the school woods. Following on from the circus that has surrounded St Mark's this last week, I urge you all to be as discreet with this information as possible and to ask your parents, guardians and friends outside St Mark's to also exhibit discretion, out of respect for the dead girl in question.'

It was a girl, the body. It was a girl. And Ms West was buying time . . . waffling her words when she should have been direct. Suzy and I exchanged a brief glance – we knew the news wasn't good.

'The body found in the woods this last Monday,' Ms West continued, 'is that of a St Mark's schoolgirl who went missing nearly twenty years ago. Her name was Marina Cotez. Her family have of course been informed of this disturbing development.'

It was as though someone had punched a hole in my heart and all the life was seeping out of me. My worst fears were confirmed. My eyes welled with tears and all I could think about was Seb. Finally he knew what he must have always suspected – that his sister was dead, and she had died at St Mark's all those years ago. He must have known when we met him in the graveyard.

That was the moment I realised how deeply I cared about him. I couldn't bear the thought of him being in pain. Whatever connection I had with him ran deeper than the time we'd spent in the woods. I was sure that he had wanted to tell me about his sister when we'd met in the graveyard. I ached to be near him – to know he was OK.

Ms West carried on speaking, but her words just fell away from me. Her voice was drowned out by the sound of Suzy's breathing. She was wheezing, having some kind of asthma attack. Through my tear-filled eyes I turned to look at her and gasped. She was grey, as if her blood had frozen in her veins.

'Suzy!' I said too loudly. Everyone turned to look at me and Ms West stopped speaking.

'It's her, Frankie!' Suzy croaked. 'It's her!'

The moment was hazy. I don't remember the words of the housemistresses as they shouted at us to sit down. I don't remember how I struggled to break free of Ms Thurlow's spidery grasp as she tried to stop us leaving.

I remember dragging Suzy to her feet and leading her

through the horrified glares. I remember running, running so fast I thought my legs would fly off. Holding Suzy's hand so tightly I thought my fingers would explode. We ran along the main school corridor, up five flights of stone stairs, opened the Newton Dorm door and rushed towards Suzy's room.

The door flung open with such force it crashed into the wall, ripping a hole into the *King Lear* poster sitting behind the door.

We stopped dead in our tracks. Staring at the room we'd left only minutes before.

It had changed.

Everything had changed.

The bag we'd collected the soil in sat in the middle of the floor, ripped to shreds, as if someone had fed it through a wood chipper.

The soil we'd collected from the graveyard had been smeared around the room, on the bed, the floor, the windowsill.

Suzy's mirror hung on the back of the open door. I caught sight of my reflection out of the corner of my eye – it didn't look like me. I'd never looked so pale. That was when I saw the writing. There was a word, smeared clumsily in mud across the mirror:

RUN.

'She's been here,' Suzy said, still holding my hand so tightly my fingers were numb. We stood together in the silence, listening to the sounds of our breathing, the sound of the world we knew crashing down around us. 'Marina Cotez.'

# 16

Before that night there had been moments of light among Suzy's darkness, but they vanished. Now Suzy lived in eternal midnight. She was convinced that the spirit of Marina Cotez wanted to do her harm.

'Why else would she trash my room like that?' she pointed out hysterically. 'The way the bag was torn up,' she sobbed. 'She must have used a knife, or scissors, something sharp. It's a sign, Frankie. Marina wants me dead.'

I sat on Suzy's bed, nervously twiddling the remains of the shredded plastic bag between my fingers. Suzy's erratic behaviour disturbed me nearly as much as the spilt soil. Her mood switched back and forth from sorrow to anger, disbelief to denial. I couldn't keep up with her – it was all I could do to watch on in horror as she flipped from one extreme to the next.

Desperation bubbled in my veins as I tried to find an explanation, something that might pull Suzy back to me. But nothing came. The time had come for me to accept the glaringly obvious.

The evidence was there: the small burn marks from the holy water, the cold hands in her bed, the scratching, the tapping, the dreams of Marina's face. And the graveyard soil. My brain scrambled to find a link between them all, but it kept drawing me back to the one terrible conclusion.

Something was haunting her.

Standing in Suzy's room, trying to ignore my rising sense of dread, all I wanted was Seb. I wanted to see him again. He'd take me away from all of this fear, bring me back to what really mattered. His sister. She'd been lying dead in the school woods for years and years. This was about her, not Suzy, not some stupid bag of soil.

Marina was dead. She was never coming back.

'We should tell someone,' I panicked, as Suzy tried to sweep the dirt from the floor, smudging it further into the carpet in the process.

'Who?' she said sharply, scrubbing at the brown smudge with a damp cloth. 'No one believed me the first time I said anything. Now they'll think that I'm totally insane. I can't cope any more, Frankie.' Her voice trembled. 'It's ruining my life. I can't even look in the mirror any more cos I'm terrified at what will be looking back at me over my shoulder.'

'OK,' I said in a tone Mum used when she was being serious. 'How about this . . . someone overheard us talking about going to the graveyard to collect soil. They thought it would be hilarious to then tip the soil all over your room and freak you out. That explains everything.'

'Who would bother?' Suzy said bitterly. 'No one hates me that much – no one cares that much. Besides, everyone was in the chapel at the same time we were.'

She was right. I was making excuses – grasping at straws

to explain the unexplainable. No one would do this to us, and there was no one we could tell. Not even Seb; especially not Seb. He was in enough pain; I wanted nothing more than to keep him away from whatever we were dealing with.

'Maybe the wind knocked the bag on the floor?' I said meekly.

'And did this?' Suzy snatched the torn and shredded bag from my hands. 'Look, Frankie, I know you're just trying to help. But the best thing you can do is just believe me, and help me find a way to get rid of this thing.'

'Holy water and graveyard soil didn't work,' I said unhelpfully. 'What next?'

'We try to contact her,' Suzy said, lifting her eyes to meet mine as she stopped scrubbing the floor.

'Contact who?' I asked, dreading the answer.

'Marina Cotez. The dead girl. I don't know what she wants, but there must be something. I need to find out what. I need to make her stop.'

'It just doesn't make sense,' I mumbled. 'Why would Marina haunt us when her brother lives down the road? Surely if anyone can help her it's –'

'Don't you see?' Suzy said impatiently. 'This isn't about Seb. It's about me – about St Mark's. She's trapped here!'

I stayed quiet. Suzy went back to violently scrubbing the floor. My mind raced as I watched my best friend hunched over the soil stains on the carpet, like a mad woman possessed. Whether ghosts were real or not, one thing was certain. I had to help Suzy, otherwise she was on the way to a secure mental health unit – fast.

'OK,' I said. 'Here's what we'll do . . .'

She listened closely as I quickly constructed a plan, studying every inch of my face as I spoke.

'OK,' she agreed. 'Tomorrow evening – no one will be in the school office then.'

'Tomorrow's Saturday – we've got the whole day to figure things out,' I reminded her. 'I'll meet you after breakfast. I'll bring the clippings with me.'

That night, after the dorm lights had been turned off, I took the photocopies out from my bedside drawer. I re-read the newsletter about Marina Cotez under the moonlight that streamed through my horsebox window.

Marina Cotez had been missing for over twenty years, and all this time she'd been buried in the school woodlands. I looked at the picture of the young schoolgirl staring back at me. Black hair tied in a lopsided ponytail, dark eyes, bright smile. She had her whole life ahead of her – why would anyone want to kill her? There must have been a reason for her death. Maybe she knew something she shouldn't, maybe she'd done something to make someone hate her so much they wanted her dead.

I stared harder at the picture. 'What are your secrets, Marina?' I whispered so quietly my lips barely moved. 'What do you want us to know?'

I scanned over the other photocopies in my hand as a dark cloud passed in front of the moon. There had to be a connection. A connection between the girls, and something that connected them to me, to Suzy.

My phone buzzed on my bedside table. My first thought was of Seb – he wanted to speak to me. But it wasn't him.

It was a message from Mum, asking how I was. I ignored it and hurriedly opened up another message to Seb. I didn't really know what to say, but I wanted him to know that I was thinking about him:

*I'm so sorry about your sister. X*

As soon as the message had sent my phone started to ring. I held it stupidly in my hands, looking down at Seb's number flashing on my screen. Exhilaration and panic swept through me all at once. After what seemed like hours, I finally pressed the green button.

'Hi,' I whispered shyly, afraid that the other girls in the dorm might be listening in.

'Thanks for your text,' he said gently, the pain in his voice so clear it shattered my heart. 'I wondered when they'd tell you.'

'When did you find out?' I asked.

He breathed deeply. 'My housemaster pulled me out of French this afternoon. A policeman had come to the school to speak to me.'

'You should have said,' my heart pounded, 'when we saw you at the graveyard this evening.'

'I wanted to. But there wasn't much time. And Suzy was acting kind of strangely . . .'

Guilt swept through me. Seb wasn't the only one keeping secrets. If he only knew what was going on within the cold stone walls of St Mark's, that his sister's spirit wouldn't rest . . .

'I'm so sorry,' I offered pathetically. I really had no idea what else to say. They don't teach you what to say when someone's sister has been found dead after twenty years.

He stayed quiet on the other end. There was only the soothing sound of his breathing in my ear. 'Honestly, it's a relief,' he said sadly. 'I always knew, deep down, she would never come home. I guess some things you just know, you don't need to be told. You know what I mean?'

'Yes.' I knew exactly what he meant. I knew it as well as I knew that life had led me to St Mark's for a reason. It was fate, to meet Suzy and Seb.

'I need to go,' he said. 'We've got prefects prowling around outside my dorm. I'll get blasted if they know I'm on the phone after lights out. Are you around over half-term?'

'Yeah. Mum's leaving me here to rot,' I winced as soon as I said it. The image of Marina's rotting body buried in the woods drifted through my stupid brain.

'Me too.' It sounded like he was smiling, much to my relief. 'I guess I'll see you then.'

I grinned at the phone in my hands after we had said goodbye. Despite all that had happened, and all that I now knew, I felt nothing but happiness, knowing I would soon see Seb again.

The next morning, after breakfast, I took the photocopies from the tin under my bed and brought them to Suzy's room. No one paid any attention to me going into Newton; school wasn't its usual self that Saturday. Instead of ordering pizzas and watching movies, everyone was given the opportunity to speak to Father Warren or Nurse Pippa, and the housemistresses opened the doors to their flats and offered hot chocolate and biscuits to anyone who needed to chat about what had happened.

As everyone else queued up for biscuits and prayers, I sat quietly, counting the burn marks in Suzy's room (I counted thirty-six in total) while she re-read the articles.

'We need to find whoever put these out for you to read,' Suzy said eventually. 'If we find them then we find the answers we're looking for.'

'Maybe,' I agreed. 'But maybe it's easier if we just do some research ourselves. If we end up bumping into the phantom smoker on our way then it's just a bonus.'

Suzy threw the photocopies down onto the bed and paced around her small horsebox room. She chewed at her fingernails as she started to think aloud. 'Three girls, centuries apart, dead. And another girl missing. All St Mark's girls. All military daughters. And you're right, Frankie.'

'About what?'

'There's something about this first girl,' she said, picking up the oldest document. 'Her story sounds just like the Blue Lady.'

'I guess a rumour has to come from somewhere,' I offered.

'Yeah.' Suzy shrugged, unconvinced. 'But there's no such thing as the ghost of the Blue Lady. It wasn't the Blue Lady we contacted that night on the Ouija board. It's not the Blue Lady haunting me, it's her.' She held up the picture of Marina.

'Maybe,' I continued. 'But Isabelle Marshall died because St Mark's let her freeze to death on the front steps. It's the school's fault that she died.'

Suzy nodded in understanding. 'Good detective work, Frankie, but not really relevant to what we're dealing with.'

'No,' I agreed. 'But maybe that's what connects all these girls? Maybe the school was in some way responsible for what happened to them. And maybe that's why something – or someone – is haunting you?'

'Frankie!' Suzy gasped in realisation. 'Think about the messages the ghost has tried to communicate so far,' she said with horror. 'First there were the letters burned into the ground of the shack . . .'

'NEXT,' I said quickly.

'And the word RUN smudged on my mirror. And everything else . . . it's like they're trying to scare me more than hurt me. If they wanted to kill me they could have done it easily by now.'

'They're trying to scare you into running away,' I added.

'Because I'm next,' Suzy said quietly.

'Next for what?' I mused.

'Next to die,' she said simply.

'I wonder if there are other girls who died or disappeared. I bet Marina and Isabelle weren't the only ones,' I said, slotting the pieces of the puzzle together.

'So now we know what we're looking for when we break into the school office,' Suzy said with a wicked glint in her eye. 'We need to find evidence of more cases like this. More girls who died or went missing at the school. Then we're going to contact Marina and ask what she knows!'

Suzy flung herself onto the bed dramatically and laughed manically. The sound sent cold shivers through me. 'The curse of St Mark's, Frankie. And I'm next . . .'

* * *

168

I waited until after lights out, like we'd planned. Then I snuck out of my dorm and headed towards the stone staircase to meet Suzy. She was already there, waiting for me.

'Where've you been?' she whispered angrily.

'I waited until ten thirty, like we agreed.'

'Well, you need a new watch,' she snorted. 'You're late.'

'How are we going to find a key?' I asked, following Suzy down the dark staircase, my feet burning as they touched the cold, cold stone. 'I forgot my slippers, my feet are freezing.'

'There'll be one in the staffroom,' Suzy replied. 'I had to meet Ms Thurlow for detention in there one time – I saw a load of keys hanging up on the far wall. One key for every room of the school.'

She was right. The staffroom was unlocked and we pushed back the heavy oak-panelled door. We crept across the carpeted room to the hanging keys. Science block, drama department, gym, school hall, school office – we lifted off the office key and snuck back out.

We tiptoed along the corridor. I looked around nervously, wondering if the ghostly figure I'd seen before would return. Maybe they were watching, maybe this is what they wanted me to do. But I didn't see anyone – we were completely alone. My heart raced as Suzy turned the key in the school office lock and pushed open the door.

We both pulled torches out of our dressing-gown pockets.

'First we need to find keys to the cabinets,' I whispered.

We pulled open the desk drawers in the office and soon found a bunch of keys mingled in with elastic bands and bent paper clips.

The keys fitted the cabinet locks.

Drawer by drawer we searched the cabinets. There was a file on every girl in school. Suzy had a quick look at hers – nothing exciting, just old school reports and her parents' contact information. I searched in vain for a file on Marina, or any of the other girls mentioned in the documents I had – but it looked like all files were destroyed after girls left the school.

Eventually we came to a drawer that contained a large file named ARCHIVE.

I peered over Suzy's shoulder expectantly. It was one of those old files, where hole-punched papers were held in place by pieces of string.

This was it, surely. This is where the school would keep its dark secrets hidden. This is where we could finally read about the girls who had died or disappeared.

Suzy opened it and shone her torch down onto the open file. It shook in her trembling hands.

There was nothing. Nothing but the string that once held papers in place, and fragments of torn paper. The file had once been full – and someone had ripped out its contents in a hurry.

Someone else had got there first.

## 2nd Battalion Mess Wives' Newsletter
### 19th April 1890

*Mrs Robert Shows has given birth to a healthy baby boy, who has been named after his great-great grandfather, William. The Christening will be held in the Mess Chapel a week on Sunday.*

*Fundraising has now begun for the annual Summer Ball, which will be held in the Mess. The theme for the event is The Empire. A committee has been assembled to organise costumes, food and decorations – any wife wishing to participate should speak to Mrs Webster before the end of the month. Tickets can be purchased and donations can be made to the Master of Ceremonies.*

*On a more sombre note, Captain Lakers' youngest daughter, Meredith, has been reported missing from her school. Meredith was last seen at St Mark's College a fortnight ago and there has been no trace of her since. Many of you may remember Meredith's 'Once in Royal David's City' solo in last Christmas's carol concert. Our prayers are with Captain Lakers and his family at this difficult time.*

## 7th Battalion Mess Wives' Newsletter
### 12th December 1910

*Military hero Brigadier Walter Forbes returned home to England from heavy fighting in India to the tragic news that his daughter, Margaret, had suddenly died.*

*Margaret was a pupil at St Mark's College, a girls' boarding school famed for its schooling of military daughters. Young Miss Forbes was in her third year at the school, under the tutorage of Headmistress Conner.*

*Reports are that Margaret died from a fatal head injury, sustained while falling from a great height. It is unclear from where she fell, although the understanding is that it was within the school grounds.*

*Hope is that this tragic incident does not deflect from the marvellous victory of 7th Battalion, Brigadier Forbes' regiment, which fought bravely in India these past five years.*

## 17

The half-term holiday came around too quickly. I watched from my horsebox window as countless cars came and went, each taking away excited schoolgirls and driving them to freedom. I was stuck at St Mark's.

Every other girl in my year was leaving for the holiday, apart from me. Saskia was leaving to stay with her aunt in Italy, Claire was going on a riding holiday in Devon and George was visiting her brother at university. The other girls in my dorm sniggered as I told them I had nowhere to go – as if my life, or lack of it, existed solely for their amusement.

There were only five of us left in school: myself, two girls in the first year, an Italian girl called Carla in Suzy's year and one of the sixth formers. Two of the teachers stayed on: Ms Barts and one of the first year housemistresses. We were the dregs of the school, the unwanted, the forgotten.

But Seb was around too. Just the thought of seeing him made me glad that my mother had abandoned me at school.

'Are you sure you're gonna be OK?' Suzy asked, poking her head around my horsebox door. 'My taxi comes in five minutes.'

'I'll be fine,' I said with confidence, assuring myself as much as Suzy. 'Text me when you get to Cyprus.'

'Will do,' she smiled. It was obvious how much she was looking forward to leaving the school. That whole week she'd been on countdown to half-term. 'Let's hope you-know-who doesn't decide to follow me!' she joked.

'Not unless you're flying Ghost Airways,' I kidded.

Suzy threw her arms around me, locking me in a tight grip. 'I love you, Frankie,' she whispered seriously.

'Love you too,' I squeezed back.

'I gotta go,' she muttered, pulling away from me. 'Stay safe.'

'The only thing I'm in danger of is dying from boredom.'

I stared out of my horsebox window until I saw Suzy lugging her suitcase through the door below. I watched as a black taxi pulled up and she bundled her bags into the boot and climbed in clumsily. As the taxi pulled away, she turned and waved up at my window from the back seat. I didn't have time to wave back before the taxi turned the corner and slipped out of sight. It was the last glimpse I'd have of Suzy for a whole week, and as soon as she'd disappeared I felt a dull sinking in my stomach, and I suddenly felt very alone.

With a heavy breath I turned away from the window and slumped back down on my bed. I checked my phone: no messages from Mum saying she'd changed her mind and I didn't have to stay in school. Nothing from Seb asking me to meet him. The lonely evening ahead of me suddenly felt as though it might stretch into eternity.

I stared into my horsebox room and listened to the world

outside my window as it bustled and continued without me. Sounds of car horns, heavy footsteps and revving engines filled the autumn air – a sharp contrast to the stillness inside my friendless room. But the chaos soon died down, the steady stream of cars dwindled and everyone who was leaving had left.

My eyes glazed over as I stared into space and ran over the itinerary for the next week. School had arranged an outing for us into London to see Buckingham Palace. Ms Barts was taking us out for an Indian meal one night, and then there was a cinema trip next weekend, but other than that I had nothing to do for the next seven days. I needed to spend some time investigating the strange disappearances and deaths of girls at St Mark's. But that was a distraction from what I really wanted to think about.

Seb.

I hadn't heard from Seb for a few days. I tried not to let that bother me. The last week must have been unimaginably painful for him. I wondered if his family had held a proper funeral for Marina yet, if all of this meant Seb wasn't spending half-term at school any more. Surely his family would want him close to them at such a terrible time. I buried the thought as quickly as it had appeared.

In a moment of bravery, I picked up my phone and dialled his number without thinking. Just when I thought the call would click to answerphone, I heard his voice. 'Frankie.'

'Hi,' I said simply, suddenly unsure of what to say. 'How are you? I was just wondering if you're still about at St Hilda's?'

'Yeah, I am,' he said quietly. He sounded brighter than I had expected him to be. 'Want to meet up?'

'Sure?' I said, unable to keep the smile off my face. 'When are you free this week?'

'How about now?'

'Now?' I repeated with surprise. 'Um, OK.'

'I'll see you in the woods in ten.' He hung up at the other end and for a moment I sat dumbly on my bed, the phone still pressed against my ear. I quickly leapt up, rummaged through my drawers and picked out the best outfit I could find. Black jeans, a dark red jumper and my woollen black beanie. I wore the hat slouched at the back of my head like I'd seen models do in magazines, and styled my loose dark hair around my face, framing it.

I pulled on my coat and wrapped a scarf around my neck.

It was already growing dark outside.

The school felt deserted. There was no distant hum of schoolgirls, no evidence of life at all. As the final taxi drove off into the distance, St Mark's seemed to morph into another place entirely. Everything that made it a school – the teachers, the pupils, the lessons and the gossip – evaporated and left a residue of such stillness. The school was a phantom of its former self.

I walked alone through the desolate car park with nothing but grey sky, cold brick and the puff of my warm breath for company. Expectation prickled my insides. It felt as though I had lightning running through my veins. The anticipation of seeing Seb was a heady mixture of gut-wrenching nervousness and blistering excitement. For every step I wanted to run, I wanted to take a step back, delaying the moment I'd see him again.

The woods were still roped off. Now that the police had finished excavating the site, the workmen were due back any day. So many trees had already disappeared, but there were still enough to lose yourself in. I lifted up the police tape and climbed underneath. As I stepped into the cordoned-off zone I felt a surge of exhilaration. I was in forbidden territory, and I was completely alone.

I had no idea where I was walking to. Seb hadn't told me where to meet him, so I wandered aimlessly in the rising darkness. My feet led me on an old, familiar route – towards the shack.

I hadn't meant to go looking for the grave. I hadn't even given much thought as to where in the woods it might be. But before I knew it I was standing at the foot of where Marina Cotez was buried. It wasn't far from the school sports fields, and Suzy and I must have walked over it a hundred times before. Yellow police tape stretched around a shallow pit filled with nothing but puddles of water from the recent rain.

I stared down thoughtfully. It wasn't deep, not as deep as a grave should be. I wondered how many other girls had trod that path before – girls sneaking out for cigarettes, girls out on runs, girls who just needed fresh air and came to the woods to escape from the suffocating school halls. I circled the grave and stared at its rough corners and jagged edges. I wished that the earth would give up its secrets, I wished that the soil, the trees and the rocks could whisper in my ear and tell me how Marina had ended up buried there.

There was a crackle of twigs, and I knew Seb must be close. It suddenly felt intrusive, standing at his sister's grave. I had no right to be there. I paced forwards, trying to distance myself from the gaping hole in the earth, but suddenly felt stupid walking away from Seb so I paused and waited for him to come into the small clearing.

'You found it then?' was all Seb asked when he saw me. He was wearing a black jumper, dark jeans and a heartbreakingly shy smile.

'I was on my way to the shack,' I mumbled apologetically. 'I'm sorry, it must be horrible for you to be here.'

'It's OK.' Seb shrugged, his eyes flashing wearily to the flooded grave. He leant up against a tree and pushed a hand through his mop of dark hair. The sleeve on his jumper pulled down as he raised his arm, and there they were again – the bands tied around his wrist.

'Where did you get your bracelets from?' I asked, walking towards him. He pushed up his sleeve and looked down at his wrist thoughtfully. 'Er, this one I got when I had a holiday in Spain with Dad a few years ago,' he said, pulling at a multi-coloured string. 'And this one's from a music festival James and I went to last summer. Um, this one here was a string that came off a balloon at my cousin's party, and this one,' he pointed to a thicker red band, 'was a ribbon from one of my sister's dresses. It seems quite morbid . . .'

'No,' I said quickly, seeing the discomfort in his eyes. 'You never knew her. I guess you just wanted to feel close to her somehow.'

'Exactly,' he smiled gratefully. 'You know, it's kind of a

relief . . . finally knowing that she died. She's been here all along.'

There was a moment of silence. It wasn't awkward. It was still, calm. Somehow, now felt like the right time to talk about his sister. 'When you first asked me to borrow that library book for you, you told me your sister had died at St Mark's.' His blue eyes studied me intently but gave nothing away. 'How did you know she was dead if they'd never found her body?'

He tilted his head back and raised his eyes to the shivering trees, 'It was just the way my dad talked about her. Dad's first wife – Marina's mother – left him after she went missing. She couldn't bear the way Dad held onto the thought of her coming home. But even I knew, from the way Dad spoke about her, that Marina wasn't the kind of girl to just disappear. I knew something had happened to her, that she wouldn't just turn up on the doorstep one day and play happy families.' He looked at me. Words seemed to be forming on his lips but he couldn't bring sound to them.

'What?' I pressed.

'You'll think I'm crazy,' he said carefully, his eyes burning with intensity.

'I won't,' I assured him. There was nothing Seb could say that would make me think he was crazy. I knew crazy, I was living through it inside the school walls, and it had nothing to do with Seb. 'Tell me.'

He bit down on his lip and my heart thudded as I listened to his careful words. 'I've been at St Hilda's for five years now. Five years in the shadow of St Mark's. Every day I look up at it looming down on us, and there's something about it that just feels so . . . wrong. I don't know, I can't explain it. I just always thought that there were secrets there, and that they had something to do with my sister, and why she died.'

Now the ghosts of words were dancing on my lips. I wanted desperately to tell him everything that had happened to me, and to Suzy. I longed to tell him about the Ouija board, the holy water, the soil, the words burnt in the shack floor and the feeling that something terrible was waiting for us. My lips moved, pressing together to form words, but they wouldn't come.

'There's something you should know,' said Seb.

My heart froze, dreading whatever he was about to say.

'It's about James,' he said carefully.

Confusion tightened my eyebrows together as I looked at Seb's clear blue eyes sparkling in the fading twilight.

'He's been seeing another girl in your year. A girl called George. I've been saying to him for ages that he needs to tell Suzy, but I guess he's just chicken. Either that or he likes stringing girls along.'

'Oh,' I uttered stupidly. That wasn't what I was expecting. 'Thanks for telling me. Suzy definitely has the right to know.'

'That's what I thought,' he agreed. 'Look, I kind of need to get back for dinner, but maybe we could meet again this week?'

'Sure,' I smiled, failing to hide my disappointment. 'I don't know about St Hilda's but only the seriously socially challenged have been left at St Mark's – I'll go mad with boredom if I'm stuck with them all week.'

'I'll call you?' he asked hopefully.

I nodded, and we both stood there for an awkward moment. I longed for him to reach out and touch my hand again, as he'd done when we met outside the school gates. I wondered if he felt it too, because he inched nervously towards me and then stopped, shuffling his feet and staring at me hopefully. But the moment wasn't there. With a silent nod he turned around and headed off, into the darkness and away from me.

I dug my hands into my deep coat pockets and made my way back towards the school. It was bitterly cold and the light was fading by the second. All the time my head hung low, staring at my feet as they moved and thinking of nothing but Marina. But I knew she was only one piece of the puzzle. There was more, much more.

I crossed the school fields quickly and turned the corner into the car park, the main school building towering down over me. I'm not sure what it was – intuition perhaps – but something pulled my head up and made me look towards my bedroom window.

That was when I saw it. There was someone in my room, looking out of my window.

A girl. Dark hair. Pale features. A uniform of some kind – one I'd seen somewhere before. Eyes that stared right back at me.

In the blink of an eye the girl was gone. As quickly as she'd appeared to me, she'd vanished.

I stood still in the car park, looking up at my bedroom window. I had to remind myself to breathe. My heart was lurching and blood was rushing to my head so quickly that

I struggled to think. I ran towards the school entrance, and then through the corridors and up the stone staircase. The piercing sound of silence rung around my ears as I bolted through Raleigh Dorm. I came to my horsebox, the last room on the left, and held the doorknob in my quivering hand. I'm not sure what I expected to see when I opened the door – another girl, a teacher, the ghost of Marina staring back at me. I felt sick, so sick I could have curled up on the dormitory floor and writhed around in pain.

I pulled the handle towards me and flung open the door with one swift jolt.

The room was empty. There was no one there.

There were no hiding places for me to check – no room under the bed for someone to hide, no wardrobe, no large cupboards. If someone had been in there they'd long gone.

Backing out of my room I then stormed over to the horsebox opposite mine. I pushed the door open – there was no one in there either. I worked my way down the whole dorm, opening doors one by one. Every room was empty. I was completely alone.

Bewildered, I went back to my room. Closing the door behind me and staring at it, I waited for it to burst open and for someone to come in. But no one did.

I must have been sitting there for hours, because before I knew it the dinner bell was ringing and it was time for me to head to the dining hall. I walked there in a dream-like state, my legs still shaking and my mind still whirring like a fairground ride. I hadn't imagined it. Someone had been in my room.

Ms Barts sat with me and the four other girls who had

been left in school over half-term as we ate. As hard as I stared at the girls, I couldn't make them look like the girl I'd seen at my window. Whoever she was, she wasn't sitting round that table.

'I love your hat, Frankie,' Ms Barts said kindly. I realised I was still wearing my woollen hat slouched at the back of my head. I reached for it and self-consciously pulled it from my head. 'It's OK,' Ms Barts smiled. 'I know you're not meant to wear hats in the dinner hall but it's the holidays, and I always liked a rebel!'

We forced out conversations about the weather and told our own stories of why we were staying at school over the holidays. But the mindless chat couldn't take me away from the face at my window. The memory echoed through my mind. The more I thought about it, the more I was certain that I recognised the girl.

After dinner, I headed back up to Raleigh Dorm. My sketchpad sat on my desk, in the same position I'd left it over a week ago. It had been the longest I'd gone without drawing since I could remember. Looking at my unloved sketchpad I felt a twang of self-hatred. Drawing was my passion. I was letting myself get caught up in everything around me – I'd almost forgotten who I was. It was such an obvious and easy way to escape from the myriad of thoughts whirling around in my head, I almost laughed as my eyes rested on it.

I picked up my pad with a violent thrust of my arm and opened it so hard I tore the spine. My hand absently reached for the first thing I could find to draw with – a black Biro pen. As the nib of the pen hit the paper I felt a rush of peace and silence swirl around me as shapes began to fill the empty page. Feelings of anger and frustration emptied from me like swelling water breaking free of a great dam. Suddenly I was free, free from the niggling horror that something terrible was about to happen, free from the chains that Suzy and her dramas had bound me in, free from Marina Cotez.

I wasn't even sure what I was drawing. It was only after the picture had taken shape that I sat back to admire what I'd created.

It was a girl.

The girl I didn't want to recognise. Dark hair, pale skin. Just like her brother. The same girl I'd seen at my window that evening.

Marina Cotez.

Her black, black eyes stared back at me from the sketchbook. Wisps of black hair swept over her face, just as they did in her picture in the paper, just as they'd done when she'd stared down at me from inside my room. But it was her eyes, those dark, dark eyes that fixed my gaze and wouldn't let me escape. It was like her eyes were screaming at me from the pad – begging, pleading.

I felt sick.

I ripped the page from the sketchbook, screwed it up tightly and threw it across the small room. It bounced off my horsebox door with the smallest sound, and rolled onto the floor next to my bed. Just like the thoughts of her in my head, the picture of Marina was like some kind of boomerang – however hard I tried to throw it away, it only came back.

My hand started to jolt around the page again, but this time I paid attention to what I was drawing. I forced myself to draw things that would take me away from St Mark's – I drew animals, beaches, forests and waterfalls. I drew for hours. I ignored the darkness in the sky outside and the terrible pounding of the wind hammering at my horsebox window. I ignored the sound of the autumn rain thrashing at the ground outside, whipping my window like a horse running to war.

I only stopped because the ink in my pen had run dry. I tossed the sketchbook to the floor and leant back against the windowsill. With my feet on the bed, I pulled my knees to my chest and sank my forehead between them. My breathing was ragged, rasping, as if I'd run for miles and miles. Suddenly it felt as if there wasn't enough air in the room to breathe. Reaching behind me for the window, I pulled it open and stuck my head out into the cold night air. The chilling, rushing wind felt wonderful against my flushed cheeks. I closed my eyes and let the starless darkness penetrate my eyelids.

When the time came, I couldn't sleep. I rolled over and over in bed, trying to empty my mind of all thoughts and give myself over to sleep. It didn't work. Nothing worked. How could I sleep in that room after what I'd seen staring down at me from the window? After what Seb had said about St Mark's having dark secrets?

I pulled myself onto my feet and wrapped my duvet around me. Quietly, I shuffled out of my horsebox, out of my dorm, down the corridor, up the stone staircase and out onto the floor above me. Newton Dorm was empty. I tiptoed in the darkness to the third door on the right – Suzy's room.

I lay down on her bed, my eyes running over the darkness in her room, making out the shapes of her posters and pictures. Moonlight snuck through cracks in the curtains, illuminating the burn marks that pockmarked her room – scars of something that I didn't understand. The sight left me cold.

I closed my eyes tight shut and tried not to think about what the small burn marks might mean, and what – who – had put them there. Eventually, my eyelids felt heavy, and I let sleep drag me into darkness.

# 18

Something woke me not long after I'd fallen asleep.

A noise. I'm not sure what. Maybe something in a dream. I woke up in a cold, clammy sweat, my heart racing in my chest. I sat up in bed, closed my eyes and listened to the darkness for some sign of movement. But there was nothing. No rattling pipes, no distant slamming doors, not even the sound of the wind. Nothing but the stillness and emptiness of the abandoned Newton Dorm.

I lay back down and tightened the covers around me so only my head poked out. The silence was burning my ears and I was suddenly very aware that I was completely alone. Of all the twenty or so horsebox rooms, this was the only one occupied.

Keeping my eyes tightly closed I tried to force myself back to sleep. I tried to still my mind of all thoughts, so I could drift off to sleep again, but the face I'd seen at my bedroom window kept floating into my head. Dark hair, pale skin, sad eyes. I tried to think of others things: Mum, Suzy, school work – anything to distract my busy brain from the image that kept pushing itself at me. Nothing worked. Even thoughts of Seb couldn't take me away from the vision that haunted me. Marina's picture was glued to the inside of my eyelids.

As I lay awake wrestling with the lingering image inside my head, the window next to the bed began to rattle. Gently at first and then ferociously. The wind beat against the glass, whipping it frantically.

I pulled the covers around my ears, trying to drown out the sound of the wind. But the freezing breeze seemed to creep through the rattling window and find its way into bed with me. I suddenly felt so cold. My body shivered and my head felt numb with frost. Once again I pulled the covers closer around me, hoping they would warm me and keep out the wind.

It didn't work.

A sudden gust of wind flung open the widow violently. My breath caught in my chest as I felt the bed covers peel off me, as if someone was ripping them away. My eyelids bolted open, and I stifled a scream in my throat. I expected to see someone there – someone standing at the end of the bed with the bed cover in their hands. But there was no one in the room. The covers sat in a crumpled heap at the end of the bed and the curtains flapped wildly in the cold midnight breeze. The open window swung about and knocked loudly against the wall. I could feel tears welling up in my eyes, and as a bitter, cold gust of wind filled the room a shudder of horror crept up my spine.

I'd never felt so petrified. I tried to tell myself it was just the wind pushing open an old window. The wind had blown the covers from the bed. It was the wind that was making me so deathly cold.

I reached down and gathered the covers. I pulled them back onto the bed and wrapped them tightly around me.

I got onto my knees, knelt on the bed and reached for the banging window. As I pushed it closed I made sure the catch was secured. Perhaps it hadn't been fastened properly before – perhaps that was why it had flown open.

I lay back down in the bed and listened to the wind rattle the window once again. In that moment it was the worst sound I'd ever heard – the urgent clatter of the hinges, begging to burst open – like someone violently shaking a dead bolt that just won't budge.

Swallowing hard, I closed my eyes. I muttered nursery rhymes inside my head, trying to cover up the sound of the wind. The wind grew louder and I found myself humming songs, and then singing them out loud. I put my fingers in my ears and sang louder, louder, trying desperately to drown out that terrible sound.

But then the scratching started.

Something was scratching at the bedroom door. It sounded like fingernails dragging down over the wood. My mouth fell paralysed and I stopped singing. I tried digging my fingers deeper into my ears but it didn't work. The scratching got louder.

Coldness flooded the room – it was colder than the wind. The wind felt natural; there was nothing natural about this. It wasn't the chill of winter rain, or wind or ice, but a poison that filled my veins.

If I lay in bed much longer I'd die of fright. I had to do something – something to make it stop. Slowly, I pulled my fingers from my ears and sat up in bed. My shaking hand pulled the bedclothes off me and I swung my legs over the edge of the bed so my feet touched the floor.

My legs felt numb as I stood up and walked towards the door, towards the scratching. Trembling hard, I reached for the door handle.

'Who's there?'

There was no answer. The scratching stopped for a short moment and there was silence. The silence was almost more terrifying, more unnatural than the sound of the scratching. Unexpected relief swept over me as the scratching started once again.

There was no way I was imagining it. My mind wasn't capable of such tricks – Suzy's maybe, but not mine.

With a swift jolt I pulled open the door.

There was nothing there. No one standing outside the door. No signs of scratching in the woodwork.

I slowly closed the door again. Resting my hands against the wooden door, I closed my eyes and tried to recover my breath.

Before I opened my eyes again I knew I wasn't alone. Something was there in the room with me. That feeling you get when someone stands behind you, when you can feel them at your shoulder, that was how it felt.

My eyes peeped open. I was still facing the closed door. There was a stream of light flooding the room, escaping through a crack in the curtain. Silver moonlight flooded over my shoulder, lighting up the patch of Suzy's bedroom door upon which my hand still rested.

I took a shaky step back, then two steps, then three. I stood in the middle of the room. The window and bed were behind me, the bedroom door and mirror in front of me.

The mirror.

I knew what was waiting for me in the reflection before I had the courage to lift my head and stare back at it. A horror and dread gripped my heart and squeezed the blood from within it. Every nerve in my body felt as though it was on fire, so pained with terror I was numb. I felt a single tear fall down my face – its warmth reminding me that I was still alive. My life hadn't yet been stolen from me by whatever dark, dark force was pinning me to the spot like a marble statue.

I could feel it behind me, cold. The smell of flowers and putrid rot burned my nose.

Something unspeakable standing at my shoulder.

I raised my eyes to the mirror.

She was standing behind me. Tangled, filthy hair knotted around her drawn face. Her skin was sickly and pale and her eyes so dark and terrible I knew I was looking into the very face of death.

'Marina,' I mouthed into the mirror. Paralysed, catatonic.

'RUN,' the apparition croaked back at me. 'RUN.'

# 19

I couldn't see. My eyes were blind with tears and glazed with fear and dread. I couldn't hear the sound of my own screams as I ran through the school corridors, mad with panic.

My feet carried me far, far away from Newton Dorm. I thought I'd been running for hours, but only seconds had passed when Ms Barts caught me in her arms and shook me violently, 'Frankie! Frankie!'

I tried to speak but nothing came out apart from sobs and howls. I buried myself in her arms and cried into her pyjama top. She stroked my hair and whispered something in her familiar lisp about a bad dream.

'Not a dream,' I managed to stutter.

She pulled me away from her and her duck-like mouth formed a sympathetic grin. 'It's OK, Frankie.'

I shook my head from side to side. Panic started to well up inside me as I realised that no one would ever believe me. They'd think I was insane. They'd write me off as nothing more than a hysterical teenager, just like they'd done with Suzy.

I didn't want that – I didn't want to be known as crazy. Standing in the school corridor in the midnight darkness, my limbs still shaking and my head still spinning with something worse than fear, I knew I had to somehow make Ms Barts believe me. I had to make her realise what was going on. She had to know I was telling the truth, that Suzy had been telling the truth – something was out there, it was after us.

I straightened my back and cleared my throat. I tilted my head up and looked Ms Barts right in the eye, squaring up to her as an equal. 'I saw her,' I said, my voice as calm as I could possibly manage. 'I saw Marina Cotez. Her ghost.'

I waited for Ms Barts to laugh at me. I waited for her to stroke my hair and offer me a hot chocolate while she called Nurse Pippa away from her holiday vacation. But she didn't. Instead she stared back at me, locking my eyes into hers.

'Come into my room, Frankie,' was all she said.

Her flat was small, and piled high to the ceiling with books. Dusty books, old books, books that smelt like damp paper and dirty fingers. Piles of unopened letters stacked up clumsily on the coffee table in the middle of the room, each addressed to Ms F. Barts. There were piles of crumpled clothes on the floor, and old coffee mugs and plates scattered about carelessly. I sat down on a small couch covered with colourful rugs. Something stuck into my back and I reached behind me and pulled out a high-heeled shoe.

Adults should be tidy. But Ms Barts wasn't. Junk and clutter was strewn over every available surface. Half-drunk cups of coffee made the place stink like Starbucks and the quiet hum of fruit flies hovering above an ignored fruit bowl filled my ears.

I sniffed away the last of my tears and steadied myself for the inevitable phone call to Mum. Ms Barts passed me a box of tissues and slipped out of the room. I listened, expecting her to pick up a phone, but I heard nothing. As I waited for her to reappear, my eyes scanned the room and noticed a pile of art books stacked next to the couch. They were strange books – books about artists who drew death and disease and war. I'd never seen anything so dark and disturbing in print before. I was about to pick one up and study it further when Ms Barts strolled back into the room with a packet of biscuits and a glass of milk.

I've always hated milk. Horrible, stale cow juice. But at that moment my throat was as dry as a desert, and I swallowed the cold milky glass in two large gulps. I brushed my milk moustache off with the back of my hand and stayed quiet, preparing myself for the inquisition that was sure to come.

'I was in her year, you know,' Ms Barts said unexpectedly.

'Sorry?' I asked, slightly bewildered. Ms Barts watched me, expressionless, pressing her large lips together. She let out a deep sigh, relaxing her mouth and once again reminding me of a cartoon duck.

The howling wind shook the window and my eyes darted towards it in horror. The sound alone evoked a sick sense of panic. Any calm I had found suddenly fled, and I curled my toes and clenched my fists, on high alert, half expecting the rotting corpse of Marina Cotez to open the door, come to finish me off.

'I was in the same school year as Marina Cotez,'

Ms Barts continued, unaware of the speed my heart was beating below my ribs. 'Here at St Mark's.'

She pushed the packet of biscuits towards me. I looked down at them in horror. The last thing my dry mouth needed was a crumbling biscuit. I'd choke.

'She went missing when we were in fifth year.'

'Were you friends?' I asked, trying to sound casually interested, but the rate at which my heart was still beating made my words sound like shattering glass.

'No. I hardly knew her,' she said sternly. She seemed for a moment to be taken aback by the tone in her own voice. She must have seen the look on my face, the look that told her that at that moment I could snap and cry and break into a thousand pieces. The next time she spoke she sounded softer. 'But we were in the same dorm. Newton actually – or, what's now called Newton. It was called Willow when I was a girl. Back then the dorms were all named after trees.'

I've always been good at hiding my feelings. Good at building up walls, being polite and playing along. But at that moment I felt my brows tighten together and the corners of my lips lift as my face contorted into a mask of bewilderment. Ms Barts had caught me crying and screaming in the middle of the night. I'd told her I'd seen a ghost. And all she wanted to do was eat biscuits and talk about the names of trees.

'I was in the first room on the left. Marina was in the third room on the right.'

'That's Suzy's room!' I whispered in horror, understanding creeping through me. 'Suzy's sleeping in Marina's old room.'

Ms Barts nodded her head solemnly.

'I was there this evening,' I continued, tilting forwards on the sofa and leaning towards her. 'I was sleeping in Suzy's room when I saw Marina's ghost.'

Ms Barts stared at me for a moment. The sound of the wind rattling the window made me want to scream and break the silence.

'Tell me what you saw,' she said eventually. She seemed to chew on each word, saying them carefully, thoughtfully. She knew she was treading on dangerous ground.

I told her about not being able to sleep in my own room. About moving to Newton Dorm and falling asleep before being woken up. I told her about the window flying open and the scratching on the door. I told her about seeing Marina and what her ghost had told me to do: Run.

When I finished talking Ms Barts stayed quiet. So quiet and pensive that I felt like crying. The sound of silence, and the wind that punctuated that silence, blistered my ears. I waited for her to speak. To laugh at me. To come over and sit by me. But she did nothing.

'Do you believe in ghosts?' I whispered, desperate to break the silence.

'Yes,' she replied without emotion. 'Did you know that that room, Suzy's room, also belonged to Laura Niever?' she asked.

My mind went blank. For a moment I couldn't remember who Laura Niever was. She was just a name. A faceless name that Ms Barts was wafting about in front of me.

Then I remembered.

'She was the girl who killed herself,' I said quietly. 'She has a sister at the school today.'

'Sarah Niever,' Ms Barts nodded.

'So what are you saying?' I asked, accusingly. 'That that room is haunted and whatever's haunting it killed Laura Niever and now wants to kill Suzy too? It could have killed me this evening?'

'No –' Ms Barts started to say.

'But Laura Niever was crazy, everyone says so,' I interrupted.

'Yes, but why? What might have driven her crazy?' She spoke without irony or humour, without emotion, without anything that betrayed what she might be thinking. Her eyes gazed coldly at me from behind her thick glasses and her hands sat steadily in her lap.

My words stuttered from my lips as I tried to understand what she was saying to me. 'What do you mean? Were you here then too? Did you know her?'

She nodded absently, her voice taking on a far-away quality, as if she was remembering. 'She was so special. Clever. She saw things . . . things like you've seen tonight.'

'Marina?'

Ms Barts shook her head. 'I've said too, too much!' She got up to leave, picking up a blanket from the far end of the couch and passing it to me gently. 'You can sleep here tonight, or for what's left of the night.' I took the blanket from her and stared at her disbelievingly. 'Don't say anything about this to anyone,' she said sternly. 'I won't do either.'

Ms Barts left me alone in the chaos of her cramped living room. I lay down on the sofa, covering myself with the blanket she'd given me, leaving on the small lamp beside the sofa. I was afraid to be in the dark. I was exhausted, drained of all sense and energy. My eyes fluttered closed and thoughts spun in my head like a twisted spider's web, tangled and unwanted. Amid the images that floated in my numb mind, images of Marina and the force of the wind against the window, I saw a woman's face. It was the woman I'd met in the graveyard the night Suzy and I snuck out to steal soil. It seemed so long ago. I don't know why her face came to me, but as I remembered her I recalled how she'd been a girl at St Mark's once too. I wondered if she'd known Marina. She was about the right age. I wondered if there was anything she could tell me about her that Ms Barts couldn't. My mind tried to form a plan, of how I would visit her and ask her questions. But then I fell into a deep, dreamless sleep, and I forgot all about her.

*Hertfordshire Observer*
*3rd February 2006*

### Tragedy Hits Local School

Schoolgirl Beatrice Soells, age fourteen, was found dead on Monday morning in the dormitory she shared with ten other girls at St Mark's College. The alarm was raised when Beatrice failed to attend breakfast and her body was then discovered by a fellow pupil. Beatrice was in the fourth year at St Mark's and had been a pupil at the school for three years.

Preliminary reports are that there was no history of illness and no evidence of foul play.

No members of staff or family were available for comment.

## 20

I wear it like a scar, my memory of that night. No matter how hard I try to forget, it will remain with me always. When I look in a mirror, over my shoulder or gaze out of a window – I'll always see her face, staring back at me.

I couldn't bring myself to tell Seb. I couldn't bear the thought that it might drive him away. He didn't need that burden – what would he possibly gain from knowing what I saw? This wasn't his problem, she wasn't haunting him. It was my problem, mine and Suzy's.

I didn't hear from Suzy once during half-term, and honestly I was pleased to have some distance. Distance to think about what had happened, to try to make sense of it. And the space from Suzy only seemed to bring me closer to Seb.

Seb and I met in the woods every day that week. At first I thought I'd struggle to keep such a secret from him, but the time we spent together were the only moments I found I could escape the horrible memories of that night. And even though it was hard to look at Seb's striking face and not see Marina, being with him was the only thing that brought me comfort. Each day I ran towards the woods without looking back.

'I thought we could just hang out, you know . . . read, sketch, chill.' Seb shrugged as he greeted me the first day. He had a large book tucked under his arm. 'I'm guessing you're really into your sketching. So if that's how you want to spend your time, you can spend it like that with me. I don't mind.'

'I'd rather be here sketching next to you than alone in my room,' I admitted shyly.

'And I'd rather be here reading with you than anywhere else.' He pushed his dark hair away from his eyes, revealing a nervous, hopeful expression.

I felt my cheeks burn red. I loved how he seemed to understand me so easily. I loved how I could just be myself with him. I could sit quietly and sketch and not say anything at all. We didn't need words.

Every day that week we would meet and listen to music from our phones, he would read books and I would sketch. It was so easy to lose myself in my drawings whenever Seb was around. I sketched for hours without noticing where the time had gone. Pictures of Mum and Suzy, and scenes of woodland tangled with flowers and leaves.

'Can you turn this song up?' I asked him one day. 'The wind is so loud.'

'You don't like the sound of the wind?' he asked casually.

I didn't reply and he looked up at me as he fiddled with his phone. The smile fell from his face as he watched the colour drain from my cheeks. 'Frankie?' He looked concerned.

'No,' I said quietly, trying to hide my unease. 'I don't like the sound of the wind.'

Seb flashed me a sad smile and turned up the music. He didn't ask me to explain myself, or accuse me of being weird. He just understood.

Every day I looked forward to seeing his scruffy head of hair approaching through the trees. He brought me other books he thought I'd like, and CDs and films. He even made a mix CD of his favourite songs to share with me. It was mostly guitar music, with mellow baselines and soulful lyrics – poetry to music. In return I sketched him a picture of the Sandman walking through woodland. 'This is awesome,' he beamed. And I made him a playlist on my iPod and we played it as we sat in the shack.

'I really like that Bob Dylan song on there,' he enthused, as we sat opposite each other on the shack floor, our backs pressed against the ivy growing through the cracks in the walls. 'I'd never think of listening to anything that old, but it was actually kind of cool.'

'Dad's record collection was pretty much the only thing Mum kept after he left. My real dad,' I explained. 'Not my new stepdad. Mum was out a lot when I was younger, I used to put on Dad's old records while I taught myself to draw. It's all I know about him really.'

'Where is he?' Seb asked carefully.

'Dad took off and left us before I was old enough to hate him,' I told him. 'Haven't heard from him since. Mum says I look like him. I wish I didn't. Sometimes I imagine Dad died.' I'd never told anyone that before. 'And that's why he's never been in touch. But in my heart I know he just doesn't care. But I guess it's a good thing he left. Otherwise Mum would never have met Phil, and I'd never have come to St Mark's.'

'And you'd never have met me,' he smiled and my heart skipped inside my chest. 'And I like the way you look,' he mumbled so quietly I wondered if he'd wanted me to hear.

Seb was thoughtful for a moment. 'I can't imagine not knowing my dad,' he admitted. 'I mean. I don't really *know* my dad – he's always been like a ghost to me.' The wind screamed slightly in my ears, and his words made me shiver. Seb watched me carefully as I reached for the music and turned it up. The wind stirred up the woodland floor outside the shack, sweeping rotten leaves in and around our feet. I tried to ignore the earthy, rotten smell – the smell that reminded me of Marina. 'I imagine he was different before Marina disappeared. He was really high up in the army, fought in loads of conflicts and had friends. But after she went missing . . . he vanished too, I guess. And that's how I've always known him. Vacant.'

It was sad. Seb was sad; even when he smiled I could see it in his eyes. Sometimes that was how I felt when I looked in the mirror; all I could see staring back at me was uncertainty and sadness. Maybe that's what he saw in me, maybe that's why he seemed to like me. Maybe he knew what I knew, that we were joined by shadows.

On the third day of half-term, as we sat in silence in the shack, I looked up from my sketchpad and caught Seb staring at me. He flashed me a shy smile and then looked back down at his book. 'You're so talented,' he muttered, without looking up.

'Thanks,' I grinned.

'Would you . . .' He looked up and smiled at me again. 'Would you draw me?'

'I'd love to,' I said, rather too quickly. He put down his book and sat up straight. 'No, don't.' I gestured to the book on the floor. 'Carry on reading, I'll draw you like that.'

My stomach tightened at the excitement of being able to stare at Seb so freely. I flipped open my sketchpad onto a new page and my eyes moved over the strong contours of his face, taking in every inch of him. The haunting resemblance to Marina was impossible to ignore.

I've always been good at drawing, but even a masterpiece could never do Seb justice. To me he was perfect – his dark, wild hair, pale skin, the peppering of freckles on his perfect nose, and lips that curled into a gorgeous smile every time he looked up and saw me studying him.

'You need to keep your eyes on your book,' I teased. 'Stop distracting me.'

It's strange that sharing silence with someone can make you feel so close to them. Maybe, sometimes, silence can bring you closer than words. But the closer I felt to Seb, the more intense my guilt became. Not only was I holding back the terrible story of his sister's restless spirit, but worse than that, I couldn't be honest with him about how I felt. Sitting on the shack floor, watching him lose himself in his book as I studied his face and struggled to translate his handsome features onto my sketchpad, my feelings became crystal clear.

There could be no confusion.

I knew, as sure as I had known I was looking into the face of death that night in Newton Dorm, that I was completely in love with Sebastian Cotez.

I couldn't tell him.

How can you possibly find the words to tell someone you love them? As my pencil drew darkened strokes onto the page, I imagined every possible reaction he could have to my confession, and each one felt unbearable. The thought of him laughing, or walking away without a word tore a hole right through my heart. But even worse than that was the thought that he might feel the same. The very thought of it was so electrifying that it terrified me more than the thought of rejection. So I stayed quiet.

He messaged me on the Thursday night that week:

*How about a walk into town tomorrow? Meet by the graveyard at 11? X*

Seb was waiting for me in the crisp mid-morning air, his heavy coat wrapped tightly around him as he shivered slightly in the cold. 'Winter's definitely on its way,' he greeted me.

'I feel like it's been here since the start of term,' I mused. 'Does Martyrs Heath even have any other seasons but grey skies and frost?'

'So where do you want to go?' he asked.

'I thought you had a plan?'

'There's not much here,' he said, pointing out the obvious. 'There's a small bookshop in town, and a coffee shop.'

'Well, that's as good a plan as any,' I shrugged.

The bell chimed softly as Seb pushed open the door to the bookshop. It smelt delicious, like musty old books and dust and coffee, and it was warm too, a relief from the snappy cold outside. 'I love to look at travel books,' he said softly, picking up an old book about America. 'I definitely want to travel when I've left school. Maybe take a gap year or something . . .'

'I'm just going to look over here,' I said shyly, edging away from him. A dark corner of the bookshop had caught my eye. There was a shelf marked MIND, BODY AND SPIRIT. I walked over to it and ran my eyes over the dozen or so books that sat wedged against each other. My eyes rested on a spine embossed with the words *English Ghosts*. I quickly glanced over my shoulder to see Seb deeply absorbed in another travel book. I pulled the book from the shelf and opened the cover. The list of chapters read like a journal of my life so far at St Mark's: *Summoning the Dead, A History of Hauntings, Signs of Poltergeists, Banishing Unwanted Spirits.*

After the night I'd spent in Suzy's room I was desperate to learn anything I could about ghosts. I had just about enough money in my purse to pay for the book. I shuffled over to the counter and silently placed it down. The old man behind the cash register looked at me over the top of his glasses and gave me a nicotine-stained smile.

'Just this one?' he croaked.

I nodded, hoping that Seb hadn't heard the old man speak. I handed over my money and as the man reached for a bag Seb's hand brushed past my arm and picked up the book.

'*English Ghosts?*' he said thoughtfully. He put the book down on the counter. I could feel him staring at me and my face flushing red as I refused to meet his eye. 'I didn't have you down as a girl who believed in ghosts.'

'I'm not.' My voice shook slightly. 'It's for Suzy,' I lied.

We went to the coffee shop and he treated me to hot chocolate and cake. I tried to talk about the weather, about music, art and travel books. But I knew from the way he looked at me that he could see I was hiding something.

I wanted to tell him. I did. But I didn't know the truth about what was going on; I didn't even know where to begin looking for it.

Silence fell between us and I glanced up into his searching eyes.

'Do you believe in ghosts?' I whispered.

He stared at me curiously for what seemed like an eternity. 'No,' he said finally. 'But I believe the dead can have secrets, and that no secret stays hidden forever.'

I looked down at my empty mug, studying the patterns left behind by the dregs of my hot chocolate. 'How can the dead give up their secrets?'

'Frankie.' He said my name so gently I felt as though my heart would shatter into a thousand pieces. I hated lying to him. 'I need to find out how she died. Will you help me?'

'How?' I said, the feeling of desperation flooding through me.

'I'm not sure yet. I trust you, you know that, don't you?' He pushed the hair out of his eyes, 'You know, I feel . . . I feel . . .' I held my breath, waiting for his next words. His eyes locked with mine and it felt as though he was looking straight into my soul. 'Frankie, when I need you, will you be there?'

'Always,' I replied.

Seb sat back and exhaled deeply, his eyes never leaving mine. Our silence was broken as the waitress came and laid our bill down on the table. Seb stood and walked to the counter to pay for our drinks, leaving his winter jacket draped over the back of his chair. I so desperately wanted him to know how I felt, but I couldn't say the words. It didn't seem enough to just say them out loud. Then I remembered something I had read in *Wuthering Heights*. Emily Brontë said it better than I ever could. Quickly, I took a pen from my pocket and scribbled on a napkin. While his back was turned I put the napkin into his coat pocket, so he could read the words later:

*Whatever souls are made of, yours and mine are the same.*

'Thanks for the hot chocolate,' I said shyly, watching as he picked up his warm winter coat and shrugged it on. My heart skipped as I saw his hand reaching for his coat pocket. Feeling suddenly embarrassed, I just wanted to get away. 'I'll go and put some money in the tip jar.'

I took my purse up to the counter and fumbled about for some change. After I'd dropped it in the jar I headed back to our table to find Seb holding my coat. He watched me closely as I took my coat from him, smiling in thanks.

We said goodbye at the bottom of the hill and I walked back up to St Mark's alone.

When I got back to my horsebox room I slipped off my coat. As I hung the coat on the hook on my wall I noticed a small corner of white poking out of the pocket. I reached in and pulled out a familiar white napkin. The words from *Wuthering Heights* were still scrawled across it. For a moment I wondered whether I'd imagined slipping the note into Seb's pocket, except I knew that I had. Before my heart could sink inside me, I turned over the napkin to see a note written on the other side.

*I know, I feel the same. X*

## 21

'I saw her,' was the first thing I said to Suzy as she walked through my horsebox door after half-term. No niceties, no greetings, no time wasting. I'd waited all week to tell her – she needed to know the truth.

'Why didn't you tell me before?' was all Suzy could say, shutting the door behind her and perching on the edge of my desk. 'You could have texted or called.'

'I needed to figure things out,' I said. I'd been expecting Suzy to ask me such a question. 'And it was something I needed to say in person.'

I told her everything. I'd never seen Suzy sit so still before, and she'd never before let me speak for so long without interrupting. She didn't even flinch when I told her she was sleeping in Marina's old room – the same room from which Laura Niever had leapt to her death.

That week away from school hadn't replenished Suzy's energy. She didn't look rested. She looked defeated. Her skin had broken out into dozens of pimples, and her dyed red hair had faded to a rusted orangey-brown. And there was a sadness in her eyes that followed her around like a shadow. The girl before me wasn't the Suzy I knew. She was a ghost of the vibrant creature my friend had once been.

'Have you told Seb?' she asked flatly. I shook my head, my stomach tightening at just the sound of Seb's name. 'Why not? I thought he was around over half-term too. Did you see him?'

'He was. I did,' I said carefully. 'But I didn't tell him. I don't know why,' I lied. I knew exactly why I hadn't told Seb, but I didn't want to admit anything to Suzy. I didn't want to tell her how I felt about him, and that I didn't want to taint him with this horror. Whatever was happening to us was happening within the walls of St Mark's, and that was where it needed to stay.

Suzy stared at me, her eyes narrowing in suspicion. She wasn't stupid; she knew I was holding something back from her. Taking a deep breath, she closed her eyes and exhaled, too exhausted to care.

'At least we can trust Ms Barts,' Suzy said eventually.

I nodded my head. 'I think she knows more than she's letting on.'

'What do you mean?'

'I think she knows something about the connection between Marina Cotez and Laura Niever, and between the other girls that died.' I'd taken the photocopied documents I'd found in the school office weeks ago out of my secret tin and spread them on my bed. I ran my hands over them thoughtfully. My eyes skipped over the picture of Marina, pretending it wasn't there. Even from the corner of my eye I could see her staring up at me. The sight of her sent cold shivers down my spine.

'A curse, maybe?' Suzy said in a low whisper.

'Maybe?' I shrugged. 'I don't really believe in curses, but

then I don't really believe in ghosts either – well, at least I didn't used to.'

'Maybe it was Ms Barts who led you to the school office that night? Maybe it was her that stole the other documents in the archive file?' Suzy said quickly.

I'd already thought of that.

'I don't think so,' I replied.

'Why not?' she asked. Frustration crumpled her face. She looked tired, beaten, ready for answers – whatever they might be.

I didn't want to tell her that the more I thought about that night, the more certain I was that whatever led me to the school office wasn't human. That was my suspicion, my secret, something I wanted to hold close to me. The longer I didn't tell Suzy, the longer I could pretend that it wasn't real.

'It didn't look like Ms Barts,' I said carefully.

Suzy fell quiet for a moment and looked at me with a tortured expression. 'I haven't heard from James for weeks.'

I took a deep breath. 'There's something else I need to tell you. It's about James.'

'What?' she said quickly, her voice quivering.

'He's seeing a girl in my year. George.'

A single tear fell down Suzy's cheek and she shrugged with exhaustion. 'Bitch . . . but really, James is the least of my worries . . .'

'What?' I asked. 'What's wrong?'

She looked away suddenly. I could see tears welling in the corner of her eyes. Her fingers curled around the hem of her bright purple skirt and gripped it tightly. She seemed hollow, broken.

'What's wrong?' I asked again, this time putting my hand on her shoulder lightly.

'I made a decision over half-term.' Her voice trembled as she drew in a deep breath.

I waited for her to speak again, but when she remained silent I prompted her. 'What?'

'Promise me that we'll always be friends, always,' she said, her eyes pleading with me as she took my hand in hers.

'Of course,' I answered instantly. 'Suzy, what's all this about?'

'I don't want to be here, Frankie,' she said, fighting back tears. 'You're the only thing worth sticking around for in this dump. And I know we'll be friends forever, until the end, no matter where we are or how far apart we have to be.'

She was starting to scare me. 'Suzy, what are you talking about?'

'I've decided I'm gonna leave school,' she said resolutely.

She may as well have told me she was going to fly to Mars or become a professional rugby player, the idea seemed so ridiculous and impossible. St Mark's was our life – it was our home. 'You can't just leave!'

'Why not?' she challenged me. 'I begged my parents to take me away from here, but they wouldn't listen. I cried for hours and wrote a ten-page letter but they didn't even bother reading it.'

'So what?' I asked, not even attempting to hide the tone of annoyance in my voice. Suzy couldn't just abandon me at St Mark's, leave me with no friends and no one to help me escape the mess I was in. The mess that she had got me in to. 'Now you're back here you're just gonna run away?'

She shook her head. 'Not run away, no. It won't work. I've thought it through – they'd just find me and bring me back. I need to leave this school and know that I'll never ever come back.'

I watched her take a deep breath and prepare to tell me her plan.

'I'm going to get myself expelled,' she said calmly.

My mouth dropped open and I felt my blood rush to my head like some kind of tidal wave. Expelled? I'd never heard anything so crazy before. It was a stupid idea, even for Suzy.

'I know what you're thinking,' she said quickly.

'No, I don't think you do.' I threw her hand back at her and began to pace frantically around my small room. 'You're insane.'

'That's exactly what I thought you'd say.' She rose from the edge of my desk and grabbed my arm. I flinched away from her and pulled my arms tight around myself so she couldn't touch me. My eyes glued themselves to the panelled carpet floor so Suzy's green stare couldn't penetrate them.

'Frankie, don't be like that,' she pleaded. 'Please try to understand.' I let out a loud snort of indignation. 'I'd rather try my luck as an actress in London than stay here and let some kind of curse kill me off before I have a chance to do anything with my life.'

'And what about me?' I shouted loudly. 'You're just going to leave me here alone? Have you even thought about me in all of this?' I brought my voice down to an angry whisper, afraid that the other girls in my dorm would hear and think I was mad. 'I don't want my life to be over because of this "thing". I want to grow up and go to art school and have a future!'

'Then come with me,' Suzy said. 'You and me, Frankie. We'll leave this place forever. We'll move to London. I have a cousin who has a house in Camden –'

'No!' I said through clenched teeth. I didn't want to run away. I wasn't stupid enough to run off into the polluted London sunset. 'You might want to throw your life away but I don't. Stay here, please.' I was begging now. 'Nothing's going to harm you, Suzy, I promise.'

'You can't promise me anything,' she shook her head. 'You know as well as I do that it's only a matter of time before that . . . thing . . . comes after me again. Tonight? Tomorrow night? How much longer have I got, Frankie, before I fall out of a window, or break my neck playing hockey or just disappear?'

She started to sob, and threw herself down on my bed, burying her head in my pillow and blubbering loudly. Suddenly I just wished she'd go away, pack up her theatrics and leave me in the bubble I'd created for myself over half-term. I'd rather sit in a mouldy woodland shack with Seb every day than spend time listening to Suzy whine and cry. I took a deep breath and tried to bury my uncharitable thoughts, Suzy was clearly sick and she needed a friend. I was all she had.

'Suzy, Suzy,' I said, sitting down on the bed wearily. 'Just listen to me, please.'

'You won't listen to *me*!' she shouted angrily, lifting her head off the pillow. 'Why should I listen to you?'

'OK, OK,' I conceded. 'Fine. I'm sorry, Suzy, you're my best friend forever. I've got your back always and I promise I'll support you, whatever you do. But before you do anything stupid please hear me out. I have a plan.'

Suzy lifted her head again and twisted her body so she lay on her back, her head rested on my pillow, staring at me. She sniffed. 'I'm listening.'

'After what happened that night,' I began. 'After I saw Marina in your room, I went to the bookshop in town and bought a book about ghosts and hauntings –'

'They all say the same thing,' she interrupted. 'Holy water, graveyard soil, blah, blah, blah. Been there, done that, Frankie. It's all worthless.'

'Yes, but there's something else,' I said quickly. I'd read the whole book that weekend, cover to cover. 'There's something we haven't tried.' I turned around and opened my desk drawer. I pulled out my copy of *English Ghosts* and flicked to the bookmarked page. 'We hold a seance. We burn sage and light candles and ask the ghost to leave.'

'So after everything that's happened, you think the ghost is just gonna go if we ask it nicely?' Suzy said angrily. 'And what if it's not even the ghost I need to worry about? What if there is some kind of curse?'

'It's worth a shot,' I said.

Suzy shook her head from side to side, silent tears running down her pale cheeks. She closed her eyes and took a deep breath, resolving herself to what was to come. 'OK,' she agreed. 'But if it doesn't work then you'll help me get expelled?'

I nodded slowly. There was no way I was planning to help Suzy get herself expelled. I'd think of another way to stall her if the seance failed. I thought I knew Suzy well enough to know that she'd soon get bored of the idea of expulsion, and find something else to fixate on.

'Where do we get sage from?' Suzy sat up and wiped her face.

I reached back into my desk drawer and pulled out a bundle of sage leaves. 'Ms Barts took us into London to see Buckingham Palace and I managed to sneak away to do some shopping.'

Suzy snatched the bundle of leaves from me, lifted them up to sniff them and then thumbed them thoughtfully. 'Tonight, Frankie. We do this tonight.'

# 22

I went to Suzy's room at 11 o'clock that night. The lights were out in Newton Dorm, but as usual no one was asleep. Girls were in each other's rooms, bedside lights were on and the air was full of whispers and giggles.

'You brought the sage?' Suzy asked. I passed the bundle of leaves over to her.

'I've got these too.' I pulled a handful of tea lights out of my dressing-gown pocket. 'We need to light them when we summon the spirit.'

Suzy pulled a packet of cigarettes and a cigarette lighter from her coat pocket. She placed the cigarettes carefully on her desk and handed me the lighter. I cautiously lit the small candles, passing them one by one to Suzy, and she in turn scattered them around the room. When all the candles were lit, we sat on her bed opposite each other and held hands, just like we'd done the time we'd played with the Ouija board.

'Spirits come to us. Spirits come to us. Spirits come to us,' we whispered.

I let go of Suzy's hand, picked up the sage and lit it on a nearby candle.

Suzy took the smouldering bundle of leaves from me

and waved them gently above her head. 'Marina Cotez, Marina Cotez, Marina Cotez.'

Above the steady drones of whispers and giggles, the distant wail of the wind began to fill the room. As the wind grew louder and the candles flickered, it felt as if the rest of the world was falling away from us. All that existed was us, the candlelight, the smell of smouldering sage and the sound of the whispering wind.

Suzy passed the sage to me and I did as she had done, waving it above my head. 'Marina Cotez, Marina Cotez, Marina Cotez.'

The sound of the wind got louder, its eerie song almost human, as if it were carrying hordes of distant voices.

'Your spirit is unwanted here,' I whispered into the candle-lit room. 'We ask you to leave.'

'We ask you to leave,' Suzy repeated. 'We ask you to leave, we ask you to leave.'

The wind roared like a wild beast and we felt the heavy force of flowing air on our faces as the window burst open, just as it had done that night I'd spent in Suzy's room, and knocked a small candle from the windowsill onto the bed. The bed sheet began to smoke and soon a small flame appeared by my leg. Another gust of wind fanned the flame and soon half the bed sheets were on fire. Smoke and heat blazed around us; it had all happened so quickly. I panicked, jumped off the bed and looked for something – water, anything – to suffocate the flames.

Suzy reached for her pillow and frantically beat out the flames. Finally the last flicker of light died out, but she hadn't been quick enough. The sound of the school fire alarms blasted into the air.

'Put the candles out!' I shouted at her. We both frantically stumbled around the room, puffing out the candles, and Suzy flung the smouldering bundle of sage out of the open window into the damp night.

'Everybody get out!' cried a voice from the other side of the dorm.

Without a word, our faces pale with shock and confusion, Suzy and I tripped over one another to get out of her room and out of Newton Dorm.

Lines of girls filed down the stone staircase, following the fire drill we'd been taught.

I was halfway down the stairs when I realised, 'I'm a fire marshal!'

'You can't go back,' I heard Ms Barts' voice. 'Just evacuate the building, Frankie.'

We all walked along the path outside to the school hall, and waited in the cold until Ms Thurlow appeared with the keys to the school hall. Her mass of grey hair was tied askew on the side of her head and her pursed lips were stained with red wine.

I turned to Suzy. 'Someone's hit the bottle . . .' but Suzy wasn't there. She was nowhere to be seen.

Ms Thurlow clapped her hands and shouted loudly, shuffling us into the school hall. 'Fire marshals, please count the girls from your dorm and let your housemistress know if anyone is missing.' There was a waft of booze as I walked past Ms Thurlow and headed towards the gaggle of Raleigh

Dorm girls. Everyone was there. The girls, the housemistresses, even Ms West.

But no sign of Suzy.

Panicking, I looked around for any sign of her. The glare of fire engine lights flooded the school car park. Their loud sirens pierced the night air and what seemed like dozens of uniformed men ran purposefully into the school. Everyone pressed their faces to the school hall windows and watched in excitement.

I moved through the commotion in the hall, desperately searching for Suzy. And then I saw her. She was standing alone in a corner, her face emotionless and pale.

I shuffled towards her, through the dozens of girls crowded in the hall. Suzy's eyes rested on me for a short moment – there was something fierce and determined in them, something that made me feel instantly uneasy. She walked away, heading in a straight, unwavering line towards Ms West. Suzy walked straight up to her, brazenly tapped her on the shoulder and started to say something. My heart leapt into my throat as I watched Suzy enter into some kind of strained dialogue with the headmistress. Ms West's face twisted in anger and confusion as Suzy spoke. Whatever Suzy was saying to her, Ms West did not want to hear.

Soon I was close enough to overhear. Close enough to see the pain in Ms West's usually expressionless face. 'Are you sure, Suzy?' she asked sternly.

'Yes, Ms West,' Suzy replied calmly. 'It was me. I set the fire alarms off. I was smoking in my room. You can go up there and see for yourself. My cigarettes are still on my desk.'

Horror filled my veins at the sound of Suzy's words. She was putting her plan into action. She was getting herself expelled.

# 23

There was a text on my phone when I woke up the next morning:

*Will you meet me in the graveyard after school tonight? xx*

Hating myself for it, I just couldn't text back. I was so worried about Suzy, and so sick of lying to Seb. I didn't know how to tell him what was happening to Suzy without telling him the truth. There was so much he didn't know – so much that I had kept from him. I feared he'd hate me if I told him now, after so long.

I skipped breakfast that morning so I could find Suzy. I headed straight for Ms West's office. I waited and waited outside the closed oak door, listening to the deep murmurs coming from inside. Eventually the door swung open and Suzy walked out, accompanied by the headmistress.

'I'm afraid Suzy can't speak to anyone, Francesca,' Ms West said coldly. 'Besides, it's time you headed to your first class.'

I watched, speechless, as Suzy was marched away from me towards the school office. I studied her face, looking for clues as to what had happened, but she was unreadable. She wouldn't even look at me. All I could hope was that Suzy hadn't got her way, and Ms West hadn't expelled her.

As the school office door closed, the bell began to ring and I had no choice but to scuttle away to my first lesson of the day, French. I'd taken to carrying my phone around in my pocket all day. I felt it buzz as I made my way to the lunch hall:

*Will you meet me tonight? I need to see you. xx*

I felt sick with guilt as I thought about how I'd have to lie to Seb. I put the phone back into my pocket without texting him back. Of course I wanted to see him, but I owed it to Suzy to help her in any way that I could., I couldn't just desert her now. But Suzy wasn't at lunch that day, which made me even more concerned. As soon as school was over I ran up to Newton Dorm, pushed the door open without even knocking and headed straight to Suzy's room.

She wasn't in there.

'She's moved all her stuff out,' said a voice behind me. This wasn't true – her posters were still on the walls and there was an open drawer with clothes spilling out of it.

I turned around and stared defiantly at the tall, freckly fifth year behind me. 'Maybe now Suzy isn't in Newton we won't have to worry about annoying little fourth years invading our space!'

'Where is she?' I asked, battling not to rise to the insult.

The girl folded her arms and paused for a moment before

saying, 'She's been moved to San. She has to stay there until her parents pick her up.'

'Parents?' I asked, my heart lurching within me. 'She's been expelled?'

'Suspended,' the girl said with a satisfied grin. 'Until next term.'

I turned and bolted as fast as I could out of the main school building and towards San.

Nurse Pippa caught me running into the cold, tiled San corridor. 'Francesca!'

I stopped and pressed my back into the chipped bile-green wall, trying to catch my breath. I'd forgotten about Nurse Pippa – I wasn't expecting her to get in my way. Seeing her there irritated me. Everything about the San irritated me. The smell of bleach burnt my nose and the mindless hum of a TV game show coming from the office was enough to make me want to smash my head against the tiled walls.

Nurse Pippa shook her head, her monk-like hair swinging around her face as she gave me a pitiful look. 'I can't let you see her I'm afraid. Headmistress's orders.'

'Please,' I begged impatiently.

'Absolutely not,' she said firmly.

My brain raced, trying to think of some sort of plan. 'OK,' I said as loudly as I could, hoping Suzy would hear me. 'But I really need to pee, can I use the toilet before I head back to school?'

'OK. Be quick.' Nurse Pippa sighed, exasperated, before slipping back into her office.

I pushed open the bathroom door and waited in there,

hoping Suzy had heard me and had understood to follow. My breathing finally evened out, and I became aware of a retching noise coming from one of the toilet cubicles. Someone was throwing up.

'Are you OK in there?' I asked quietly, tapping on the cubicle door.

The toilet flushed, the cubicle door sprung open and out came a tiny sparrow of a girl. Sarah Niever.

'Don't eat the chicken in the salad cart,' she joked. I didn't laugh.

I watched silently as Sarah washed her hands and mouth with tap water. She was small for her age, but otherwise she looked so normal. Her sister had killed herself – for some reason I felt like this should have made Sarah look different, like she should have a sign around her head saying 'Handle with Care'.

Sarah turned around slowly, catching me staring at her. I looked away, feeling rude.

'I'm not crazy, you know,' Sarah said calmly.

I looked up at her, taken aback. 'No one thinks you're crazy.'

'My sister Laura wasn't crazy either. I bet you've heard the story about how she jumped out the window?' I shrugged my shoulders, unsure of what to say. 'She didn't jump.'

'She was pushed?' I said quickly, without really thinking.

Sarah nodded. 'It got her.'

I opened my mouth to speak again but the bathroom door flew open and Suzy stormed in. 'You're stupid coming up here, Frankie, unless you want to get yourself kicked out as well.'

232

Sarah Niever slipped out of the bathroom door without another word, leaving me and Suzy alone.

'They've suspended me,' Suzy admitted, bitterly. She tightly closed her eyes and pinched the bridge of her nose as if trying to stave off a headache.

'I know,' I said, trying to sound kind. Suzy needed sympathy and understanding, but at that moment giving those things to her couldn't have been farther from my mind. All I wanted to do was push her out of the way and chase after Sarah.

'Sarah Niever is in the San too,' I said urgently. 'She's eaten something bad . . .'

'She's bulimic.' Suzy rolled her eyes. 'It's nothing she's eaten. She makes herself puke up.'

I swallowed hard. 'She said something about her sister, about Laura . . .'

'Frankie, she's messed up, don't listen to her!'

'Everyone thought you were crazy, Suzy. I listened to you! What if Sarah Niever is telling the truth too?'

Suzy's green eyes narrowed, 'Sarah Niever is a four-foot tall bulimic who'll say anything to get attention!'

'Suzy . . .' I argued.

'No, Frankie, just leave!'

I tried my hardest not to shout. 'Why are you being such a bitch? I'm only here to see if you're OK!'

'Of course I'm not OK!' she screamed. I flinched and tried to shush her – the last thing I needed was Nurse Pippa hearing Suzy freak out.

'I won't be quiet! My life is over. Ms West doesn't have the guts to kick me out properly so instead she's just kicking me out for the rest of term. I have to come back after Christmas. And I'm stuck in the stupid San until my parents can be bothered to get on a plane and come and collect me. My life couldn't get much worse, and all you want to talk about is some stupid cow putting her fingers down her throat! I don't need you and I don't want you here, Frankie. Just go.'

'Suzy, I'm sorry . . .'

Nurse Pippa pushed open the bathroom door and glared at us. 'Francesca, leave now please,' she said sternly.

'Please, Nurse Pippa –'

'Now!'

I ran out of the bathroom, and into the tiled San corridors. My cheeks felt burning hot as tears started to stream down them. I stormed out of the San building into the moonless twilight. The sky was growing darker, deep purple shadows gathering threateningly on the horizon as the sun sank in the sky. I let the door slam loudly behind me, hoping Suzy would hear it and realise how angry I was. I'd gone up there to see if she was OK because I cared about her. I wondered if she'd have done the same thing for me. Probably not.

The thought made me senseless with anger. As I marched back to the main school building, I was aware of my jaw and fists clenching in rage. It just wasn't fair. Why did I have to feel things so deeply?

I wanted to just walk back to school, to forget about Suzy and Marina and the whole sorry mess. I wanted some peace, some quiet where I could just be me. Not some stupid existence where I chased Suzy around and danced along to whatever twisted tune she felt like playing. But I couldn't escape. I was already in too deep. I couldn't shift the urge to do more – to help Suzy, even if she didn't want me to. There had to be a way I could stop the school from sending her away.

By the time I pushed open the door to the main school corridor I was devoid of all sense and emotion. My mind was made up. My plan was in place. I was going to storm into Ms West's office and plead with her to change her mind. I had it all worked out – I was going to tell her everything – about how special Suzy was, and about the ghost and the burn marks in Suzy's room, and that I'd seen Marina's ghost and that Ms Barts believed me.

If Ms West knew the truth then she'd understand that making Suzy leave school wasn't the right thing to do. In that brief moment of blind panic and fear I actually believed that I could save the day, save Suzy.

My feet marched through the stone corridor, towards Ms West's office. I lifted my hand to knock on the door and realised it was already ajar. I pushed it slightly, ready to storm in.

That was when I heard voices.

It was a man's voice, not a voice I recognised. 'Preliminary reports suggest that she was buried alive.'

'I see, Inspector,' said another voice. This time I recognised the voice. It was Ms West.

The man, the police inspector, spoke again. 'This new evidence will of course be made available to the media in due course as part of an appeal for further information into the killing.'

My feet inched backwards, away from the office door.

I stood alone in the corridor, tears still rolling down my face.

Marina Cotez had been buried alive.

*Mrs Niever*
*26 Engineer Regiment*
*Tedworth House*
*Tidworth*
*1st April 2009*

*Dear Ms West,*
*Thank you for allowing us the opportunity to hold a memorial service for Laura in the school chapel at St Mark's. However, we feel that it would be wrong to do so, given the nature of Laura's death and the questions that are still left unanswered for us. Instead we will hold a smaller, private ceremony for Laura where only close friends and family will be welcome.*

*I respectfully ask that neither you nor any other members of staff from St Mark's College attend this service.*

*Yours truly,*
*Margaret Niever*

# 24

Buried alive.

My mind crawled with images of Marina being pushed into a shallow grave, soil hurriedly thrown on top while she still drew breath. It was too much to bear. I imagined her gulping down earth, clawing at the soil. Begging to escape her terrible fate.

The sickness and pure horror that rose within me could not have hurt more if I had been hearing news about my own family. Marina and I were two girls, a lifetime apart, but so horribly linked by fate. Marina had chosen me, me and Suzy, to haunt and warn – warn that we needed to run, that we were next. In that horrific moment, the path ahead of me became so clear – I needed to finish this. I needed to know what we were running from. We couldn't be next; this had to stop. And I knew that I would do whatever it took to put Marina to rest.

As realisation struck, a hideous wave of nausea swept through me like a plague. I lurched forwards, dry retching and gagging for air.

'Is someone there?' Ms West said sternly from within her office. There was a shuffling of chairs and footsteps coming closer. I knew I had to run, had to get away.

I couldn't let them catch me there, listening in to their conversation.

I bolted down the corridor, not looking back. The door to the outside world was nearer than the staircase to my dorm so I escaped through that. My breath caught in my throat, and as I ran outside into the cold evening air I let my sobs out into the wind with a howl. It felt like I was choking, I couldn't breathe. All I wanted was to be far, far away.

Was this what Marina had wanted us to know? She had been murdered in the most brutal, cruel way imaginable. Moments away from the school, from the place that was meant to keep her safe.

I stopped running at one of the science blocks. I leant my back against the wall of the building and bent forward to catch my breath. I couldn't look up; just the thought of seeing the school made me feel sick. Everything about it seemed evil. All I wanted were answers. I wanted to understand why Marina had met such an unbearable fate. I wanted to speak to someone who had known her.

Then a thought hit me like the crashing of a falling tree.

The woman I'd met that night in the graveyard. The church warden. She must have known Marina. She'd been a schoolgirl at St Mark's and was about the right age to have known her. As soon as the seed of thought had taken root in my brain I knew I had to speak to her.

I had enough breath in me to carry me away from the school, down the winding hill and through the misty streets of Martyrs Heath without stopping. It was pitch black; only the faintest moonlight lit the way. Shadows caught the corner of my eye and I thought every tree branch would reach out and choke me.

Her cottage sat next to the church. Inviting, soft light seeped out from cracks in the curtains and sweet-smelling smoke billowed from the chimney into the velvet-black air. I was out of breath and shaking violently as I reached up to ring her doorbell.

There was a flush of hesitation on her face as she opened the door and stared at me. I must have looked like something conjured up out of hell, deathly pale and shaking all over. Then she placed my face, realising where she'd seen me before. Worry flushed her cheeks. 'Come in,' she beckoned, opening the door wider.

Inside her house couldn't have felt more different from the dark, cold night outside. Pictures hung on the walls, colourful landscapes and photos of smiling faces. An old, black Labrador padded softly into the hallway, its tail wagging lazily at the sight of me.

'You're one of the girls who were strolling in the graveyard not that long ago? With Sebastian?' she asked me.

I bent down to pet the dog, gripping its warm fur with my shaking fingers. He felt so warm, so alive. After a while I realised she was still waiting for me to answer her.

'I'm Frankie,' I told her.

'I'm Tina,' she said. Her face was furrowed with worry. I wondered if she was going to even let me speak before she called the school and told them I'd run away. 'Do you want a drink?' she asked kindly. 'A hot chocolate, maybe?'

Tina's kitchen was warm and smelled like cake and butter. A huge old Aga sat proudly by the far wall, taking up most of the kitchen. I watched, shivering in silence as Tina boiled a kettle until it whistled on the hob. She poured me out a sweet, thick, piping hot chocolate. I sipped at it greedily, not caring that the sweet liquid burned my lips. Tina's Labrador lay obediently by her feet as she sat down on the opposite side of the kitchen table.

'Are you going to tell me why you're here?' she asked softly.

'Did you know Marina Cotez?' I blurted out, without warning.

Tina took a deep breath and looked worried for a moment before answering, 'Yes, yes I did.'

I put down my hot chocolate. This was good, it was what I'd wanted – someone to ask about Marina. But now I sat there, I didn't know where to begin.

The distant rumble of thunder shook the windows to Tina's cottage. We sat in silence as we listened to rain begin to beat down against the windows.

'I was in the year below her,' Tina said slowly. 'I didn't know her well. But I knew of her – everyone did. She was very popular.' She smiled a kind, understanding smile. 'What happened to her was awful. I know it must be very upsetting for everyone at St Mark's at the moment . . .'

'She was buried alive,' I told her, once again the words leaving my mouth before I could think them through.

'I didn't know that,' Tina said quietly, obviously shocked.

'No one knows. The police have only just found out. I heard them telling Ms West this evening.'

'And then you ran here?' she asked.

I nodded, picking up my drink and taking a loud slurp.

My hands were still shaking, and I splashed the hot chocolate all over me as I lifted it to my mouth. I wiped the mess from my face with the back of my hand, hating myself for being so clumsy.

'Do you want me to open the church?' she asked sympathetically. 'Would you like to pray? I know the school chapel doesn't feel peaceful at times –'

'No,' I interrupted her. Being alone in an old stone building with nothing but the sound of rain for company was the last thing I needed. 'I came here because I wanted to ask you about her. About Marina. I guess I just wanted to understand what happened to her.'

'Frankie,' she said softly, as if she were speaking to a child. 'I don't know what happened to her. I know her father was in the army, I know she did well at school from the prizes she won at Speech Day. I know she was captain of the netball team. I know that she disappeared. I know that her body was buried in the school woods. I know as much as anyone else –'

'But you *knew* her,' I cut in, sounding emotional. I tried to calm myself, steady my voice and breathe easily, but I couldn't manage it. Coming to speak to Tina was my only hope of shedding some light on what had happened to Marina all those years ago. 'I could have asked Ms Barts – she was at St Mark's then too – but she's already told me that she hardly knew her and –'

'You asked Ducky?' Tina said quickly.

My eyebrows twitched in confusion.

'Sorry,' Tina apologised, looking mildly embarrassed. 'That was Felicity – Ms Barts' nickname at school. Girls can be so cruel, can't they?'

243

I nodded my head, knowing only too well.

'I don't know why Ms Barts would say she hardly knew Marina. They were best friends at school,' Tina said softly. 'They were inseparable.'

I stared at Tina blankly, wondering if I'd heard her correctly, or if I was remembering wrongly what Ms Barts had told me. 'She told me she hardly knew her,' I said, feeling confused.

Tina shook her head. 'Maybe she felt like she didn't know her at all. Sometimes it feels like that when you look back and remember someone you knew so long ago.'

I nodded, although I didn't understand what she was saying. I had no idea why Ms Barts would have lied to me about being friends with Marina. 'That night in the graveyard,' I said hesitantly. 'You recognised Seb. How do you know him?'

She sighed sadly. 'Sebastian came to me with questions about his sister, just as you have now. He wanted to know anything I could tell him about her – any clues I might have as to what happened to her.'

'What did you say?'

'Only what I've said to you. Until they found her body I didn't know for sure that Marina was dead, and I still don't know how she died. Or why. It's late, Frankie. You shouldn't really be here,' Tina said, reaching down to pat her dog. 'I'm sorry I couldn't tell you more about Marina,' she shrugged. 'But if you ever want to come here again, just to chat or to go into the church, then my door will always be open to you.'

Tina lent me an old jumper, which was dry and warm.

'Do you want me to come back with you, in case anyone asks questions?' she asked softly.

'No,' I said, bending down to give her dog a comforting hug. 'I'll be fine on my own. And it's not that far to walk. I'll be OK.'

Tina suddenly lurched forwards and wrapped her arms tight around me, enveloping me in a warm hug. It made me want to cry – I suddenly missed Mum so much I thought my heart was ripped in two. All I wanted was to stay there in that moment, feeling safe in Tina's arms, feeling like somebody cared.

'Remember,' she said, as she gently pulled me away from her. 'You're always welcome to come and chat.'

As I left the warmth and safety of Tina's house I felt numb. Everything was falling apart and I had no way of knowing how to repair it. I felt so lonely I could have laid down in the dark and never got up again.

The rain began to fall heavily. My feet picked up the pace, taking me past the church and its vast graveyard. A figure ran towards me in the darkness. 'Frankie! Frankie!'

It was Seb, soaked right through and shivering.

The sight of him made my heart burst, my veins rushing with a myriad of emotions in a single moment. My legs shook, my stomach tightened, my cheeks burned and my throat tightened painfully. 'Why are you here?' I shouted, angry at seeing him when I felt so wretched.

'I came to meet you,' he said with concern. 'I've been waiting here for you. I thought you weren't coming.'

I'd forgotten about meeting him, I'd never even texted him back.

Staring at his pale, sad face I felt my shoulders begin to shake and tears stream from my eyes without warning. He looked so lonely, as lonely as I'd felt my whole life. My breath was ragged and pathetic sobs began to escape me.

'Frankie.' He came closer to me. We were standing in the shadows, the graveyard behind us and the winding hill leading to St Mark's ahead. 'What's wrong? I saw you coming out of Tina's . . .'

'Please,' I sobbed, turning away from him and running up the hill. 'Just leave me alone!' I shouted back. But Seb ran after me, his feet slapping heavily down in the puddles. He pulled at my sodden jumper sleeve and swung me around to face him.

'Tell me what's going on?' he demanded. 'I know there's something you're not telling me. I know it!'

My head shook desperately from side to side. I was so tired of being strong, keeping secrets and trying to figure everything out alone. 'Oh, Seb,' I sobbed. 'She's still there . . .'

'Who's still where?' He shook me, confused. 'What are you talking about?'

'It's Marina,' I said without holding back. 'She's still there. At the school. Haunting it. Suzy saw her, I've seen her.'

His grip stayed firm on my arm and he looked deeply into my eyes. 'What do you mean, you've seen her?'

I told him.

I told him everything.

Finally, the words came out of me like a great dam bursting with a flood. I told him about the Ouija board, and the fire in the shack. About Suzy's dreams, the holy water, the graveyard soil and the face that stared back at me in the mirror. It felt so good to say those things out loud, and not once did he flinch as I told him. Not once did he let me go.

'But that's not all, Seb,' I whispered, frightened to tell him this last part more than anything. 'There's more. I know how she died . . .'

He looked at me, the rain falling hard around us, both of us shivering and shaking from the cold night and the words spoken between us. I could hardly believe I was telling him this. But I had to tell him everything, the whole truth. 'She was buried alive.'

I wasn't sure if it was rain or tears, but rivers fell down his cheeks as he nodded in understanding. 'Who did that to her?' he whispered. 'Why?'

'I don't know,' I said honestly. 'But I'm going to find out. I promise, Seb. I promise I'll find out for you, and we'll let your sister rest once and for all. I promise.'

He was still holding me. Still staring deep into my eyes. Still inches away from me.

'Why did you want to see me this evening?' I asked.

His hands moved slowly up my arms, brushing past my shoulders and then stroking my neck. Then he held my face between his hands, so gently, as if I was the most precious thing in the whole world. He ran his thumb over my lips before pulling me into him.

His lips met mine. Warm and soft, gentle yet urgent.

There was a perfect moment where I was lost to him. Where the world fell away from me and all that existed was me and him, kissing in the rain. The way his lips felt so tender against mine. The way his hands ran so easily through my hair. The way his skin smelt when I breathed him in.

But it was his smell that pulled me out of whatever I'd been lost to.

He smelt like earth. Like the woods after it's been raining.

My heart sped up so quickly I thought I'd fall down. I pulled away from him in horror, nothing but thoughts of Marina and her angry spirit in my head.

He moved towards me again, 'Frankie, please . . .'

I ran as fast as my legs could carry me. I didn't look back as I sped into the pitch black of the night. Up the winding hill and through the school gates.

I ran past the San, past the science blocks and towards the main school building. As I came nearer to the car park my heart stopped in my chest.

There was someone walking across the car park. A sharp bolt of fear ran through me – I half expected the figure to disappear as soon as I'd spotted it. But the figure walking through the car park wasn't like the face looking down at me from my bedroom window, or the mirror in Suzy's room. This figure was solid, real, alive.

I recognised her instantly – her red hair looked like mud in the darkness, her white nightdress like some kind of hospital gown.

'Suzy!' I cried out.

She didn't turn around, she kept on walking. Heading through the car park, away from the main school building, through the cold night rain and towards the sports fields.

'Suzy!' I tried again, exhausted.

Rain hammered down hard around me as I ran further into the night. My heavy school shoes smacked the puddles of water and the cold rain splashed up at me, soaking my legs as they moved.

Soon I was standing at the edge of the car park. I paused and looked around for Suzy. She was nowhere to be seen. The rain was falling heavy and hard, the wind whipped me like a slave and my bones started to shake with chill.

Eventually, I spotted the small white figure moving through the darkness.

I didn't dare call her name for fear of someone else hearing me. I had to keep out of sight and earshot of the teachers – I couldn't risk them seeing Suzy. They wouldn't understand why she was roaming around in the rain, they'd think she was rebelling; they'd use it as an excuse to expel her for good. I couldn't let that happen.

Closing in on Suzy, I watched how she moved through the rain. She looked clumsy, careless, as if she were sleepwalking. Her bare feet trod through the mud, taking her towards the school woods, towards the building site, towards Marina's grave.

Up until that movement I'd thought that Suzy was making a well-planned escape. But there was something about the way she was moving through the rain that told me that wasn't so. She seemed possessed.

I ran after her, my footsteps taking me from car park tarmac onto wet grass. The ground beneath me was frozen, and it hurt my lungs to draw breath in the icy rain.

Suzy didn't move any faster as I closed in on her. She

slipped between the machinery and once again I lost her from sight.

As I arrived at the edge of the woods I looked around urgently. Rain beat down angrily on the sleeping machines, flooding the cavernous foundations of the new sports hall. That was when I saw her, climbing down into one of the deep holes.

'Suzy!' I called into the rain. I was close and she must have heard me, but she didn't respond.

Standing on the edge of the hole I looked down at her, her nightdress filthy and soaking. She was kneeling in the mud, her bare hands scraping away at the wet earth. Her face was expressionless – a sleepwalker acting out a dream.

I yelled her name once more into the wind, and once again she didn't look up. I jumped down into the hole. Trampling through the sloshing rain and mud, I was soon next to her.

'Stop!' I cried, feeling my heart thump so hard my ribs felt like cracking. My shaking hands reached out and grabbed her soaking nightdress. I pulled at it, toppling her over into the mud. 'Please stop!'

Suzy pulled herself up and continued to claw at the mud. Grazes and scratches opened up on her hands and blood fused with the rain and mud. My hands desperately reached over hers and held them tight. I shook her hard, but still couldn't wake her from her trance. She stared down at the ground, her eyes glazed over.

Frantic, I slapped her hard across the face. I didn't know what else to do.

It worked.

Her muddy hand raised itself and gripped her cheek where I'd hit her.

'Frankie!' she gasped, as if recognising me for the first time. 'Oh, Frankie!' She let out a terrible scream. Her scream ran through the trees, harmonising with the wind. It sounded like the last cry of someone drowning at sea.

'It's OK,' I said, throwing my arms around her. 'I'm here.'

## 25

I dragged Suzy through the rain and wind, back to the San. I didn't know what else to do. I was desperate. A diver lost at sea, running out of air beneath crashing waves. My best friend was slipping away before me. I was losing her to a darkness that I didn't understand and couldn't penetrate.

The door to the San was wide open, blowing in the wind – the way Suzy must have left it as she escaped. I helped her climb the stairs. She was shaking and sobbing.

Nurse Pippa ran out into the tiled corridor with disbelief on her round face, an old dressing gown flapping madly about her. 'What on earth . . .'

She didn't say any more than that. Horror filled her eyes and all life drained from her face as her eyes ran over Suzy's pathetic figure.

Suzy's drenched gown clung to her body. Her hair was bedraggled and wild and her face was streaked with tears and snot from crying. Blood oozed from the scratches and cuts on her hands.

'Get her in to the bathroom,' Nurse Pippa instructed as she tried to swallow her horror and take some kind of command.

I heaved Suzy towards the bathroom as Nurse Pippa led the way and began to run a hot bath.

'Sit her down there, Francesca.' Nurse Pippa pointed to a small wooden stall in the corner of the cold room. She held up Suzy's chin and looked into her eyes. 'What happened?' Nurse Pippa asked me in a whisper

I was silent for a moment, hoping that some wonderful excuse would come to me. I wanted a plausible story to give her, some way to explain the madness that I'd just thrust before her, but I could think of nothing.

'You can't shock me, Francesca,' Nurse Pippa said, holding her hand under the running taps to measure the water temperature. 'I used to be a midwife.' Something about Nurse Pippa's eyes told me that in all her years as a midwife she'd never seen anything like this.

I sank to the bathroom floor and hugged my knees tightly. I was so sick of feeling scared. All I wanted was for someone to understand. At that moment I didn't care if Nurse Pippa thought I was mad, I just wanted someone to listen to me. I needed to talk, and I had nothing to say but the truth.

Nurse Pippa sat listening, forgetting about the hot water filling the bath, so I had to reach over and stop the taps before the bathroom flooded.

When I'd finished speaking Nurse Pippa gathered her thoughts and looked at me with worry. 'Wait out in the hall, please, Francesca,' she asked. 'I need to give Suzy a hot bath before she catches her death.'

I got up to go.

'You can stay here tonight,' Nurse Pippa added. 'I'll

phone Ms Thurlow and let her know you're here. I'll come and see you're OK once I've got Suzy sorted.'

I nodded, feeling exhausted.

As I closed the bathroom door behind me and stepped out into the corridor, my school shoes echoing on the tiles, I saw a girl standing by an open door, peering out at me.

Sarah Niever.

'Hi,' she said nervously. 'You OK?'

She was wearing pyjamas and had her long hair braided at the sides of her head. She looked much younger than she really was.

'I'm staying here tonight,' I told her.

'Why are your clothes so wet and muddy?' she asked, tilting her head to one side curiously.

I looked down at my sodden school uniform and the jumper that Tina had lent me. They were dripping mud and rainwater onto the tiles beneath me. My head shook helplessly from side to side. I had no words to offer.

'I have spare clothes here, if you want to borrow?' Sarah smiled sweetly.

I looked at her, knowing that anything such a small girl could wear would never fit me. But I was suddenly so cold, and I noticed I was shivering, my teeth chattering. Even a tiny T-shirt seemed appealing.

'OK,' I said.

She gestured for me to follow her into the San bedroom where she was staying.

Inside, the room looked like any girl's bedroom. There were posters and pictures on the walls and clothes spilling out of a chest of drawers in the corner. Sarah obviously spent more time there than in her own dorm.

Sarah's bird-like legs skittered over to the chest of drawers and pulled out a large T-shirt. 'Here,' she said, throwing it over towards me.

I pulled off Tina's sodden jumper and my numb fingers began to unbutton my school shirt. Sarah passed me a clean towel and I dried myself off and got changed.

'Thanks,' I said, my teeth still chattering. 'You've got a lot of stuff up here,' I said, looking around.

'I stay up here a lot,' she confessed.

I nodded, not wanting to ask why.

'They say I have an eating disorder,' she smiled sadly. 'They like to keep an eye on me. Nurse Pippa stays here too. She doesn't have a family of her own. We keep each other company.'

There were two beds in the room, one with Sarah's pink bed clothes on and another with plain white sheets. I sat down on the white bed and crossed my legs, looking at Sarah sitting on the bed opposite me.

'I saw you come up here with your friend Suzy,' Sarah said. She jumped off her bed and started to move the bedside table away from the wall.

'Ah ha,' I nodded, watching as Sarah crouched down and slid a loose floorboard across the floor. She pulled out a packet of chocolate biscuits from a hole in the floor. She then slid back the floorboard and placed the bedside table back on top of it. She offered me a biscuit and I took it hungrily. Then I took another, and another. 'Thanks,' I smiled. 'I didn't eat dinner this evening.'

Sarah looked at the biscuits thoughtfully before folding up the end of the packet, leaning towards the bed I was sitting on and tucking them under the pillow. 'If Nurse Pippa asks, these are yours, OK?'

I nodded.

'I ate dinner with Suzy this evening,' Sarah continued in her dream-like way. 'We ate here, in the San. Roast beef and mashed potato.'

I nodded again, unsure of what to say to the strange little creature talking to me. I felt numb.

'She told me she's in Newton Dorm normally, in my sister's old room. The room that Laura fell from.'

'Yeah,' I answered, looking down.

'Have you ever heard of the Blue Lady?' Sarah asked.

My eyes flicked up and suddenly my numbness began to fade away. The sound of the Blue Lady's name sent a warm jolt through me, an electric current bringing me back to life once again. 'Yes, I've heard the story of the Blue Lady.'

'Do you believe in ghosts?' Sarah asked carefully. There was a fervour in her eyes that transported Sarah beyond her years. The caution in her voice sounded so familiar. It was a tone I'd heard and used so many times over the last few weeks. She didn't want to be labelled crazy.

'I didn't used to believe,' I told her, echoing her careful tone.

'There's something horrible in this school,' Sarah said. 'Something evil and rotten. Something that wants to harm people. It got my sister.'

'I believe you,' I said truthfully. 'But I don't know what

to do about it. Whatever it is . . .' I stopped myself, swallowing hard, thinking I might cry. 'It's coming for my friend too.'

Sarah studied me intently. Weighing up whether she could trust me.

'It's the Blue Lady,' Sarah nodded, confirming my fears.

'How do you know?' I asked, astonished that she was talking about it so freely.

'Before Laura died,' Sarah said, looking into my eyes. 'She begged my parents to let her leave St Mark's. She cried on the phone to them every night but they wouldn't listen. Laura told them that she could hear whispering. Voices that were speaking to her from beyond the grave. Voices of girls who'd died here at St Mark's. She said that something had killed them, and that something wanted to kill her too. One night I picked up the phone without my parents knowing and listened as Laura cried and begged them to save her. But they didn't. It wasn't their fault, I know that now. They didn't believe her. And who would? But if they had believed her . . .' She shrugged and looked away from me.

'They, my parents, didn't want me to come here – to St Mark's, they wanted to send me somewhere else. They said it would be bad for me to come here when this was where Laura had killed herself. But she didn't kill herself, she didn't mean to. I told them, I argued with them until I won. This is where I needed to be. Being here makes me closer to my sister. Every day I wonder if it will come for me too. But I don't think it's me it wants.'

'Suzy,' I said with dread. 'It wants Suzy. Why?'

Sarah whispered thoughtfully, 'I wish I knew.'

I stared at her hard, reading that blank little face for clues, but I got nothing. 'I think I know a way to find out.'

Her eyes opened with intrigue.

'I think something . . . someone . . . has been trying to warn us about whatever's trying to do Suzy harm,' I said carefully.

She blinked at me and nodded, urging me to go on.

'The body they found . . .'

'Marina Cotez?' she asked. 'She was one of the other girls that died. Apparently her younger brother's at St Hilda's.'

'She's been haunting us. Haunting Suzy,' I said.

Sarah's eyes opened wider and she nodded in understanding. 'She knows. Marina knows.'

An awful realisation dawned on me. 'We need to contact her. Then she can tell us the truth.'

'How?'

The words danced on my lips for a heavy moment; I was afraid to give them voice. Once I said it there was no going back. But it was the only way. I had to take Sarah along a dark path I'd promised myself I'd never revisit. I had to go back to where this had all started; maybe then Marina's spirit could finally be put to rest.

'The board,' I whispered. 'We reach her through a Ouija board.'

# 26

Safe in the knowledge that Nurse Pippa would be occupied looking after Suzy, I set about creating a Ouija board. I made an exact replica of the one Suzy had made all that time ago in the abandoned Gibson Dorm: paper with letters around the side and the words YES and NO in the centre.

'We need a coin,' I said to Sarah.

She ferreted around in her bedside table drawer and pulled out a small purse, handing me a single coin from it.

'That'll do,' I nodded. 'Have you done this before?' I asked, expecting that she hadn't.

'Yes,' she replied.

I looked up at her, startled.

'I've tried everything I could think of to contact Laura. Nothing's worked,' she added sadly.

'We should do this quietly,' I whispered. 'Nurse Pippa will flip if she knows what we're up to.'

'Agreed.'

We both sat on Sarah's bed and held hands over the board, summoning the spirits of the dead with the well-versed phrase, 'Spirits come to us.'

A cold shiver ran through me. Hearing those words again felt like holding my hand too near a flame. Only I wasn't just playing with fire – I was dancing in the flames, letting them scar me with every touch.

Silence surrounded us as we opened our eyes and looked at each other. We both placed fingers over the coin.

'Is anyone there?' Sarah asked into the dark room, her calm voice telling me she'd done this a thousand times before.

The coin moved, just as it had done that time in Gibson Dorm, towards YES.

Sarah looked up at me with an excited smile, thrilled at what had just happened. 'I've never got this far with it before.'

'Are you The Blue Lady?' I asked the board, wanting to press on and get it over with as quickly as possible.

The coin moved again, this time towards NO.

'Are you my sister?' Sarah asked, the hope in her voice wrenching my heart.

The coin shuffled slightly, but didn't move from NO.

I took a deep breath and asked the question burning on my lips. 'Are you Marina Cotez?'

Slowly, the coin began to slide across the sheet of paper. It settled eventually on YES.

I looked up at Sarah and nodded my head in acceptance, not at all surprised by what was happening. Suzy and I had contacted Marina the first time we played with the Ouija board. Since that day Marina had been trying to get through to us, to tell us something, to warn us. Now I was about to find out what it was that Marina was so desperate to communicate.

'Are you going to hurt us?' Sarah said, her voice starting to tremble.

The coin moved towards NO. I let out a long exhale.

'Are you going to hurt Suzy?' I asked.

The coin hovered on NO.

'Is something else going to hurt Suzy?' Sarah asked.

The coin moved towards YES.

'The same thing that hurt my sister?' Sarah asked, her voice shaking heavily.

The coin stayed on YES.

'I knew it!' Sarah said, to me this time, not to the board. 'I knew it!'

The coin started to move again, this time away from the YES and NO, towards the letters surrounding the side of the board.

Slowly, the coin began to spell out a word – a word that wasn't prompted by a question. It was a word that the spirit of Marina Cotez was desperate to communicate to us.

M-U-R-D-E-R.

I felt a stab in my chest as blood drained from my head and filled up my heart as if it were about to burst. The coin moved again, again unprompted. It was moving so fast, it was almost difficult to decipher the words it was spelling out.

S-T-I-L-L H-E-R-E C-O-M-I-N-G

'What's coming?' Sarah asked urgently. 'What's still here? A spirit?'

C-O-M-I-N-G the coin spelt out again.

'Who's coming?' I asked, my heart thumping like a battle drum. The coin began to move again.

D-U

The door to Sarah's San room began to creak open. Someone was coming.

As the coin continued to move wildly about the board I picked it up and threw it to the floor. The door to the room pushed open. Sarah looked at me with horror-filled eyes. I felt blind and sick with panic as I screwed up the paper and threw it at the floor.

I swung around on the bed and saw a figure standing in the doorway. All the time I'd been panicking, destroying the board and all evidence of what we'd been doing, I thought I'd turn around to see Nurse Pippa standing over us. But it wasn't Nurse Pippa who'd pushed open the door to Sarah's room.

Standing in the doorway, dressed casually in jeans and a jumper, was Ms Barts, a soft smile balancing on her thick lips. My mind felt numb with confusion – she was the last person I'd expected to see.

Ms Barts quietly stepped into the room, closing the door behind her. She took small, slow, considered steps towards us. My heart began to beat faster. I knew something wasn't right. Ms Barts reached out her hand towards me.

'It's time to come with me now, Frankie.'

# 27

Suzy was outside in the corridor, shivering – her hair dripping with bath water. Ms Barts tugged at Suzy's dressing-gown sleeve and whispered something I couldn't hear in her ear. Everything seemed wrong – there was no way Suzy should be leaving San. I quickly turned around to see the door to Sarah's room shut behind me, her small confused face disappearing as it closed. As Ms Barts pushed me towards the San door I spoke up.

'I think Suzy needs to stay –'

'Shhh!' Ms Barts hissed at me.

Before I knew it we were outside the San block and walking through the cold, drizzling night towards the main school. I held my sodden clothes to my chest, trying to find warmth – I was only wearing Sarah's T-shirt and I was freezing.

Ms Barts gripped Suzy's arm, tugging her forwards like an angry mother shepherding a naughty child. Suzy looked over at me, her eyes petrified. I wanted nothing more than for Suzy to think everything was OK. But I knew it wasn't.

As the wind howled in my ears, and my numb feet plodded forwards in my wet shoes, I tried to think of how I could get away from Ms Barts. I wanted to be with Sarah; I wanted to finish what we'd started.

'I've just found your boyfriend prowling around the school grounds,' Ms Barts said suddenly. I looked over at her, startled. 'He seemed very upset.'

'Seb?' I asked, my teeth chattering as I spoke. 'Is he still here?'

Ms Barts wouldn't look at me – her eyes were fixed on the dark towers of St Mark's looming above us. Her voice sounded strained. 'He'll be expelled from St Hilda's for this. Lurking around St Mark's like some kind of alley cat. Talking rubbish about his dead sister being murdered and haunting the school . . .'

My heart jolted slightly. 'What do you mean?' I asked quickly.

'You know what I mean,' Ms Barts replied flatly. I stared over at Suzy, hoping she'd say something to take the pressure off me. But Suzy seemed oblivious, with no idea what was going on.

'Sebastian told me how you've filled his head with nonsense. How you've been terrorising the local community, sticking your nose in where it's not wanted and prying into Marina's death. You think Marina's come back because she has something to tell you? Some great secret to share? It's none of your business, Frankie. Let the dead stay sleeping.' She turned to me and looked me straight in the eye. 'Don't you see what you've done to him? Sebastian will hate you for this, for filling his head with poisonous rubbish!'

Ms Barts pushed open the door to the main school and held it without looking at me. I couldn't bring myself to catch her eye. I hated the idea that she might be right, that Seb would hate me for telling him about his sister. I wished

I'd just stayed quiet. My racing heart sank in my chest and I felt my eyes begin to itch with tears.

I followed Ms Barts and Suzy up the cold stone staircase, and when we came to the fourth floor I went to walk out into the corridor, towards Raleigh Dorm.

'Where do you think you're going?' Ms Barts said quietly.

I wasn't sure what to say. 'Umm, to bed.'

'Come with me,' she instructed, pulling Suzy up the stairs with her.

I trailed behind until we reached the door to her school apartment on the fifth floor. The lock clicked open and she led us into her dimly lit, messy flat. There was music playing quietly in the background – something old, from the 60s, like the records Dad left behind. As the door locked shut behind me, the smell of old coffee hit me and made me feel sick.

My heart lurched like a tidal wave. 'Seb!'

He was slumped back on an armchair between piles of clothes and books. 'Frankie,' he said quietly.

'What are you doing here?' I said, running over to him.

'Enough!' Ms Barts shouted at me. 'Frankie and Suzy, over here, please.' She pointed to the couch opposite Seb. 'And you're not to talk to Sebastian. His housemaster will be here any minute to take him back to St Hilda's. He's in a lot of trouble.'

Seb gazed up at me vacantly. Something seemed wrong. He should have been angry, frightened, annoyed – but instead he just looked numb. Between his hands he was holding a glass of water that trembled slightly. I looked at his face, into his pale blue eyes, trying to understand what had happened since I'd left him at the bottom of the hill. But he gave nothing away.

Ms Barts clicked her fingers and pointed down to the couch. I obediently sat down, worried about Seb and psyching myself up for the biggest telling off I'd ever had in my life. 'Ms Barts, I'm sorry,' I trembled, fighting back the urge to cry. Suddenly thoughts of ghosts, Marina Cotez and Ouija boards couldn't be further from my mind. I knew I was in serious trouble; we all were. I could be expelled, sent away from St Mark's forever. I'd never see Suzy or Seb ever again, and I'd never know the truth about Marina and how she died.

'Stay here,' Ms Barts said flatly. 'You both look frozen. I'll make some hot chocolate to warm you up. Then we'll talk.' She disappeared into her kitchen and I listened to the sounds of the kettle filling up with water and Ms Barts shuffling about, clanking mugs together and opening cupboard doors.

'What's going on?' I whispered, wide-eyed and terrified that Ms Barts would hear. Suzy turned her head towards me at the sound of my voice. Her eyes were dull and her face was as blank as a new sketchpad. Suzy just shook her head.

'Seb?' I pleaded, my voice so quiet it was barely a breath.

The glass of water began to shake violently in his hands, which made my heart quicken with panic. 'She knows,' was all he managed to say.

I shook my head, not understanding what he meant. 'There's something I forgot to tell you before,' I said quickly. 'When you were waiting for me in the graveyard I went to visit the church warden, Tina. I wanted to know more about Marina, but all she could tell me was that Marina and Ms Barts – Felicity – had been best friends.'

I paused for a minute, suddenly feeling unsure of myself. There was a memory of something Tina had said to me that itched inside my head like a rash. But as soon as the thought had appeared, it escaped me.

'Did you know that already? You never mentioned it.' Seb stayed silent and his eyelids blinked heavily. 'And now Ms Barts knows I ran out of school and I'm gonna get in so much trouble. What if she tells Ms Thurlow? Ms West? I'm dead!'

Suzy just stared at me, as if I were speaking a foreign language. She pulled her head away and focused on something sitting on the coffee table. Something within the mess and madness had caught her eye.

'I don't understand why Ms Barts lied before,' I continued, whispering as quietly as I could. 'She told me she hardly knew Marina . . .'

Suzy lent forward and picked up whatever was bothering her on the coffee table. It was a book of some kind. She started to leaf through the book, ignoring everything I said.

Seb's sleepy eyes followed Suzy's movements with interest, and then looked up at me. His lips began to move but before he could saw anything I continued to whisper, 'Is that what you mean, Seb? That Ms Barts knows something about Marina, about how she died? Maybe she knows something about the other girls that died? Maybe –'

I heard footsteps and my heart begun to ache with panic as Ms Barts came back into the room carrying two steaming mugs. I watched her move through the room, studying her profile in detail. Maybe I could read her expression, work out just why she had brought us up here. As I stared at her she pouted her lips, pressing them into a beak-like pout.

Suddenly, the memory of being in Tina's warm kitchen overwhelmed me. Ducky – Ms Barts' cruel nickname at school. Somehow that seemed important, although I couldn't work out why . . .

Ms Barts' eyes fixed on Suzy. 'Yes, I thought you might find that interesting.' Ms Barts didn't take her eyes from book in Suzy's hands as she steadily put the two mugs down on the coffee table.

Suzy was holding some kind of scrapbook. Blank pages had been filled up with newspaper clippings, letters and articles. On each page were handwritten notes and arrows pointing to things in the articles. Without thinking I snatched the book out of her hands. My heart was racing so fast it felt as if it was going to jump out of my throat. I instantly recognised the letter glued into the first page – it was the original of the photocopy I had – the letter from the St Mark's headmistress in 1786 informing Brigadier Marshall that his daughter Isabelle had died on the school steps.

The sound of water splashing on the floor pulled me away from the book. I looked up and saw Seb's head flop towards his knees. The upturned glass in his limp hands fell towards the carpet with a soft thud. I watched in horror as his body slumped to one side, crashing into a stack of books and pushing them to the ground.

'Seb!' I shouted, springing to my feet.

'Sit down!' Ms Bart's voice boomed. 'He doesn't need your help,' she said coldly.

'What's wrong with him?' I panicked. 'He's just –'

'Shhh,' Ms Barts hushed me as if I were a child. 'He'll be fine. I told you before that he was very distressed when I found him. That's your fault, Frankie. You made him like that.' I felt my eyelids flutter quickly. 'I just gave him something to calm him down, that's all.'

'You've . . . drugged him?' I stuttered in disbelief. I reached towards him. 'I can help him –'

'Frankie!' she said sternly. 'Leave him alone. He'll be fine.' I felt sick. Seb looked very far from being fine. 'If you want to do something useful then read that book you're holding . . .'

I looked down at the scrapbook I still held. My hands began to tremble and I couldn't think to do anything other than sit back down. I cast another desperate look towards Seb, utter hopelessness flooding through me. I had failed him. I'd failed everyone. Tears began to fill my eyes.

'Read the book, Frankie,' Ms Barts said steadily.

My fingers began to turn the pages of the scrapbook.

Suddenly the sound of Seb's heavy breathing fell away from me, so did every other sound, smell and colour in Ms Barts' flat.

The originals of the four documents I had were all in there – and there were more. Headlines popped out at me from the pages, hitting me like a sharp slap in the face: *Schoolgirl Dies in Mysterious Circumstances, Tragedy Hits Local School, Schoolgirl Dead, Schoolgirl Missing.* Words and letters leapt from the page and made the world around me

271

spin. I slammed the cover of the book shut and slowly raised my head towards Ms Barts.

Her eyes were boring into me from behind her glasses. I could hear Suzy start to sob beside me.

'Why do you have this?' I asked, my voice shaking violently.

'Did you know, Frankie,' she asked in a steady voice, 'that since that first letter, since Isabelle died on the steps of the school with her newborn baby in her arms, there have been a total of eight unexplained and tragic deaths and disappearances of St Mark's girls? Slightly higher than your average school, wouldn't you agree?'

Acid rose in my chest, burning my throat and lungs. I couldn't breathe and I had the overwhelming urge to vomit. 'I don't know what you mean.'

'Of course you do, Frankie,' Ms Barts smiled. She leant forwards and pushed the cup of hot chocolate towards Suzy. 'Drink this, it'll make you feel better.' Suzy lifted the mug and put it to her lips.

'No, Suzy, please . . .' I pleaded, watching on helplessly as Suzy lifted the drug-laced drink and drank. I reached out desperately, grabbing at Suzy to stop her drinking.

'Sit still, Frankie!' Ms Barts commanded. 'Do as you're told or you won't see either of them again.'

I repressed a sob rising deep within me. What did she mean, never see either of them again?

When Ms Barts spoke again her voice was softer. 'Just listen and you'll understand, Frankie. You're clever, just like me.'

'I'm nothing like you,' I bit back angrily.

Ms Barts' eyes fixed on me like a snake swaying in a trance. 'You know, Frankie, that all those girls, all those tragic accidents and disappearances are all linked to one another.'

'How?' I asked, desperate for an answer to the question that had been spinning through my mind for weeks. I looked over at Seb, wishing he was able to hear this.

She sat back, her eyes narrowed, and she drew in a deep breath. 'The Blue Lady,' she said slowly.

'There's no such thing as the Blue Lady,' I laughed, feeling almost hysterical. 'It's just a story made up to scare first years.'

'But where do stories come from, Frankie?' Ms Barts' lips twitched at the corners, raising her mouth into a twisted smile. 'Stories can come from nowhere – invented for pleasure and amusement. But some stories come from truth, from things that happened so long ago that they're no longer memory but legend.'

I look at Suzy incredulously, wanting to see the same look of bewilderment on her face. But Suzy sat slumped over, her shaking hands clutching her hot chocolate.

Ms Barts smiled at me. 'You might not want to think you're like me, Frankie, but you're just like me. And I was just like you when I was young – desperate to be special, to be different. I've seen the way you are with her.' Her hand waved in Suzy's direction. 'You worship Suzy as I worshipped Marina. Marina was so magical – so full of life. So beautiful, clever, popular – everything I always wanted to be. And Marina liked me because of the way I made her feel – I understood her.

'Just like you, every evening we'd run into the woods, share

273

secrets and plan our futures. One night we were late for dinner. I can't remember why. We came into the dining hall late. Of course we were both given detention. Our punishment was to help re-file all the personal records of St Mark's girls. A boring task until we stumbled across the archive file.'

My mind flashed back to the empty archive file Suzy and I had found in the school office. 'You stole the archives?'

'Not then, no. There were only a few letters then. Everything else in there . . .' she pointed to the scrapbook, '. . . I've found through years of research: local papers, libraries, personal records. But what we saw that day in detention was enough to make me curious. I realised that all those tragic accidents weren't accidents at all. They weren't coincidences – there's no such thing as coincidence. They were all linked somehow. A curse, maybe? I wasn't sure at first. But the legend of the Blue Lady was something all St Mark's girls knew – it didn't take long for me to realise the truth – that she's real. She never sleeps – she haunts this school, taking the lives of those in it as revenge for what happened to her.'

'You're crazy,' my voice croaked painfully. 'It's not the Blue Lady haunting this school – it's Marina Cotez. I've seen her, Suzy's seen her. She's been trying to warn us that something . . . someone is after us.'

Ms Barts paused before answering, carefully considering what she should say next. Eventually she shook her head in frustration. 'So typical of Marina. The brightest star in the darkness. Why worry about the Blue Lady when all you can see is her? And she's been trying to warn you about the Blue Lady . . .'

'No. Not the Blue Lady,' I said quickly, 'It wasn't a ghost that killed Marina. A ghost can't bury someone alive.'

I'd said something to anger Ms Barts. 'It's not that simple, Frankie,' she said bitterly. 'If it wasn't for the Blue Lady then Marina would still be alive. And once I'd figured out that she was the connection between the dead girls I knew she'd come for one of us. For me or Marina. And it couldn't be me – I wasn't ready to die. I hadn't learnt to be special yet – not like Marina.' She paused, watching me as her words sunk in and I started to understand what she was telling me. Drawing a deep breath she continued steadily, 'Throughout history there are so many cultures that realised human sacrifice was the only way to achieve what they wanted. If one person dies to save another, is it so wrong?'

'You killed Marina?' The words caught in my throat as if I'd swallowed shards of glass. Marina had tried to tell me – she'd tried to spell out Ducky on the Ouija board.

Ms Barts nodded slowly. 'She was the first one I offered to the Blue Lady, yes.'

My mind raced to think who else she could have killed in the name of sacrifice. 'And Laura Niever?' I said with horror, thinking of Sarah back in the San, desperate to contact her sister and find out the truth about her death.

'Laura would have killed herself if I hadn't got there first – the Blue Lady would have seen to that. The Blue Lady finds ways to pull people into darkness they'll never claw their way out of.'

My blood ran cold as the horrible truth swarmed around me. My hand reached for Suzy's. I gripped her fingers tightly in mine but her hand hung limp.

'Suzy!' I said desperately, reaching over and shaking her. She murmured something but didn't open her eyes, Her half-drunk hot chocolate sat cold on the coffee table. I'd been listening so intently to Ms Barts I hadn't noticed Suzy slip into a drug-induced sleep by my side. I was on my own.

'Suzy, please, wake up!' I shook her as hard as I could but she didn't stir. Tears poured down my cheeks and from the corner of my eye I was aware of Ms Barts standing up and walking towards the window. I bolted to my feet and tried to pull Suzy up but she wouldn't move. 'Suzy, please, please!' I sobbed.

A cold gush of wind blasted into the flat as Ms Barts pulled open the window as wide as it would go. She turned to me and offered me her outstretched hand, beckoning me over to the fifth-floor window.

I could hear the call of the wild wind outside and the rush of the cool night air on my skin. I had no way to escape. Every day I'd spent at St Mark's had been leading me to this. Numbness swept through me. For a second I felt calm, and at peace in that horrible moment. I found myself walking over to the window, and peering down at the hard ground five floors below.

I felt Ms Bart's hand rest gently on my shivering shoulder. 'If we don't give her Suzy then she'll come back. She'll come back for you.'

## 28

My blood pumped cold.

'There's no such thing as the Blue Lady.' The lack of conviction in my voice shocked me. 'The police will find drugs in her body – they'll figure out you pushed her. And Seb's housemaster will be here any minute . . .'

'Don't be an idiot, Frankie!' Ms Barts laughed. 'Seb's housemaster has no idea where he is. No one's coming, and if they did I'd only tell them the truth,' she said sinisterly, holding open the window and letting the freezing wind whip my face. 'I'll tell the police that Suzy came to me wanting to talk. She was wild and unhinged – clearly under the influence of something. Screaming about her boyfriend dumping her. And when her boyfriend came to find her, he was deranged too. Everyone knows how much pressure Sebastian has been under recently with the discovery of his sister's body. It won't take much for people to believe he turned violent towards his girlfriend. I went to get help, and when I returned there was nothing I could do. The star-crossed lovers had both jumped to their deaths . . .'

I shook my head. 'They'll never believe you!'

Ms Barts narrowed her eyes at me and allowed herself a smile. 'They believed me before, about Marina.'

I stood motionless by the open window, shivering in the night breeze. The world suddenly seemed so silent; even the gushing of the wind and the window creaking on its old hinges were lost to me. I only had one thought in my head.

Survival.

Ms Barts was crazy. She'd killed before and she was about to kill again.

'What happened?' I asked, my voice sounding collected and calm. I needed to keep her talking – distract her while I figured out what to do. 'How did you kill her?'

Ms Barts looked at me intensely, and then looked back over at Suzy slumped unconscious on the couch. Without a word she walked slowly towards the couch, bent over and listened to Suzy breathing. She perched on the arm of the sofa and started talking.

'It was the last night of term. School had finished and the girls still here were waiting for flights or boats over the next few days. Marina and I were the only girls left in our year. Without everyone else around I had her all to myself that night. But all Marina wanted to do was spend the evening reading. I managed to persuade her to come out to the woods with me after dinner. You see, ever since we stumbled across the school archive file I *knew* there was a supernatural connection between the accidents. And I thought Marina and I could do a Ouija board and try to contact some kind of spirit – someone who might know more.

'We went to the shack in the woods. Back when we were girls it was a nice little shed, not the half-rotten hovel that the workmen are tearing down. I'd read about Ouija boards, and I knew how to make one – I thought it could be fun. But you know as well as I do, Frankie, that Ouija boards aren't a game – they work. And the board worked for us that night. It spelt out the name "Isabelle" – I didn't know what it meant then, but now I do. That was her name before she died – Isabelle.'

'Isabelle Marshall,' I said in a whisper, remembering the oldest document I'd found that night in the school office. 'Isabelle Marshall is the Blue Lady.'

Ms Barts spoke again. 'Isabelle Marshall was expelled from this school over two hundred years ago for giving birth to a bastard child. All her life she had been loved, adored, worshipped and suddenly she was alone. She had nowhere to go, no one to help her. It was bitter midwinter and she had nothing but the clothes on her back and the memories of her last meal in her belly. I can't imagine the anger and despair she must have felt. And in those final hours, when all hope had left her and she knew that she would die, she sat down in the blistering cold and swore to take revenge. As her life slipped away from her, she sat on the school steps clutching her dying child and plotted how she would take that revenge. Ever since her death she's been haunting this school – punishing the girls who came here, dragging down their souls so she's not alone in her torment. She has made St Mark's pay for what it did to her.'

'Then what?' I asked. Exhilaration tingled in my blood, and I felt like I was standing on the edge of a cliff – desperate to know what would happen if I jumped. 'That night you and Marina contacted Isabelle through the Ouija board, what happened next?'

Ms Barts spoke with anticipation, as if we were two girls sharing secrets in the darkness. 'Marina became hysterical. She said we were messing with things that we should have left alone – she said we'd awoken something evil and now it would come for one of us. I knew she was right. I shook her to calm her, but it only made her worse. She was screaming, crying – wild with panic. Then I started hitting her, softly at first to snap her out of her frenzy, but then harder, with intent. She fell and hit her head. I thought she was dead – she was so still. I panicked. I dug a grave for her, and I dragged her into it. Then she started to wake up, started to cry again. She promised to keep our secret and not tell anyone. But I knew Marina – she was terrible at keeping secrets. I knew that my life would be over if Marina told anyone what I'd done – and worst of all I knew she'd never be my friend again. I'd rather she were dead than out there in the world without me. So I grabbed a rock and hit her again and again until she stopped screaming. Then I threw earth over her and covered the grave with leaves and rocks.

'She wasn't dead,' I told her simply. 'She was still breathing when you buried her.'

Ms Barts didn't seem to register my voice and continued talking as if I weren't there. 'The next day everyone at school assumed she'd caught a flight home. And when she didn't arrive home everyone supposed that she'd run away. Her body was never found, until now.'

'But you must have known that one day they would find

her,' I said, shivering as the wind from the open window blew down my back. 'You must have known your secret wouldn't stay buried forever?'

Ms Barts snapped out of whatever dream world she was lost in and let out a horrid snort of indignation. 'Why do you think I came back here? Of course I knew that one day they'd find her, and I wanted to be here when they did. I wanted to see what they knew – but they know nothing. But more than that, do you know why I came back here, Frankie?' I shook my head. I had no idea why Ms Barts would want to come back to the scene of such a horrific crime. 'I wanted to be near *her* – near Isabelle, near the Blue Lady. I wanted to make sure that when she struck again I could be here – that she took the right people. You see, Frankie, no one's ever cared what I thought. I've always been invisible. I've always been nothing. But with her . . . the Blue Lady . . . finally I had power.'

I stared at her. 'You're crazy – she's not real!'

'Wake up, Frankie! Of course she's real . . .'

'There's only one ghost in this school and it's Marina!' I shouted. 'And you killed her!'

'Listen to me, Frankie,' she shouted back. 'Why did I kill Marina? Why have so many girls died here? She takes them. And she's hungry. I can feel her restlessness.'

Ms Barts stood up and faced Suzy. Leaning forwards she pulled Suzy's limp body towards her and hauled her onto the floor. Ms Barts looped her arms under Suzy's shoulders and began to drag her towards me, and towards the open window.

'Frankie, help me. She's heavy.'

'Are you insane?' I gasped, feeling choked for air. 'You're asking me to help you hurl my best friend out of the window.'

She raised her eyes to meet me – she was puffing with strain and struggling to move Suzy on her own. 'If you don't help me you know what will happen, Frankie. She'll come for someone else – for you!'

'Marina's been trying to warn us about you. You're crazy,' I said, reaching for the window and trying to push it closed. Before I knew it Ms Barts was standing next to me, with Suzy limp at her feet. 'Please!' I begged. She caught the window as I tried to force it shut, her eyes narrowing with purpose.

'Seb!' I screamed at him for help but he still lay unconscious on the armchair.

His legs were twitching slightly. A glimmer of hope.

'Typical Marina – trying to outshine me.' Ms Barts forced the window open again and reached down for Suzy. 'And now her little brother comes along, trying to get in my way . . .'

I screamed so loudly I thought my throat would explode. I reached for Suzy and tried to wrestle her out of Ms Barts' arms. Ms Barts slapped me hard around the face and I felt myself falling backwards from the blow.

My head smashed into the edge of the glass coffee table and I heard a loud crack. Pain blinded me as I reached around the back of my head. My fingers tingled like pins and needles as I tried to find the spot that had hit the table. But every inch of my head throbbed. Blood oozed from my scalp and my temples pounded so hard I thought I was going to be sick.

My legs kicked at the floor, trying to find the strength to stand as I watched Ms Barts pull Suzy up towards the open window. My mouth was moving, words, sobs and pleas pouring out, but they made no sense. All I could hear was the throbbing inside my own head.

Ms Barts' flat started spinning around me, and colours and stars filled my vision. Nothing seemed real, and I couldn't remember where I was or why I was there and who the people by the window were. I wanted to run away but my legs wouldn't move. I wanted to scream but I'd forgotten how.

I could feel myself slipping away. There was nothing but stillness, and peace and a smell so strong it hurt my nose. As all my other senses abandoned me, my sense of smell heightened and all I was aware of was that horrible, horrible smell. It smelt like flowers, weeds, and earth after rain. I could smell rotten leaves and tree bark and the stench of death.

That was when I saw her – she appeared from nowhere. Marina.

She was standing by the window. Her dark, muddy hair hung about her face and her dark eyes studied Ms Barts' strained movements as she heaved Suzy's lifeless body up onto the window ledge.

The putrid, rotting apparition held out its hand towards its murderer.

'You,' croaked Marina's lifeless and hellish voice. She reached for Ms Barts. 'Next.'

Ms Barts was next. Not Suzy. Not me.

In the haze between consciousness and sleep, I thought

I was alone with Marina. I thought no one else could see her. She was appearing before me, as I slipped from this world into the next.

But Ms Barts could see Marina too. Screaming, she spun around and dropped Suzy to the ground. Suzy slumped and slid down the wall, landing in an awkward heap on the floor. Ms Barts backed up against the windowsill and stretched her arms out so she was holding the sides of the window frame.

'Marina!' she gasped.

There was a murmuring from the corner of the room. A shape was moving from the armchair – Seb. He was muttering something but I couldn't understand what.

The smell of death grew stronger, and the sound of Ms Barts' petrified screams forced my eyes shut with pain. I fought with every scrap of life I had left – opening my eyelids so I could watch the scene before me.

I knew that this was the end. The story I'd been a part of since coming to St Mark's was playing out its final chapters right there in front of me.

'Join us,' croaked Marina. Her jaw hung limp as she spoke, her muscles rotted away after so long in the ground.

Ms Barts shook her head furiously and backed away from the ghost of the girl she'd murdered. There was nowhere for her to run, and she perched up on the open window in desperation.

Through my blurred vision I saw Seb's figure move towards the window.

My eyes were so heavy they ached. I felt the sleep of death tug on me, seductively pulling me away from the horror around me into eternal stillness. I had no energy to fight, and I let myself fall into darkness.

The moment before the world went quiet I saw something. I saw the truth. There was a blinding flash and suddenly Marina wasn't alone. She stood shoulder to shoulder with the others, the girls who had died at St Mark's. There were too many to count in that final moment – each one of them a snapshot of the time of their death.

And standing at the front of them, like some kind of Queen of Shadows, was her.

I saw her.

The Blue Lady.

## Hertfordshire Observer
### 28th November 2012

**Teacher Arrested in Schoolgirl Murder Probe**

The Metropolitan Police have confirmed that a 32-year-old woman has been arrested in the ongoing investigation into the death of Marina Cotez. It is widely believed that the woman arrested is Felicity Barts, a Biology teacher at St Mark's College, where the girl's body was recently discovered.

Felicity Barts is currently in intensive care in hospital, suffering from extensive injuries as a result of a fall from a fifth-floor window at St Mark's College.

Two unconscious girls, both said to be pupils at St Mark's, were found in the fifth-floor flat from which Ms Barts allegedly jumped. It is not believed that either of the girls was responsible for the fall. Both girls are currently being treated in hospital for their injuries.

A further teenager, said to be a pupil at St Mark's brother school, St Hilda's, was also reported to have been at the scene. The boy is currently being held by police for questioning.

# Epilogue

It's been months since I left St Mark's. Months since I last saw Suzy or Seb. All this time I've lived with the knowledge that ghosts are real, that their secrets won't stay secret forever. I've never told anyone else about what happened at St Mark's, about Suzy, Seb, the Blue Lady, Marina or Ms Barts. No one would ever understand.

I spent a week in hospital – concussion, a cracked skull and six stitches in my head. Mum flew over from Germany on the first available flight – leaving Phil to attend an important military dinner alone. Of course Mum and Phil didn't last. Mum came back to England for good and I left St Mark's and went back to a normal school. She didn't say anything at the time but I knew she blamed me.

Suzy was discharged from hospital before me. Her parents took her straight back to Cyprus to recuperate. She didn't even visit or call to say goodbye. The doctors thought she'd had some kind of nervous breakdown and just needed to rest. To my amazement Suzy didn't argue with them. 'I don't want to talk about it, Frankie. I think we should just try to forget,' she mumbled down the phone, when I eventually called her. 'I'm leaving St Mark's for good.' She sounded relived. 'I'm never going back. I'm going to live with my aunt and go to a regular school next year. She lives in this big, ancient country mansion, with a river running through the grounds – it's amazing. I think I'm going to join a local drama club, maybe do some more acting. You should come and stay with me, Frankie.'

I haven't spoken to her since.

There had been a time when the thought of losing Suzy had been painful. But when the moment came, it wasn't as horrible as I had imagined it would be. But Suzy's not the same girl I once found so captivating. But how could she ever be the same? We are both forever changed.

Ms Barts lived, but only just. She'll spend the rest of her life as part-vegetable part-prisoner. I hated her at first for what she'd done. I thought she was evil. But to be truly evil you need to know the difference between right and wrong and turn your back on what's right. And Ms Barts didn't see the world like everyone else – she really believed in what she was doing. I still visit her from time to time. I take her flowers and books on artists I know she'd like.

And then there's Seb.

Beautiful, mysterious, blue-eyed Seb. He tried to visit me in hospital but Mum wouldn't let him in. He'd been taken in by police for questioning but soon released without charge. Mum said he was a bad influence, and that I needed to focus on getting myself better and not some teenage crush. But Seb's not a crush; he's so much more than that.

You see, no one else gets me. It used to bother me – it used to tear me up inside and make me feel so alone. But I've learnt to be strong. I'm a survivor. I'm not the loudest, brightest flower in the jungle. I'm not like Suzy. I'm quiet,

I blend in; no one ever notices me when I walk down the street. But my roots go deep and nothing can ever shake me.

Seb and I wrote to each other every day while I was in hospital, and every day since. I've kept every one of his letters. I put them in the green tin Gran gave me, where I still keep the documents about the dead and missing girls.

I'm amazed Seb's father let him stay at St Hilda's. And I'm surprised Seb wanted to stay. I thought once he knew the truth about his sister then he'd find some peace, and want to leave. But I don't think Seb will ever be at peace.

'I like being here,' he admitted to me on the phone one night. I was sitting at my bedroom window, staring out into the dark night at the crescent moon. The same moon that sits above Seb. 'It makes me feel closer to her.'

There isn't a moment in the day when Seb isn't on my mind. I miss him so much it hurts, and I've been counting down the hours until I see him once again. We're meant to be together, me and Seb – like Romeo and Juliet, Heathcliff and Cathy.

He doesn't like it when I talk about Marina or Isabelle, or any of the other girls that died. 'And I wish you'd stop visiting her,' he said to me, when I went to see Ms Barts on her birthday. 'Please let it go,' he begged.

But I can't let it go, and I don't see how he can.

He saw her too.

You see, Ms Barts was right. I knew it as soon as I closed my eyes and let sleep take me away that night in her flat.

The Blue Lady is real.

She'll come again. She never sleeps.

At night I close my eyes and imagine the moment I'll go back to St Mark's. The moment I'll be closer to Seb again, and closer to her. I'll pretend I don't know my way around the cold corridors, the stone staircases and the sprawling grounds. I'm sure the woods are long gone. Once I'm back I'll listen for her on the wind, look for her in mirrors and window panes.

But if I could just go back there, just once, maybe then I'll be free. I wish that the school was just bricks and mortar, rattling windows and draughty halls. But I know that's not true. I need to see it again. I just can't shake the feeling that it's not over, not yet.

It's half-term again, and he's coming into London to meet me. I'm meeting him at the station, where his train from Martyrs Heath comes in. I wanted to go back there, to meet him in the cafe where I first told him how I felt about him. But Seb wants to keep me away. I think he likes to keep me separate from everything back there, everything that might remind him of the dark times we shared.

I haven't seen him since the moment I slipped into unconsciousness that night in Ms Bart's flat. I don't feel nervous, I feel ready.

His last letter arrived yesterday:

*Frankie,*
*I want us to be together, but more than that I want us to be free. I want a clean slate.*
*When you come to meet me, I don't want a word said about her. Please, not a word about the Blue Lady,*

*or my sister, or any of the others. Let's leave it all behind . . .*

*I once read that the road of life can only reveal itself as it is travelled. Each turn in the road reveals a surprise. Our future is hidden. I don't know what tomorrow holds, but it has to be better than yesterday. We have to keep going, Frankie. We can't look back.*

*I can't wait to see you. I've thought about this moment every day. I can't believe it's here at last.*

*Remember, whatever souls are made of, yours and mine are the same.*

*Always,*

*Seb xxx*

I'm waiting at the train station. The train arrives in ten minutes.

I like to be alone in crowded places, to watch the faces of people around me. To wonder where they're going and who they're meeting. I wonder if any of these strangers have ever had their lives touched by a ghost, ever had their reality swept from their feet like fire destroys everything in its path.

Everyone around me seems so normal, so free. I don't think I'll ever be free. For me there can be no closure, no happy ending. Maybe there's no ending at all; maybe there's so much more.

That's when I see the departures board. I notice there's a train that goes through Martyrs Heath, which is leaving in five minutes.

It could be so easy. I could just jump on the train, go

back to St Mark's. When I'm not there to meet Seb he'll think that I couldn't see it through. I wonder how long he'd wait before he knew I wasn't coming. I wonder if he'd know where I had gone. If he could ever forgive me for returning. I wonder if that would be the end.

Seb's train arrives on platform nine, the train to Martyrs Heath leaves from platform three. One road to face my past, and another to walk into an unknown future.

I was never the sort of girl who believed in ghosts. But life changes you – it takes you on journeys that you never planned for, and leads you to places you never knew existed.

This is where my story ends. But the story of the Blue Lady still has chapters left unwritten.

I know what I have to do.

I stand up and swing my bag over my shoulder, lower my eyes to the ground and begin to walk.

# Eleanor Hawken

Eleanor Hawken spent her teenage years at boarding school, where there was many an opportunity to tell ghost stories by torchlight. After leaving school she went to university and gained a degree in Philosophy. She then worked as a children's book editor in Bath, where she was also part of the team that established the Bath Festival of Children's Literature. Eleanor devised the fiction series WILL SOLVIT and has written books under the pseudonym Zed Storm. In 2010 Eleanor left England and travelled the length of the Americas with a laptop; it was during this time that she wrote THE BLUE LADY. Eleanor has also written the SAMMY FERAL'S DIARIES OF WEIRD series for younger readers. Eleanor now lives in north London with her husband.

Find out more about Eleanor:
Twitter #ehawken
www.eleanorhawken.com